Entwined Publishing books by Jennifer Moffatt

Falling Hard
A Hard Sell
A Hard Fit
A Hard Sell

I0661673

Falling Hard

A HARD NOTE

JENNIFER MOFFATT

ENTWINED PUBLISHING

A Hard Note
ISBN # 978-1-80250-257-2
©Copyright Jennifer Moffatt
Cover Art by Kelly Martin ©Copyright July 2025
Interior text design by Entwined Publishing
Published by Entice, an Entwined Publishing imprint

Published in 2025 by Entwined Publishing, United Kingdom.

Entwined Publishing is a division of Totally Entwined Group Limited.

A HARD NOTE

Dedication

To my girls, E & H—
Always be who you are and follow the path that
makes you happiest. I'm so proud of you.
(Also, you aren't allowed to read this yet.)

Acknowledgements

When Totally Entwined agreed to publish my first book, *A Hard Sell*, they asked for a series, and I am so very grateful that they did. I absolutely loved creating more of Luka's world, and it was such a pleasure getting to know Finn, Rory, Morgan and Kazio better. In fact, if forced to choose… this book might be my favorite of the three (but don't tell Luka!). Thank you to Rebecca Scott, Anna Olson, Kelly Martin, and the entire team at TEG for helping send the Falling Hard trilogy out into the world.

To this day, I don't know how I've been so lucky to have so many ridiculously talented, kind and generous beta readers. Thank you to Hanna Kubicka, a brilliant friend and writer, for giving me 'Kazimierz Arkadiusz Złotowski', plus the adorable nickname 'Kazio' —and teaching me how to say all of it. Thank you to Andrew Padgett, head Muffin of the JMuffins, for his sharp suggestions, sense of humour, and essential Instagram reels. Thank you to John, so talented and unendingly generous with his time, for my beautiful website and for all of his help navigating the perils of social media. To Rebekah Rodriguez-Lynn, one of the sweetest people in the entire world, for enthusiastically and thoughtfully reading my work and telling me what themes I wrote. And thank you to Gwen, for always being so excited to read my drafts and spotting typos like a boss.

Thank you to my agent, Jordy Albert, and all of my family and friends who continue to be so excited for me. It feels good having so many people in my corner, and that feeling keeps me going when life gets bumpy.

And finally, thank you to you for reading *A Hard Note*. I hope it made you smile.

Chapter One

Box Full of Shit

It was all the Thai restaurant's fault.

If they hadn't forgotten Luka's order that night, Morgan wouldn't have gotten fired.

But there he was, standing on the sidewalk outside Breakpoint Advertising, holding a box full of his office shit, like a total asshole.

There was only one place to go.

He thumped the box of shit on the bar at the Bitter Exchange and slumped onto his favorite stool. Luckily, the pub had just opened for the day.

Kazio, the owner, came over and eyed the remains of Morgan's office life with distaste, as he did most things. "Morgan. What can I get you?"

Morgan scrubbed his face. "Twelve shots of tequila."

"Let's start with one," Kazio said, raising an eyebrow, "and go from there."

Morgan's brain spun as Kazio poured.

The text from Luka last night— *"I'm sorry I hurt you, Morgan. I was a jerk when I broke up with you."*

The words Morgan had blurted this morning at the meeting—*"It's true, what Luka says. I blackmailed him."*

His boss—*ex*-boss—frowning at him across her desk—*"I'm afraid we have to let you go, Morgan."*

"Taking an early lunch?" Kazio placed the tidy glass of amber liquid in front of Morgan, gaze drifting over the lamp poking out of the box.

Morgan laughed, dry and humorless. "Guess you could say that." He raised the shot. "Cheers." It vanished down his throat. "I'll take the other eleven now."

Kazio leaned on the bar. Morgan noticed his toned arms, not for the first time. Kazio's long white-blond hair was half tied back, but a few pieces had slipped out to frame his sharp nose and discerning eyes. "Were you let go?"

Morgan shifted, eyeing the only other patron at the bar, but they were oblivious. "Not so much 'let go' as fired. Thanks to Luka."

"Ah," Kazio said, as if that made sense.

"What do you mean, 'Ah'?"

Kazio wiped the bar with a rag like every bartender in the world had before him. "Luka was in here last night."

Morgan blinked. "And?"

"And…he asked why I don't like him." A smile hinted at the corner of Kazio's mouth. "Aside from his labor-intensive drink order, I might have told him about the time I saw you heartbroken over him."

"What? You told him about that?" The day after Luka had broken up with him—actually, *dumped* was a better word—about seven months ago, Morgan spent a long night at the bar with Kazio, exact same stool even, and he wasn't sure what drunken confessions he had made. He and Kazio had never talked about it again.

But now the sudden text from Luka last night made so much more sense.

"I'm sorry I hurt you, Morgan. I didn't mean to. I didn't even realize I had. I was a jerk when I broke up with you. And I'm really sorry."

That fucking text had sat in Morgan's head all night, festered there, seeped into his conscience, put down roots and blossomed into a confession for his boss that morning. *"It's true. What Luka says. I blackmailed him."* The relief at telling the truth had almost outweighed the humiliation of getting fired. Almost.

"What happened to the bartender code?" Morgan sniffed. "Aren't you supposed to be like a priest? Keep all confessions to yourself?"

Kazio shrugged and poured Morgan another shot. "I thought Luka should know he was an ass. That guy is too smug for his own good."

"Thank you!" Tears nearly sprang to Morgan's eyes. "*So* fucking smug! And everyone just adores him. Everyone but you, I guess," he corrected at Kazio's raised eyebrow.

"How did he get you fired?"

Morgan shook his head. "If he had... When Thomas..." He downed the second shot. "I don't really want to talk about it." Thomas was no doubt partly to blame too, the smoking hot VP Luka had been drooling all over since the moment he had arrived.

Another customer came and sat a few stools over, waving at Kazio. Kazio bobbed his chin at the man and collected two bar menus. He placed one in front of Morgan. "You need food. I'll come back for your order in a minute."

"I don't want any food," Morgan grumbled, but the wings were really good, and he was a bit hungry.

The man down the bar was hot, a toned silver fox type, in a nice suit. Reminded him a bit of Thomas, actually. Normally Morgan would have chatted him up. He had certainly made a go at Thomas, that was for sure—a desperate attempt to regain a sliver of confidence that had only led to further humiliation. The memory of Thomas shutting him down was enough to keep him glued to his stool. Besides…how could a man hit on someone with the sad contents of his desk sitting right there in a box?

Kazio served the man a pint, then was back.

"Can I have another drink?" Morgan asked, pretty sure he managed not to slur.

"After you eat something."

Morgan rolled his eyes. "Are you kidding me? What are you, my dad?"

"Are *you* kidding *me*? You're looking to get smashed and I could lose my license for feeding you twelve tequilas in a row."

Morgan sulked and pushed the menu back across the bar. "I'll have the chicken wings. Honey garlic."

Kazio left the menu where it was. "Be right up."

A plate of wings and another tequila shot later, Morgan's face was hot and his blazer was off. "You know the wors' part about Luka?" he asked Kazio, undoing the top button of his dress shirt.

Kazio tapped his tablet and appeared to be only half listening. "Hmm?"

"Luka…" Morgan waited for the right words to settle on his tongue. "Luka…actually liked me. They hardly ever really *like* me, you know?"

"What do you mean?" Kazio collected a signed bill, filed it into his till then went back to wiping down the bar.

"I mean... I had a chance — a real chance — and it all got fucked up."

Kazio poured a glass of water and placed it in front of Morgan. "Drink this. And how about some fries?"

* * * *

Kazio spread out his next three shots, then cut him off. "You'll thank me in the morning." He slid Morgan the bill. "Fries are on the house."

Morgan fumbled for his credit card. "Guess I'll take my business elsewhere."

"Go home, Morgan." Kazio tilted his head and studied him in a way Morgan didn't like. "Have some more water, take an aspirin and go to bed. Things will seem better tomorrow."

"Easy for you to say." Morgan shrugged his blazer back on. "You're not an unemployed loser."

"You'll be okay," Kazio said.

Morgan wished he could believe him.

* * * *

Since it wasn't quite rush hour yet, the train wasn't as busy going home as it normally was, so he used the seat next to him for his stupid box. He glared at his lamp, page-a-day calendar, sticky-note dispenser and Freddie Mercury bobblehead while the train swayed around him.

He picked up the sticky-note dispenser and turned it in his hand. An office job had never been his dream anyway. The approximately college-aged person sitting across from him looked like he used lots of sticky notes. Morgan held it up. "You want this?" he asked when the guy looked at him.

"Huh?" The guy pulled out his earbud.

"I said, do you want this thing? I don't need it anymore. I got fired."

The guy gave him a look like he was diseased. "I'm good, man." He put his earbud back in and shifted away from Morgan.

Morgan wasn't sure why that made his eyes water, but it did. He chucked the dispenser back into the box. It bounced off the lamp with a clang. Everyone on the train turned to stare at him.

An ugly smile stretched across his face as he blinked up at the destination display.

* * * *

Morgan kicked open the door to his apartment and dropped his box on the floor. The lightbulb broke when it hit the sticky note dispenser, shards of glass tinkling as they fell.

He laughed so he wouldn't cry.

More tequila.

He poured himself a healthy shot, tossed it back then stumbled down the hall to his bedroom, dragging one hand along the wall for balance. His work clothes landed in a corner and were replaced with his comfiest sweats. Back to the kitchen for more tequila. Then he cracked open a lime-flavored hard seltzer and flopped onto the couch to order a pizza.

"Fuck Luka. Fuck Breakpoint," he muttered, scrolling through his contacts. In a moment of strength, or maybe it was more like a tantrum, he deleted Luka and the other Breakpoint employees. He didn't need any of them. His screen was getting blurry, so it took him a few tries, but he sent a message to his band's group chat.

Anyone up for an extra rehearsal this week before the gig on Saturday? I'm free whenever.

"Really fuckin' free," he mumbled. It was their first gig, at The Sphinx, a shitty bar downtown, opening for a band Morgan had never heard of, but it was a start.

A message from Todd, the bassist, popped up right away.

Maybe Friday? If my wife says it's okay.

I can probably do Friday, Andre, the other guitar player replied.

Can you do Friday, Felix? Morgan asked the drummer.

Some bad news actually, Felix chimed in. *We can't use my cousin's garage anymore for rehearsal. They got too many complaints.*

Fuck. Morgan took a long pull from his seltzer. *Of course.* If he was being honest, it wasn't like another rehearsal mattered anyway. The band was nothing special, and one more session wouldn't make a difference. Andre was so blah—he never took sides or did anything interesting musically. Todd could never remember his part, plus he was like a bump on a log onstage. Then there was Felix. It had taken Morgan months to put the group together, rejecting one drummer after another until he found him. Felix was decent and pansexual, really hot—Morgan was sure he hadn't imagined the sexual tension between them—and most importantly, came with a rehearsal space.

Had come. *Fuuuuck*. Morgan didn't know what to reply that wasn't a long string of expletives. He threw his phone toward the cushion at his feet, covered himself in a fuzzy blanket and turned on some stupid show featuring gorgeous actors in loincloths. He fell asleep before the end of the first episode.

* * * *

A high-pitched noise shrieked its way through Morgan's tequila-fogged brain. He groaned. His alarm. Time for work. He sat up, fumbling for his phone in the cushions, desperate for the snooze button.

He found it, then cradled his head in the ensuing silence, stomach heaving. *Oh God. What did I do?* His mouth tasted like concrete and his head pounded like it was being jackhammered. *I cannot go to w…*

Work. The events of the day before hit him like a dump truck. *I don't have to go to work.*

The shame washed over him again.

He curled up under his blanket and went back to sleep.

* * * *

What the fuck do I do all day? Morgan wondered when he woke up three hours later.

For starters, he scrolled his phone. Four messages from the pizza delivery person—shit. They had apparently decided to leave the pizza on the planter out front of his building when he hadn't answered. No messages from anyone else except for a few in the band group chat... Oh right, they had lost their rehearsal space, too. *Terrific.*

I guess no rehearsal before the show then, he added to the chat. *But try to run through the set a few times on your own.*

He didn't feel like cleaning up his place and he sure as hell wasn't doing laundry. Probably looking for a new job should be high on his list. But who the fuck was going to hire him? He couldn't use Breakpoint as a reference and now had a year's gap in his already scant resume.

So no job hunting today. He should be allowed a day to wallow in his patheticness, at the very least. And to shop. Shopping always made him feel better.

He had a shower, then put on white cuffed chinos and a blue button down. His face looked a little tired and puffy, and he wasn't the hottest guy in the world to begin with, but the power of confidence and his light gray eyes were usually enough to reel in hotter guys — like Luka.

Morgan took the train downtown to his favorite shopping area, but as he was eying a really sweet pair of pricey Reggie Hill loafers, he realized there was a slight problem — he was no longer getting paid. Now was not the time for retail therapy. He was about to sulk his way back to the train station when the Shoe Shack caught his eye.

Felix was the manager of the Shoe Shack. Felix was hot. And a fuck sounded better than shopping. And cheaper. Morgan smoothed his blond hair and pushed through the doors. Felix was at the back, eyeing the clearance shelves with a clipboard in hand, looking yummy in tight jeans and sexy professor glasses. Morgan made his way over.

"Oh, hey," Felix said when he saw him.

"Hey." Morgan gave a casual head toss.

"What are you doing here?" Felix said.

"I...need some shoes." Morgan chuckled. "Obviously."

"Cool. Let me know if you need help finding anything." Felix went back to his clipboard.

"Okay." Morgan smiled weakly and wandered over to the men's section, pretending like he was on the hunt for some off-brand running shoes. He snuck a glance over at Felix who was chatting with another employee, but whipped his gaze away when Felix's head started to turn. *You know what, fuck it.* He grabbed the cheapest shoes he could find—a pair of flip-flops that were on sale.

He sidled back over to Felix with the sandals tucked under his arm. "So that sucks about the garage."

"Yeah." Felix puffed his cheeks up, then blew the breath out as he counted boxes.

"What if we put up some more soundproofing, or stuck to certain hours—"

"Nah, don't think so." Felix scribbled on his clipboard. "My cousin was iffy about letting us in there in the first place."

"Oh." Morgan bobbed his head, then pouted to make sure his lips were full and tilted his hips toward Felix. "So, listen, what are you up to—"

"Hang on." Felix frowned and pressed his ear piece for a second before turning his attention toward the till. "Sorry, the new guy needs me to do a return. I gotta go."

"Sure."

"I'll see you at the gig Saturday."

"Yeah…" But Felix was already gone.

Cheeks burning in humiliation, Morgan jammed the flip-flops back onto the nearest shelf and got the fuck out of there.

* * * *

Nothing much happened the rest of the week. There was some more tequila and falling asleep on the couch. The box of office shit still sat by his front door. No laundry or job hunting yet, but he did run through their set until Mrs. Bagshaw-Smythe, his upstairs neighbor, pounded on her floor.

"Fine," Morgan muttered, putting his baby back in its case. It wasn't like he actually had the guitar plugged in, and he had very thoughtfully not gone all-out on the high notes.

Saturday was even less eventful. Morgan got to the shitty bar three hours early instead of the agreed-upon two. Sure, he was bored, but their first gig was a big deal. An hour early was better than two minutes late. He had just put his gear down in the itty-bitty opening act "dressing room" slash storage closet when a message from Felix popped up on his phone.

I'm really sorry, guys, but I can't make it.

Morgan's brain took a second to process. *No, surely not.* He stared at the message in the group chat, mere hours before showtime.

I have to work, Felix continued. *Everyone called in sick and the store is slammed.*

What the fuck, was all Morgan could say in reply. *I'm already here! I'm literally in the dressing room and we go on in less than three hours.*

Don't know what to tell you. I can't leave.

Panic coursed through Morgan's veins as his dream — everything he had imagined for his band — crumbled around him.

It's our first gig, Felix! Come on! What are we supposed to do without you?

See if the headliner's drummer can sit in.

"Sit in? That selfish piece of..." Morgan's fingers flew, faster than his pounding heart.

Fuck you. You're out. Your drumming sucks anyway.

Fine. And fuck you too, you arrogant prick.

Felix left the group chat. Morgan seethed.

Todd piped up. *If Felix is out, I can't make it tonight either. My wife is sick and she's pissed I was planning to leave.*

Morgan wanted to throw his phone.

What am I supposed to tell the bar manager?

No one bothered to reply. *Fuck all of them.*

The manager was furious. "I'll tell you what—you guys are blackballed. You'll never play here again, and I'll make sure to tell all the other clubs, too."

"Seeing as how I don't even have a band anymore, I couldn't fucking care less." Morgan flipped him off over his shoulder as he stormed out, guitar on his back.

He got on the train, an equal mix of hurt and angry, and pushed through the jostling crowd, looking for a seat. He bumped the shoulder of someone seated who, out of the corner of his eye, looked awfully familiar.

"Morgan?" a voice said.

Morgan stopped and looked at the two people sitting there. "Finn. Rory." A couple from Breakpoint. Close friends with Luka. They had no doubt had a good laugh about him getting fired.

Finn's gaze roamed over him, judging. "Are you— how are you?" Finn's ginger curls were ridiculously shiny and pissed Morgan off to no end.

His gut curdled. "So great. Obviously."

There was an awkward pause while Finn stared at him.

"It's nice to see you, Morgan." Rory stepped in, as sickeningly sweet as ever.

Morgan studied their fingers woven together. "Sure... You two did it right, you know. I wish that I had..." He looked away. "Anyway. I'll see you 'round, I guess." He saluted and pushed his way through the crowded train to get as far away from Finn and Rory as he could.

Chapter Two

Take a Hike

"Morgan," Kazio said with a nod.

"Hi," Morgan muttered, stashing his guitar under the bar. He hadn't been planning on stopping at the Bitter Exchange, but after the emotional wallop of seeing Finn and Rory on top of his band disintegrating…somehow, there he was.

Kazio studied him for a moment, then poured a shot of tequila.

Morgan snorted and downed it.

The bartender let Morgan be, other than leaving behind more shots, water and, later on, fries. Morgan didn't touch the fries.

"Last call," Kazio informed him in the wee hours, when the crowd had thinned out and the sidewalk outside was dark and quiet.

"Another," Morgan replied, tapping the bar next to his empty glass.

Kazio shook his head as he poured. "So…how's your week been?"

The laughter hit Morgan without warning. Nothing was funny, but he couldn't stop. "My week..." he gasped. "My week. Let's see—I got fired and rejected, my band fell apart, I'm broke and I have absolutely nothing going for me." He punctuated his list by swallowing his shot and slamming it back down on the bar. "Still think I'll be okay?" he asked, raising his gaze to challenge Kazio's.

Their eyes met. Kazio's were a dark blue, almost indigo, like the sky before the storm hits. "I do," Kazio said.

Morgan's heart hitched. *Too much tequila.* "That makes one of us."

* * * *

The next morning—actually, afternoon—when he woke, there was a message on his phone from an unknown number. He blinked it into focus.

Hey, this is Kazio. You left your guitar behind at the pub last night. Found your number inside the case. That was smart of you.

"I fucking what?" Morgan bolted for his living room, hangover be damned. No guitar where he usually dropped it. No guitar in the kitchen. No guitar anywhere.

Shit. I can come get it now, he sent back.

He rubbed his eyes, trying to soothe the pounding behind them.

Kazio's reply came right away.

No need. I'm not working today so I brought it home with me for safekeeping. I can probably drop it off. Where do you live?

East end, near the exit to 97.

Perfect. I'm heading out that way for a hike up into the Grays. I'll be there in about half an hour?

Sure.

Thanks, he added, along with his address.

Then he eyed his disaster apartment. Dishes, half-eaten boxes of crackers, burned-out candle stumps, clothing strewn about. An empty tequila bottle in the middle of the coffee table. He hadn't vacuumed in days. Well, he could meet Kazio at the front door. Not that he looked much better than his apartment. He threw himself into the shower and sniffed through his clothes until he found a clean-ish pair of jeans and T-shirt.

He hurried to the lobby when Kazio texted that he had arrived.

Kazio was leaning against a planter just outside the door. It was weird seeing him...*not* behind a bar. He usually wore jeans or dark pants and black T-shirts, but today he was in... hiking gear, Morgan supposed. Gray pants with lots of pockets, and a long-sleeved close-fitting russet-colored shirt. It suited him. His white-blond hair didn't look so severe, like sunshine instead of lightning. A dusting of stubble suited his outdoorsy look.

"Hi," Morgan said.

"Hi." Kazio straightened up and handed Morgan his guitar.

"Thanks. Can't believe I forgot it."

"You weren't in the best shape last night."

"Yeah, not really."

They stared at each other for a moment. Morgan was acutely aware how grungy he looked next to Kazio's rugged style.

"Do you want to come for a hike?" Kazio asked.

That was about the last thing he was expecting Kazio to say. "Um...I don't hike."

Kazio did not look surprised. "Do you walk?"

"Of course I walk."

"Hiking is just walking on a mountain."

"*Up* a mountain, you mean."

"On, up." Kazio shrugged. "Come on, I'll wait for you to change."

Morgan looked down at his T-shirt and jeans. "I don't have hiking clothes."

Kazio sighed. "Anything is fine, sweats or whatever. It'll be a little bit cooler up there, but you'll stay warm if you keep moving."

"I don't have proper shoes."

"We're not scaling a cliff, Morgan. Running shoes will be fine." Kazio read the indecision on Morgan's face. "Just come. You need to do something besides wallow in your apartment all day. It'll be good for you."

Morgan opened his mouth to argue but he didn't have a leg to stand on, and Kazio knew it. "Okay. You want to come up while I change?" The invitation came out before he remembered what his apartment looked like.

"Sure." Kazio paused and pointed behind the planter. "Did you know there's like an entire pizza lying on the ground back here?"

* * * *

Morgan was in worse shape than he thought. He had dabbled in running when he'd trained for a half-marathon a few years ago — well, "trained" for a half-marathon. He had downloaded an app and bought all the gear, but it turned out he didn't actually like running all that much. When both his current fitness level and lifestyle were accounted for — a lot of tequila and little else — his present state in the Gray Mountains was not a shock. Five minutes in, he was hunched over, gasping for breath. Kazio noticed Morgan had stopped and he paused a few steps ahead.

"Sorry," Morgan wheezed.

"It's okay." Kazio shifted his pack. "The trail flattens out some after this first climb."

"Phew." Morgan pulled his water bottle out of his leather Mulberry shoulder bag and took a long drink. Kazio was surely regretting bringing his sorry ass along, probably from the moment he got a glimpse of the squalor Morgan was living in, including the box of shit abandoned by the front door.

"Do you normally hike by yourself?" Morgan asked once he caught his breath.

"Yup. I like the tranquility."

"Then why did you invite me?"

Kazio's pause stretched into awkwardness while Morgan regretted asking.

"I thought you could use some tranquility," Kazio replied.

Morgan snorted. "That's for sure."

The next time Morgan took a break, it was Kazio's turn for a tough question. "Have you started looking for a job yet?"

Morgan's insides clenched, which didn't help any getting oxygen to his lungs. "No. I don't even know what I want to do."

"What kind of schooling do you have?"

"Double major in music theory and sound design."

"What did you do at Breakpoint? Or before that?"

"I was a composer at Breakpoint, and not a very good one. Ads just don't get me excited. Before that, I worked at a radio station, mostly getting coffee and screening callers. Also not exciting."

"What is exciting for you?" The sunlight seemed brighter up in the mountains and made Kazio's skin glow. A delicate breeze lifted the tendrils around his face.

Morgan laughed, embarrassed to say. "Being a rock star."

"Hmm. And you said your band just fell apart, didn't you?"

"Yup." Morgan wiped a trickle of sweat making its way down his temple that was probably mostly tequila. "We weren't that good anyway."

"These things take practice. I'm sorry it didn't work out."

That's putting it mildly. "Me too."

"But until it does...maybe you could find a job having to do with music?"

"Like what?"

"Hmm... Sound tech at the arena? Event manager at a big hotel?"

Morgan took a drink of water while he considered. "I don't know..."

"Voice lessons?"

A wave of horror swept over Morgan. "God, no. I could never teach. Don't have the patience."

Kazio laughed. It was the first time Morgan had heard him actually *laugh*. It was low and rumbly, like it wasn't used often. "Agreed."

It wasn't until they started hiking again that Morgan realized he wasn't sure exactly what Kazio was agreeing to.

He was right about the hike though, it got easier after the first climb. Morgan was able to keep up without too much gasping for air. It felt a bit like the end of *The Sound of Music*, filing along the top of the Alps. Kazio was at least as handsome as Christopher Plummer anyway, striding along in his hiking gear...although that would make Morgan Julie Andrews. Oh well, there were much worse things. Girl could wail.

They stopped again when they came to a big, smooth boulder by the trail on a small rise. Kazio leapt to the top like a mountain goat and extended a hand to help Morgan clamber after him. His palms were rough, but the grip was strong and solid. They sat and sipped their water on the sun-warmed rock. Morgan stretched his legs out and took in the view of the city shining below, harbor glinting in the distance.

"How long have you lived in Oakport?" Kazio asked, offering Morgan a homemade protein ball. Thankfully it seemed to contain a healthy amount of chocolate chips. Morgan had no patience for raisins.

"Since college," Morgan said. "Thanks. You?"

"Moved here from Poland when I was twenty-five. Almost ten years."

Morgan popped it into his mouth and chewed. "Why did you leave?"

Kazio chuckled, but it was not a happy sound. "Poland is...not a great place to be different."

"Different? Are you...?"

"Gay. Yes."

Morgan had suspected. "It sucks that you had to leave."

"It's okay. I'm happy here. My parents owned a pub and when they retired, they sold it and gave me some of the money to help open the Exchange."

"Wow. You've really... You're an actual full-on functioning member of society."

Another chuckle from Kazio, this one more amused than bitter. "Aren't you?"

Morgan tilted his head back to bask in the sun, eyes closed. "Not really."

"What do you mean?"

Morgan filled his lungs with the crisp air. The thought that had been lurking in the corners of his brain shook off its shadow and stood in the clear mountain sunshine. Functioning members of society did not blackmail people. Functioning members of society did not lie to try and get their ex-boyfriend fired. He had tried to get Luka *fired*. After he had *blackmailed* him. Luka, a person he had been deeply intimate with — a person he had cared about. The reality of what an absolute piece of shit person he was turned his lungs to rock. He struggled for a breath.

Kazio was waiting for an answer.

Morgan sucked in a gasp of air and swallowed the thought back down. "You know, functioning members of society have jobs and all that."

"You'll find a job soon enough." Kazio stood, brushed off his trousers and offered a hand. "You ready?"

Morgan stood without taking the hand. "Sure," he said, trying to smile.

But the cold reality sat in his stomach, a lump of ice reminding him that he deserved nothing.

* * * *

When Morgan got out of bed the next day, his quads and calves screeched at him in protest. *Why, why, why did I think climbing a mountain was a good idea?* He made a mug of tea and ran a bath at lava temperatures, complete with half a bottle of bubble bath. He liked to pretend he was Julia Roberts in *Pretty Woman* all covered in suds.

I hate you, he texted Kazio once he was settled.

Kazio's reply came a few minutes later. *Sore?*

'Sore' doesn't even begin to describe it. More like 'begging for the sweet release of death.'

A bath should help.

Already in one. Morgan debated sending a sudsy selfie but decided that was probably a bit much.

Same.

You're in the bath too?

Yeah.

Morgan tried to picture the stern bartender in the tub. *Are you a bubble-bath guy?*

No, I like bath salts.

Oh.

You're sitting in a mountain of bubbles right now, aren't you?

Maybe. He could imagine Kazio's low, rumbling laugh.

Hopefully next time you won't be so sore.

Next time? The idea of a next time was...nice. Except...

How about next time we do something more my speed? Something that doesn't involve me wishing for death.

A brief pause, then Kazio replied. *Deal.*

* * * *

There was no avoiding it any longer. Morgan had filed for unemployment, but it hadn't kicked in yet. His bank account was bleeding red and he was really attached to running water and electricity. The day after the bath, he sat down at his computer and went to a local classified site looking for job openings. Searching for "musician" brought up nothing more than a high school looking for a marching band instructor. He couldn't imagine himself doing any of the jobs he scrolled through, until he saw an assistant event coordinator for the Cerulean, a fancy old hotel near the harbor. They regularly hosted weddings, conferences and other big corporate events. Experience with sound design was listed as a desirable skill.

He texted the link to Kazio.

What do you think?

Looks promising. Have you ever worked in the service industry before?

Never.

What did you do in college?

Morgan decided to go for the truth, as awful as it sounded. *Uh…partied?*

I see. Can you come by the pub around two or three when it's quiet? I can help you with your resume if you want.

That seemed like a good idea, except… One of the last things he had said to Luka was "Maybe I'll see you at the Exchange," an idea that now filled him with absolute dread. He didn't even know why he had said it—trying to play it cool or save face somehow. The fact was, he'd rather jump into the lion enclosure at the zoo during feeding time than see Luka at the Exchange. But as long as he was gone by five when someone from Breakpoint could potentially roll in, it would be helpful to have Kazio look at his resume.

So Morgan found himself at the Bitter Exchange again, except this time he shook his head when Kazio held up the tequila bottle with a raised eyebrow. "Just water for now." He turned his laptop to face Kazio behind the bar. "Here you go."

Kazio scanned it as he polished a glass. "This isn't as terrible as I thought it would be."

"Thanks?"

"You said you didn't have any service experience but…what's this—'coordinated food and beverage services for Silvercloud Studio'?"

"I got the coffee and doughnuts at a radio station."

Kazio's mouth curled. "Nicely done." He looked it over again. "So you didn't work in college at all?"

"No, er…my parents paid for it."

"That's nice."

"Mm-hmm."

Kazio's eyes slid back to Morgan. "You haven't mentioned your parents before."

"No, I have not."

Kazio nodded once. "Your resume's brief, but fine...except you didn't put any references."

"Only for the simple reason that I don't have any. I can't use Breakpoint, obviously. And my radio station manager hated me and was pissed when I quit."

Kazio frowned in thought as he reached for another glass. "What if you put me down?"

Morgan's eyebrows climbed his forehead. "You?"

"Yes."

"As a reference?"

"Yes."

"But I didn't work here."

Kazio was endlessly patient. "I'm aware. We can say you did."

It took Morgan a moment to puzzle out what was happening. When it clicked, a strange sensation crept through his chest, a warmth without even any tequila. "You'd do that for me?"

Kazio set the glass down and picked up another. "I don't mind helping you out."

"That would be... Thanks, Kaz."

"You're welcome. And it's Kazio."

Morgan blinked. "You don't like Kaz?"

"Kazio is already a nickname." He said it like it was the most obvious fact in the world.

"What's your full name?"

"Kazimierz Arkadiusz Złotowski."

It was beautiful and terrifying all at once. "Wow. I can't even... Polish is a mouthful."

Kazio's straight face was belied by the twinkle of amusement in his eyes. "Is it?"

Morgan reached for his phone. "I'm going to put your last name into my contacts. What was it again?"

"Złotowski."

"Uh... Z... Zoo..."

"Złotowski."

"Can you spell that?"

Kazio obliged, then Morgan made him say it again. He made several attempts to say it himself until it rolled off his tongue without too much trouble. "Zwultovski."

"Not bad."

"Thanks."

"Just kidding. It's actually still pretty bad."

Chapter Three

Love Me

Morgan had a dream that night that he was singing on stage. No, not singing…he was fucking *rocking it* on stage. The audience a faceless screaming mass, his voice reverberated through the stadium like he was a god astride a mountain top, hitting notes he never had before. The bass vibrated through his chest, the drums kept time with his heart. He was sweating, strutting and deliriously happy. But then the music came to a ragged stop, one instrument at a time. The crowd quieted to a confused buzz. Feedback screeched through the stadium, then Felix was on stage next to him, stupid glasses and all. He ripped the mic from Morgan's hand and let out a cold, humorless cackle that echoed through the empty air.

Panic welled up Morgan's throat. "What, Felix? What do you want?"

Felix only continued to laugh.

"Felix!" Morgan tried to grab the mic from him but Felix was too fast. He ducked and dodged Morgan's hands, dancing around the stage, still laughing. Then, the crowd started to laugh too, louder and louder, until the sound invaded Morgan's ears and nostrils and lungs and he couldn't breathe.

Morgan startled awake in a cold sweat, covers tangled around his ankles. It was five a.m. and still dark in his bedroom. "Fuck," he muttered, scrubbing his face and tugging the blankets up to get comfortable again. But even as his heart calmed, his thoughts stayed with his failed music career. His band, if he could even call it that, crumbled before they even existed. What was that line? Not with a bang but a whimper. His band was a fucking whimper, that was for sure.

The other two, Todd and Andre, had messaged him the morning after they dissolved, apologizing for the failed show and letting him know they were still available if he wanted to look for another drummer. But no. No, he did not want to look for another drummer. He wanted to *have* another drummer. He just wanted to have a band. The idea of beginning the search for a new drummer from square one… again…made him want to pour honey on his head and hide in an anthill.

He tossed over onto his other side. The thing was, a rock star needed a band. And he wanted to make music again. So badly. What if he could make it happen in Oakport…get a lucky break or two… Maybe getting fired from Breakpoint was a blessing, the push he needed. He'd never wanted to work in advertising anyway.

A memory took over—a lazy afternoon, curled up next to Luka naked in this very bed, his usually freezing-cold feet warm where they were pressed up against Luka's calf. Morgan had been lost in a daydream, a lot like the first part of the rock star dream he had just had. "Do you think you'll stay in advertising forever?" Morgan had asked, running his fingers through Luka's chest hair. Luka had the sexiest chest hair.

"Yeah," Luka had said, turning his head to look at Morgan. "I mean, it's kind of my dream job. You?"

The image was still clear in Morgan's mind—on stage, bathed in spotlights, fans screaming his name. "No. I'm not even sure how I ended up here." But that wasn't true—he *did* know why he was working an office job. It was safe, comfortable. It was a decent, guaranteed paycheck. Those were good, too. And the rock star dream was just that...a dream. He drifted back to sleep, the memory of Luka's warm body in the bed next to him lingering.

When Morgan woke up the second time a few hours later, an email from the Cerulean waited. He texted Kazio.

I got an interview!

There was no immediate response, so Morgan hopped into the shower. He was eating breakfast—a defrosted burrito, 'cause why not?—when Kazio replied.

That's great. When is it?

Tomorrow at two.

Do you want to come down to the Exchange tonight? Kazio asked. *Hang out in the kitchen a bit before we close? Might make it easier to pretend you worked here.*

I guess... Morgan replied. *But you don't actually want me to work, right?*

No, Morgan. No work. Just vibes.

He suspected Kazio was making fun of him, but he didn't mind. *Sounds perfect.*

So for the second day in a row, he pushed open the door of the Exchange, taking a quick glance to make sure no one from Breakpoint was still hanging around. The coast was clear. Kazio was behind the bar as usual, doing ten things at once and yet completely unruffled, the picture of efficiency and calm. Morgan had never really noticed Kazio's hands before, but lately they were...more noticeable—creamy skin, massive palms and long fingers. Putting away six glasses at once somehow, pouring, mixing, serving, never spilling a drop. It was like magic.

Kazio lifted his eyebrows when he saw Morgan standing there. "Hey, give me a minute." He served two rum and Cokes, pulled a pint, told off a patron who complained about the temperature of his wine, wiped a spill then tossed the rag at Tasha and came out from behind the bar, smoothing his hair back. "Follow me."

They headed through the swinging door into the kitchen. There were two employees on the line wiping down surfaces. Kazio nodded at them on their way by. They nodded back, with a second look for Morgan.

Kazio led Morgan to the heart of the kitchen and stopped. "This is it."

Morgan looked around, hands on hips. "I've never been in a restaurant kitchen before. It's weird."

Kazio looked half amused, half annoyed. "How so?"

"I thought it would look more like...you know, a big, glamorous kitchen. Not all metal counters or so...empty. I dunno."

"Hmm. Well, we're all cleaned up for the night. Usually it's busier. Here, come check out the walk-in." Kazio pulled the metal handle of the big silver door and ushered Morgan into the cooler.

Once again, not what he expected. Dim and cool, obviously, with metal wire shelves and everything in white buckets or clear bins, covered in plastic wrap and labeled with masking tape. It also looked nothing like a fridge.

"We prep what we can in advance. Everything has to be labeled and dated," Kazio explained, running his fingers along a shelf.

Morgan frowned. "This is weird, too. It feels like a shed. And it smells — "

"Don't say 'weird'."

"Okay, it smells...unexpected."

Kazio stared at him. "I take back my fake job offer."

Morgan gasped. "You can't take it back!"

"Okay, fine, but promise me you won't tell the person interviewing you that anything is weird."

Morgan tilted his head, considering. "No promises."

A smile twitched in the corner of Kazio's mouth. "I'm not sure I dare show you the freezer."

"You can show me the freezer."

Morgan had his regrets once they were inside it. The freezer was quite a lot smaller than the cooler, and, well, a lot colder. When the door swung shut behind him, it was a little bit like being shut into a frosty coffin. Morgan did not love it.

"Has anyone ever gotten trapped in here?" Morgan asked, shivering.

Kazio showed him the release button on the inside of the door. "You can always open the door by pushing this. It doesn't lock." Kazio nodded at a box on the shelf. "You want an ice cream sandwich? They were left over from a staff party."

"Sure."

Kazio retrieved two sandwiches and Morgan was relieved to follow him back out into the kitchen, which was now warm and cozy by comparison.

They sat on stools at the metal counter and unwrapped their treats.

"Are you nervous for the interview tomorrow?" Kazio asked before taking his first bite.

Morgan shrugged while he chewed. "Not really. I'm just…the way I am. Take it or leave it."

Kazio licked his finger while his eyes narrowed with amusement. "That's fine for friends, but…you don't want a potential employer to *like* you necessarily, do you? You want them to think you'd be good at the job."

Morgan shook his head. "I'm a package deal, employable skills and all. Love me, or don't." He took another big bite.

Kazio studied him a moment before turning his attention back to his sandwich. "Noted."

They finished their ice cream in a comfortable silence.

* * * *

The woman conducting the interview looked younger than him by a good five years. Her suit was clearly a knock-off, and Morgan wanted to have a chat with her about her fake eyelashes.

"Thank you for coming in, Morgan," she said as they settled at a table in a small conference room. "My name is Bennett. It's so nice to meet you." Bennett had the air of the girl at the party who kept mentioning her

Mercedes, but no one was impressed 'cause her dad owned a used car dealership.

"It's nice to meet you, too," Morgan said. She blinked a lot. Too much. Probably because of the eyelashes.

"So, Morgan." Bennett folded her hands and tilted her head with over-the-top earnestness. "Tell me why you want to be an assistant event planner at the Cerulean."

"Well, I have a degree in music theory and sound design, and I think I would be a huge asset to a place that regularly hosts large events."

She picked up a pen and held it poised over his resume. "Do you have any DJing experience?"

"DJing? No, not exactly, but I can mix —"

She clicked her pen. "Oh, we were hoping for someone with DJing experience."

Morgan furrowed his brow. "So you're hiring a DJ?"

"Not necessarily, but experience would be beneficial."

"Oh."

"Let's talk about your employment at..." She frowned at his resume. "The Bitter Exchange? Is this a restaurant in town?"

"It's a pub." Morgan's palms started to sweat.

"And the owner is Ka...Kazimir...Mr....Zuh-lo-tow-ski?"

"Kazimierz Złotowski," Morgan corrected, like he was born and raised in Warsaw. "Yes."

She gave him a smile that did not reach her eyes. "I spoke to him this morning and he had some lovely things to say about you."

Morgan's stomach lurched up into his throat at the first part of that sentence, but then with the second part it crashed back down, doing a few flips on the way. "He did?"

"Indeed. What would you say was the biggest challenge you faced working there?"

"Um." What had Kazio said about him? "Uh…" Did he make up shit about Morgan as a server, or did he just talk about…Morgan the person? "I suppose the biggest challenge for me was…balancing the trays?"

* * * *

How did the interview go?

Kazio's text popped up the moment Morgan stepped out onto the sidewalk. The doorman tipped his hat as he passed.

Morgan sighed as he typed.

Not good. There's no way I'll get it.

How come?

Can I just swing by?

Of course. See you soon.

For the third day in a row, Morgan entered the Bitter Exchange. Kazio wasn't behind the bar like normal.

Tasha saw him. "He's in the back," she said, bobbing her head toward the kitchen. "Go ahead."

Morgan pushed through the doors. Another employee in a chef's coat noticed him. "In the stockroom," he said, pointing.

Morgan thanked him and found Kazio in a storage room at the end of a short hallway.

Kazio was hefting boxes from the floor onto the shelves, biceps straining against his sleeves.

"Hey," Kazio said when he saw Morgan lurking in the doorway.

"Hey."

Kazio lifted another box with a grunt.

"Need some help?" Morgan asked.

"Sure."

Morgan stooped to pick up a box, then staggered under its weight. Kazio steadied him with a hand on his back. "Whoa. You okay?"

"I'm okay," Morgan wheezed, hefting it onto the shelf.

"Don't hurt yourself."

"I won't," Morgan sniffed.

The two of them made quick work of the rest of the boxes, then Kazio rested his arm on the last box, catching his breath. "Tequila?"

"Please."

Kazio waited until Morgan was settled on his usual stool at the bar with a shot in front of him before he asked. "So?"

"I don't want to work for some snobby hotel anyway," Morgan said, waving his hand. Right then, his phone dinged—the email notification noise. He opened up his email and had to laugh when he saw the message preview. "'Dear Mr. Di Meo,'" he read to Kazio. "'We would like to thank you for your interest in employment at the Cerulean. However...'" He stopped reading. "Jesus. Took them all of thirty minutes to reject me."

Kazio looked like he was trying to decide what to say, but instead of speaking, he reached for another shot glass. He poured a shot for himself and held his glass toward Morgan. "Job hunting sucks. Cheers."

"You got that fucking right. Cheers."

They downed their shots at the same time.

Morgan groaned. "Guess I gotta find some more places to apply."

Kazio refilled their glasses. "Do you want to go camping with me?

Morgan froze, tequila halfway to his mouth. "What? Camping?"

"Yes."

He put the glass back down. "You want me to go camping?"

"Sure. Why not?"

"First of all, we were supposed to do something more my speed the next time. This is very much not my speed."

"Come on. There's a great rec site up in the Grays, by Bell Falls. I hike in."

"Second..." Morgan shuddered. "I don't *camp*."

Kazio wrinkled his brow. "When was the last time you actually went camping?"

"Never. My parents weren't campers."

"What were they?"

"They were...golf resort-ers. I imagine my dad still is." Morgan picked up his glass again and swallowed its contents.

Kazio downed his too. "So you're good at golf then?"

"No." Morgan licked a drop off the rim of the glass. "I wasn't allowed to golf. The nanny took me to the pool. I'm really great at chicken fights and Marco Polo."

Kazio blinked. "I don't know what any of those words mean in that sentence."

"I'll teach you someday. Anyway, you saw how bad I was at hiking—what makes you think I can do that carrying a tent and...and a barbecue and stuff?"

Kazio's mouth twitched. "I'll carry the barbecue."

Morgan considered, still skeptical. "How long would we go for?"

"Just a night. I don't like to leave this place for much longer than that. Tasha can handle it for a couple days. But I had to agree to let her decorate for St. Patrick's Day."

"What?"

"I'm not super into holidays. Tasha likes to go all out... I think mostly just to torture me."

"Oh. Well, I don't have a tent."

"I do."

"I don't have a—"

Kazio held up a large hand. "Let me stop you right there. I have all the gear we need. So if the only reason you're making excuses is because you think it's too hard, fuck that. You can do hard things, Morgan."

The way Kazio was looking at him was incredibly unsettling. Morgan couldn't remember the last time anyone expected much of anything out of him.

"It's not that it's *hard*," Morgan muttered. "It's just...I like my bed. And my couch. And my fridge and...all my stuff."

"Okay, but there's something to be said for being outside your comfort zone. For trying new things."

"I'm looking for a new job, aren't I?"

"All right, fine." Kazio shrugged, all casual. "The invitation is there if you want it, though."

Morgan stuck out his lower lip. "Will there be s'mores?"

He could swear there was a little twinkle in Kazio's eyes. "We can do s'mores."

"Ugh, fine. But I don't even know what to pack."

Kazio grinned and filled their glasses again. "I'll text you a list. We leave at seven on Monday."

"*Seven?*"

"Yes."

"Seven *a.m.*?"

"No, I like to leave for camping trips at seven o'clock at night."

Morgan let the sarcasm drift right past him. "Why do we have to leave at seven in the morning?"

"It's a couple hour drive to the trailhead and a three-hour hike in." He eyed Morgan. "Well…maybe four. And we need time to set up camp, collect firewood and make dinner before it gets dark."

Morgan chewed his lip.

"No, you are not bailing now. It'll be fun."

"Ugh," Morgan replied.

Chapter Four

Timber

Morgan opened his door and glared at Kazio.

"Good morning," Kazio said, about as cheerful as Morgan had ever heard him.

"It is too early to be good," Morgan muttered. He was dressed, begrudgingly, but otherwise looked like a man who had rolled out of bed about ninety seconds ago, because he had.

"Are you ready to go?"

"Yes," Morgan said, offended at the question.

Kazio threw a skeptical glance at the clothing strewn about the living room. "Did you eat?"

"It's too early."

"You can't hike on an empty stomach."

Morgan yawned and scratched his chest. "Can we swing through a drive-through or something?"

Kazio craned his neck, looking past Morgan into the kitchen now. Apparently he didn't like what he saw. "Sure."

Morgan was less grumpy half an hour later with a hot tea and a sausage breakfast sandwich from Hole-in-

One in hand. He commandeered the playlist and scrolled more job listings while Kazio drove.

"Look at this one," he said, wiping crumbs from his fingers. "Master's degree required, and it's minimum wage." He blew a raspberry. "Next. Oh, here's something. They want a composer—wait, fuck, it's another advertising agency. Never mind. A singing stripper-gram... Well, after another month of bills, I might think about it..."

The commentary continued while Kazio's SUV wound up the foothills into the mountain range, where a thick blanket of evergreen trees gave way only to crumbling granite columns and the occasional white spray of tumbling glacial water. Kazio rolled his window down and made sympathetic noises to Morgan's lamentations, blond hair blowing in the wind and fingers tapping a rhythm on the steering wheel.

Once Morgan had finished his breakfast, he became more aware of his surroundings. "Your car is so clean," he observed, peeking into the nooks and crannies in the door and checking out the floor in the backseat. "No water bottles, gum wrappers... Not even a single crumb."

"I don't eat in my car," Kazio said.

"Oh." Morgan studied the remains of his breakfast resting on his fleece. "Shit. I probably shouldn't have gotten my sandwich on a croissant."

Kazio slid his gaze over. "It's fine. I'll vacuum after our trip anyway."

"You like things clean," Morgan observed.

"I do," Kazio said. "Usually."

Just short of two hours later, they rolled into the small dirt lot at the trailhead. Kazio's car was by far the cleanest alongside the three other mud-spattered SUVs. He opened the hatch and heaved his pack onto his back.

"You're going to carry all that?" Morgan asked, dumbfounded. The backpack was nearly as big as Morgan.

"Yes," Kazio said. He pulled an ax from the back and slipped it through a strap on his pack.

"And a whole *ax*?"

"Yes. A small one."

"That's a small one?"

"Smaller, yeah."

"Do you have a bigger one?"

A smirk played at the corners of Kazio's mouth. "Yeah, I've got a bigger one at home."

I'd like to see that gathered on Morgan's tongue, but he wasn't sure they were there yet. "What's the ax for?" he asked instead.

"Firewood."

"Oh. I was imagining you fighting off bears for a second."

"Nah, if we see a bear, we're toast. An ax won't help."

"What? I am not—"

Kazio sighed. "Morgan, I'm kidding. We won't see any bears. Or probably not, anyway. But if we do, they won't bother us."

"But—"

"It's fine. Trust me."

The funny thing was, Morgan did trust him. They hit the trail.

The less said about the hike, the better. The important thing was Morgan made it to the lunch break.

"How are you doing?" Kazio asked when Morgan caught up. He was waiting on a log, lunch already unpacked, fresh as the spring day.

"Great," Morgan gasped. "So good." He fell onto the log next to Kazio, then used the fleece that was now tied around his waist to wipe his forehead.

"I hope you like salami," Kazio said, handing Morgan a sandwich on thick, grainy bread.

"I love salami," Morgan said with all seriousness, and took a ravenous bite. "Goddamn," he mumbled through his mouthful before he remembered his manners and swallowed. "How is this so good?"

"It's probably the pesto mayo. Or the toasted bread or the rocket salad."

"Wait," Morgan said, sandwich poised for a second bite. "Did you make gourmet salami sandwiches for camping?"

Kazio shrugged. "I like to cook."

"You do?"

"Yeah. When I have someone to cook for."

"Oh." For some reason this made Morgan's cheeks warm. "Well, this may be the best sandwich I've ever had."

"And you can leave all the crumbs you want here," Kazio said with an almost wink.

Morgan sputtered, but when he was unable to come up with a snappy retort, he settled for taking an offended bite of his sandwich.

They sat chewing in silence, taking in the view of the canyon below them while the sun climbed overhead. A hawk wheeled above the craggy cliffs jutting up on the other side.

"So. Kazio," Morgan said, when he was down to his last bite. "What do you do when you're not working or hiking or making impossibly delicious sandwiches?"

"Well, those things take up most of my time," Kazio said. "I'm at the pub a lot."

"I noticed. Do you ever have time to…cook for other people?" He doubted it, since he had never seen a boyfriend hanging around, nor had Kazio brought up dating or anything. Not to mention the fact that they were tromping off into the woods alone together for a night, and he suspected most boyfriends would not be okay with that. But good to clarify…in case there was a chance said boyfriend might take that ax to his front door.

"I've had a couple long-term boyfriends over the years," Kazio said. "And I was seeing someone until recently, but turns out he was…not for me."

"How so?"

"I always date the serious types—you know, they work long hours and only want to talk about the news and their investments." Kazio lifted a shoulder. "This last guy, there was just no…spark. No potential for…being fucking knocked off my feet."

"Hmm." He could picture Kazio with that type—someone smart and serious, the two of them having deep grown-up conversations over a responsible breakfast of eggs and fruit. The complete opposite of Morgan. "It's hard to meet people, isn't it?"

"Yes, especially because I generally don't like people." Kazio took his last bite.

"That's funny because people generally don't like me."

Morgan meant it as a joke, but Kazio considered it while he chewed. "Why do you think that is?"

"Oh…" Morgan brushed the crumbs off his pants. *Because I either try too hard or not enough.* "They're jealous of my charm and good looks, obviously."

Kazio didn't smile at that joke either. He looked like he was waiting for a real answer.

Morgan laughed uncomfortably. "Anyway. That conversation requires something a lot stronger than pesto mayo."

"Fair enough. Do you want a cookie?" Kazio reached into his pack and held out a bag of chocolate chip cookies.

The aroma made Morgan's mouth water. "You made these, didn't you?"

"Yes."

Morgan took two. "I feel so spoiled."

"Don't eat too many. It's all uphill from here."

* * * *

"Not to be cliché," Morgan wheezed, "but are we there yet?" His legs were rubber, his shoulders ached, and his lungs had had enough. Hiking officially sucked. Why did people voluntarily spend their free time carrying the basic items they needed for survival up mountains?

"Almost," Kazio said, not a drop of sweat to be found on his forehead. "See that scree through the trees up there? The site is just past there."

"Cool. Quick question—what's 'scree'?"

Kazio rumbled a low laugh. "The pile of broken rocks at the bottom of a hill."

"Ah. Then yes, I do see the scree."

Kazio didn't say anything more, just smiled and kept walking.

In about another hundred hours, Kazio finally stopped.

"Here we are," Kazio said, sweeping his arm toward a patch of dirt.

Morgan staggered to a halt and looked around. There was nothing but a few small clearings with a weathered picnic table and a fire pit in the middle. "This is it?"

"Yup. It's a rec site. There's an outhouse over there." Kazio pointed down a path.

"An outhouse?"

"Well…yeah."

"Gross."

"Were you expecting plumbing up here, or…?"

Morgan sighed. "No, but…I guess I blocked that part out."

Kazio patted his shoulder. "You'll be fine. Let's put up the tent before we run out of steam."

"I hate to tell you," Morgan said as Kazio began unpacking, "but I ran out of steam hours ago, if I even had any to begin with."

Kazio handed him a bundle of nylon. "I'm guessing you've never put up a tent before?"

"Never. *Pitched* a tent, sure…"

Kazio's mouth curled. "I've no doubt."

The tent—a sleek-looking gray and blue number— was up in no time at all, thanks to Kazio's efforts, obviously, but Morgan liked to think his quips and innuendo improved morale. The tent was bigger than Morgan expected. He had been imagining a pair of little pup tents side by side, but the one they had put up had room for two people to sleep, plus their gear.

"What about the other tent?" Morgan asked, but as soon as the question left his mouth, he realized it was stupid.

Kazio lifted his eyebrows. "Other tent?"

"I… For some reason, I was picturing two tents. But…there's only one tent."

"Yeah. Is that okay? I didn't think to pack two. And it'll be warmer…"

"Oh, no, that's totally fine. Yes, of course we'll share a tent. I'm just dumb."

"You're not dumb," Kazio said. "You just haven't been camping before."

Once again, Morgan's cheeks flushed. "So...time to relax now? Gather round the campfire and roast some s'mores?"

"Not quite yet." Kazio picked up his ax. "We need firewood."

Morgan sighed. "I was afraid of that."

"Come on, I'll show you how to find some good wood." Kazio hefted the ax onto his shoulder. "Ready?"

Morgan swallowed *'I know where to find good wood.'* "I guess."

They tramped through the bushes, their footsteps crackling in the underbrush. Birds called from treetops, and sun filtered through the evergreens. Morgan forgot about his rubbery muscles and felt almost...serene.

"Ah, perfect," Kazio said when they came across a small fallen pine tree. It had been there a while and had already been partly scavenged for firewood. The stump was ready to use as a chopping block. "I'll chop off a piece first, then you can help me split it." He paused to put on his sunglasses. "You might want to step back. You don't want to get hit with any wood."

Morgan couldn't resist the joke this time. He opened his mouth, but then every coherent thought was erased from his brain when Kazio hefted the ax.

He brought it down on the log, his sharp exhale of air in time with the *thunk* when the blade sank into the wood. He yanked it loose, then swung around for a second strike. Another *thunk*—the blade sank into the log exactly where the first cut had been. Then another swing took a chunk out of the log. Two more swings, then Kazio paused and pulled his sweater off. He wiped his forehead with his biceps then tossed the sweater to Morgan.

Morgan barely managed to catch it. It came with a whiff of pine and earth and something else warm and spicy.

"Thanks," Kazio said in an exhale. "Hot already."

Morgan made some sort of noise as a reply.

Kazio continued in his T-shirt. Another swing, biceps straining against the thin cotton. Another swing, this time with a louder grunt. His glutes flexed, visible through his pants. His forearms were taut. Three more hard, sure swings, then the trunk was clean through. Kazio leaned on the ax and wiped his brow.

Morgan was not okay.

Jesus fucking Christ, it was the hottest thing he'd ever seen. Kazio, the uptight, efficient and slightly cranky bartender was a sexy, sweaty lumberjack. *Timberrrr.*

Kazio hefted the log he'd cut off onto the stump and got to work splitting it down the middle. Bulging muscles, grunting, sweating, the sheer power in those arms as he slammed the ax head into the wood, over and over... *Fuck.* His big, strong hands could grip a different kind of shaft, with his rhythmic—

"Morgan?"

He jolted out of his daydream, face a thousand degrees, then snapped his jaw closed. Busted.

"You okay?" Kazio asked. He took off his sunglasses. A tendril of hair hung over his eye.

"Fine," Morgan said, doing his best to sound normal.

"You want to try?"

"I don't think I...can do...that."

"I'm sure you can." Despite his protests, Kazio took Morgan's hand and pulled him over to the stump. The smell of pine and earth and musky sweat hit him again. "Here," Kazio murmured, putting the ax in his hand. He took Morgan's other hand and helped him hold it correctly. "Give it a swing. This one should split with a couple more whacks."

Morgan knew he was about to humiliate himself, but he had some strange urge to please Kazio. "Like this?" he said meekly before wielding the ax in an unsteady arc. He missed the split in the log and the blade glanced harmlessly off one side.

He braced himself for mockery or at least laughter, but there was nothing but kindness in Kazio's voice. "Try again."

He looked at Kazio, cringing. "I don't think I—"

"Morgan." Their gazes met. Kazio's eyes were twin flames. "You can do it. Try again."

Morgan's throat squeezed. "Okay." This time the blade found the cleft, but the wood only split another inch.

"There you go," Kazio said. "You've got it. Another one like that, but harder."

Morgan exhaled, then tried again, with a little extra oomph this time. The wood cracked a few more inches. One more swing, and it split through.

"You did it." Kazio grinned like Morgan had actually done something impressive.

He hadn't, but a warm glow spread through Morgan's chest anyway. "I've always been good at handling wood," he cracked.

Kazio picked up one of the split halves and stood it on the stump. "Try this one."

"More? I sort of hoped we were done."

"Not quite."

"Hmm… in that case I think I'd better watch you do a few more first. Really want to study that…technique."

"I don't know—I think you're ready to handle this wood. Let's see what you've got."

Chapter Five

Fucking Intense

It was finally time to relax.

They had carried the armfuls of firewood back in two trips, Morgan still flustered by the scent and sight of Kazio in lumberjack mode. The fluster did not improve as Kazio stacked the firewood and lit the fire with no problem. Was there any manly outdoorsy task he couldn't perform with ease?

The campfire was a cheerful affair, dancing and sparking into a dusky sky as the trees turned black around them and Kazio whistled over the grill. He had carefully laid out tin-foil pouches and flipped them over a few times as they cooked. Morgan sat next to him on the picnic table bench, keeping himself busy throwing bits of wood onto the fire and occasionally poking at the embers.

His stomach was rumbling by the time Kazio handed him a steaming pouch on a paper plate. "Dinner is served."

"What's in here?" Morgan asked, trying not to burn his fingers on the escaping steam.

"Gnocchi," Kazio said, "with Italian sausage, corn and tomatoes, plus butter, garlic, white wine and a few other seasonings."

Morgan had to laugh. "You cook better camping than I do at home."

Kazio didn't say anything, just peeled his own pouch open. The firelight gave his cheeks a pinkish hue.

Morgan took a big bite and closed his eyes in bliss as he chewed. "This is amazing. I can only imagine what you could do in a kitchen."

"I'll have to show you one day."

Morgan opened his eyes and found Kazio staring at him. The heat from the campfire hit Morgan's face, but he wasn't sure why his stomach swirled. "That would be…good," he stammered.

Kazio went back to his food. "You know what kind of job you should look for?"

"What's that?"

"One where you get to eat."

"Ha. I would be good at that." Morgan took another bite. "This is actually better than anything I have *ever* cooked before."

"Just make sure you save room for s'mores."

Morgan gasped. "There's s'mores?"

"Of course. That was the deal, wasn't it?"

"I can't wait to try one."

"Wait. You've never actually had s'mores before ever?"

"No."

"Oh. Oh my God. Okay." Kazio put his plate down and turned to dig through the rest of the food supplies. "We need to rectify this right away."

Morgan laughed. "I'm still eating my dinner."

"Doesn't matter." Kazio stood and strode into the bushes.

"Where are you going?" Morgan asked, with a twinge of nervousness when Kazio disappeared into the blackness.

He didn't reply, but returned a moment later carrying two sticks. "For roasting," he explained. He sat again and began sharpening the ends to points with a knife that materialized in his hand.

Knife work. Check.

Kazio stabbed a marshmallow onto the end of one of the sticks and handed it to Morgan. "Here you go. Toast that up."

"Um, okay." Morgan put his plate down and stuck his marshmallow into the fire.

"Er." Kazio scooted closer on the bench. "It'll char right in the flame like that. What you want to do is find a little oven... See, here, this pocket of coals..." He leaned closer to point.

"Oh." Morgan slid his marshmallow into the orange glow.

"There you go. Don't let it sit in one spot too long. Just keep rotating it. You want it golden brown."

Morgan's marshmallow caught on fire anyway. He panicked. "What do I do?"

"Pull it out!" Kazio said. He grabbed Morgan's stick and started blowing.

The flames extinguished, but the top of Morgan's marshmallow was blackened.

"It's okay, it'll still taste good," Kazio said. "Just try to toast the bottom now."

The bottom caught on fire too. Morgan blew his hardest, but before he could rescue it, the marshmallow slipped off the stick and tumbled to a fiery demise.

They watched its flaming corpse turn to ash.

"That was a good try," Kazio said after a beat. "Want me to toast one for you?"

Morgan leaned back against the table, arms crossed. "Sure."

"What's wrong?" Kazio asked.

"It's just that I'm...completely helpless. You carried everything, you set up the tent, you cooked. I can't even toast my own fucking marshmallow. I'm like a child you have to take care of."

"It's just a particular skill set. You're good at lots of things I'm not."

Morgan scoffed. "Tell that to Bennett and her fake eyelashes."

"Fuck that job, anyway. You don't want to work with a bunch of snobs. You should have a job where you're appreciated."

The flames blurred under Morgan's distant gaze. "I wouldn't even know what that feels like."

Kazio handed Morgan's plate back to him. "Let's finish dinner. We can try s'mores again after."

Morgan swallowed a few more spoonfuls, mollified by the deliciousness.

"When I first arrived here from Poland," Kazio said after his next bite, "I didn't know what I was doing *anywhere*. My English was pretty rough, and I had a lot to learn."

"Well, I grew up here," Morgan muttered.

"You just have things to learn in new situations too, is all I'm saying. Put me in a recording studio and I wouldn't even know how to turn the equipment on."

Morgan sighed. "That's the *only* place I know what I'm doing."

Kazio poked at the fire. It crackled and popped, launching an ember skyward. Morgan lifted his chin to follow its progress up into the night.

"Would you sing something for me?" Kazio asked.

The meaning of the question hit Morgan slowly, like he had to process each word separately.

"Sing?" he repeated. Surely Kazio didn't actually want to listen to him *sing* right now. "I don't have a guitar."

"I don't mind. I'd like to hear it."

"Okay then, if you're sure. Um, let's see, what's good for campfire *acapella*...?" He mentally flipped through his favorites, tossing aside the ones that required belting, which was most of them. Then it came to him. "All right, here we go." He started to sing *Stand By Me*. He kept it soft and low-key, his eyes on the dancing flames. And the same magic that happened every time he sang took over. The feeling that his heart was too big for his chest...too big for the whole planet. Maybe even the entire universe. The feeling that told him all he was meant to do was perform.

When he was done, the forest around sat silent. The fire had even stopped crackling. Morgan picked up a stick and poked at the wood.

There was nothing from Kazio either. When he couldn't stand it anymore, Morgan looked at him.

Kazio was staring back like a man who had seen a ghost. "That was..." He licked his lips. "That was gorgeous."

Morgan flushed. "Nah. It's better with my guitar."

"Morgan, I mean it—you're so talented. You *could* be a rock star."

"Rock stars need a band." Morgan jabbed at the fire some more.

"Then let's get you one."

"I've been trying for years. It's so hard to find enough people who can actually *play*, who will commit to all the rehearsal *and* who don't make you want to scratch your eyes out when you spend hours at a time with them."

"Yeah, that must be hard. But I'll do whatever I can to help you find them. You need to sing."

"Thanks," Morgan mumbled.

Kazio handed Morgan a roasting stick with another marshmallow ready. "Let's try again."

And try he did. Turned out, Morgan wasn't that bad at roasting marshmallows.

* * * *

Morgan stood and let out a moan when his muscles protested. "What I wouldn't give for a hot bath right now." The campfire had dwindled to a small orange flicker.

"That would be nice," Kazio admitted. "All I can offer is a tent."

"Fine." Morgan sniffed. "But you owe me a bath." As content as he was with a full belly, it was painful leaving the heat of the campfire for sharp, cold night air.

Morgan's bedtime routine was impossible to execute without warm running water, but he did the best he could with face wipes and a few tubes of cream. It was a little awkward climbing into his sleeping bag on a mat right next to Kazio, but the awkwardness was forgotten when the thinness of the air mattress became his most pressing concern. He wiggled around trying to get comfortable, to no avail.

"You good?" Kazio asked.

"Yeah, there's just a tree root or something digging into my back…"

"Do you want to swap places?"

"No, I always have to sleep on this side."

"Good. Because this is my side."

Morgan wiggled some more. The tiny inflatable pillows were pretty awful too.

"Are you going to do that all night, though?" Kazio asked. "'Cause…"

Morgan paused to consider what natural objects were now poking into his body and decided his current spot was the best he could do. "I think this works. I just can't move at all throughout the night."

"Okay. Goodnight." Kazio rolled into his back. His profile was just visible in the darkness thanks to the glow from a gibbous moon.

A twig snapped outside.

Morgan half sat up. "Are you sure there's no bears?"

"I'm sure. I've been camping here for ten years and I've never seen a bear."

"Okay."

"A few cougars, maybe."

Morgan lurched the whole way up. "*What*?"

A soft chortle from beside him. "I'm kidding. I'm sorry."

Morgan tried to settle back down but the tree root had returned. He muttered a curse and scooted toward Kazio, but recoiled when their shoulders bumped. He didn't want Kazio to think he was making a move. "I've never slept next to a man without…you know… sleeping with him," Morgan told him.

"You haven't?"

"No. A lot of firsts for me on this trip, I guess."

"Oh. Yeah."

It was weird, actually. When Morgan was around men he was attracted to, assuming they liked men, sex was always on the table. But with Kazio, it wasn't. Kazio would not be into someone as unserious as Morgan, and deserved so much better anyway. Kazio was obviously not interested in anything more than friendship. A friendship that had, in fact, completely snuck up on Morgan, and somehow led to him lying on the forest floor.

Not that he wouldn't mind some sex. His dry spell was at a length now that was embarrassing. It had been months since his last hookups, not long after Luka broke up with him—a couple random dudes that had led to mediocre sex. The sex with Luka, though... God, they were good together in bed. Passionate and intense, grasping hands and whispered words, soft sighs and even some gentle laughter. It was the best sex he'd ever had.

Kazio shifted next to him.

Probably best not to think about sex right now. Maybe he should just focus on trying to sleep. Except...

Morgan shivered. "It's freezing."

Kazio rolled over to face him. His features were soft in the dim light. "Do you have any other clothes you can put on?"

"I think I'm already wearing them all."

"That's all the clothes you brought? What happened to the packing list I sent you?"

"I didn't think I'd need two pairs of pants."

"Okay, well..." Kazio's voice dropped lower. "Body heat helps."

"What do you mean? You want to cuddle?" That idea was not helping him not think about sex.

"No, but if you're really cold, we could zip our sleeping bags together."

"So we'd…"

"Be sharing a big sleeping bag, yes."

He was really fucking cold though. "If you're okay with it."

"I'm the one that suggested it."

"All right, fine."

Morgan crawled out of his bag, teeth chattering, while Kazio opened both bags then zipped them back together.

Kazio climbed into the sleeping bag, then held up the flap for Morgan. "Hop in."

Morgan squirmed in next to Kazio. Kazio zipped the bag the rest of the way.

Their shoulders touched and the warmth instantly comforted Morgan. "That's better," he said, scooting even closer. Kazio was so warm. Morgan tilted his head to rest it on Kazio's shoulder. "Thanks. You're hot. I mean…your body is hot. I mean…" Now Morgan's face was *too* warm. "The body heat thing is good, thanks. I'm hot now."

"Good." The smile on Kazio's face was evident in his voice.

Warm and cozy, Morgan fell asleep quickly, the scent of pine in his nostrils.

* * * *

Morgan woke, confused by the smell of nylon and the gray-blue glow around him. Then he remembered he was camping, and for another few seconds, listened to the morning bird song and the gentle rustling of wind in the trees. For five more seconds, he was aware of Kazio's warm, solid body next to him and the reassuring rhythm of his breath. Then his nervous system caught up and informed him that there was a rock digging into his spine, the air in the tent was suffocating and his bladder screamed for relief. And still worse, the air outside of their cozy sleeping bag cocoon was arctic.

He rolled over and burrowed deeper into the cocoon, trying to forget how badly he had to pee.

"Good morning." Kazio's voice proved a welcome distraction.

"Morning."

"How did you sleep?"

"Pretty good actually, but…"

"You need to pee?"

"I need to pee."

"Yeah, this is the worst part about camping."

"I don't know about *worst*," Morgan said, "but it's not my favorite." He stretched and yawned. His bladder registered its displeasure. "Okay, I have to get up."

"Go ahead," Kazio said, stretching himself. Morgan noted his angular jaw in profile. "I'll get the fire going and boil some water for tea."

Morgan relieved himself and did his best to brush some of the fuzz from his teeth. Kazio was waiting by the fire with a mug of tea and bagels toasting on the grill.

Maybe he could get used to this camping thing.

Chapter Six

I Get Off at Eight

They pulled to a stop in front of Morgan's building.

"I need a shower so badly," Morgan moaned. "I've never felt so gross in my life."

Kazio gave him the amused eye twinkle again. "We were gone for one day."

"Day and a half, at least."

"Well, you don't look gross."

Morgan shuddered. "I don't know if I'll ever get the smell of campfire out of my hair. And I don't even want to *think* about my pores."

"I'm sure you'll clean up fine."

They hopped out with the engine still running. Kazio retrieved Morgan's bag from the back and handed it to him.

"Thanks. And thanks for bringing me with you." Morgan squinted up at him in the bright sunlight. "I...learned a lot. And the food was..." He offered a chef's kiss.

"Anytime." Kazio fiddled with his backpack, sliding it over to fill the space left by Morgan's.

The urge to hug Kazio surged through his body, which was weird, because he was not a hugger. But he decided to go for it. When Kazio looked at him again, he stepped closer and slid his arms around Kazio's waist. Kazio's eyes widened for a second, then he hugged Morgan back.

Morgan had always described himself as petite, but being tucked under Kazio's chin really highlighted how small he was compared to him. Then the size difference fled from his mind as the smell hit him. Campfire, of course, but also pine, earth and sweat—the spicy, musky kind. The kind that found some chemical receptor in Morgan's brain and lit it on fire.

But the hug... It was a really good hug. Morgan melted into Kazio's solid frame, taking in every detail he could—the large expanse of back under his fingers, the strand of Kazio's hair tickling his nose, the hard chest under his cheek...

Maybe he *was* a hugger.

Maybe...it was just that he had had no one to hug for a while. Especially not since his mom had passed away and his dad had remarried a woman half his age and...left. He had never really had a lot of friends either. He had hung out with the guys in the band and people at work, and now he had neither of those.

"Morgan?" Kazio said, without letting go.

Morgan took in another deep breath of pine. "Yeah?"

"Are you okay?"

"Yeah. Sorry. I—" He started to pull him away, but Kazio held him tighter.

"Don't be sorry."

The hug continued until Morgan's eyes started to water. He pulled away, blinking back the startling display of emotion. "I, uh… Thanks."

Kazio put his hands in his pockets. "You're welcome."

"See you soon, I guess?" Morgan tried to nonchalantly wipe away the bead of liquid threatening to spill down his cheek.

"Yes." Kazio hesitated like he might say something else, then he nodded and smiled and climbed back into his vehicle.

Morgan headed inside, but paused at the front door first to watch Kazio's SUV disappear around a corner. His apartment was a welcome sight, with floors, running water and a lack of dirt…but it also felt empty.

Stripped naked, Morgan threw everything into the washing machine and went straight to the shower. He washed his hair three times, exfoliated his whole body twice and scrubbed everywhere again with his favorite citrus body wash for good measure.

After a thorough layer of moisturizer, he put on light, comfy sweats, left his pack on the balcony to air out, lit a candle and sat on his couch with a seltzer and a bowl of popcorn. He turned on the dumb show with the gods in loincloths and put his feet up on the coffee table.

He wished Kazio were there.

* * * *

Morgan's dream that night featured Kazio in lumberjack mode and he woke up with his own kind of wood. "Oh, God. What are you doing, Morgan?" he muttered. "Stop perving after your friend." He was a little slow to get out of bed, trying to refocus on more appropriate thoughts. But once he did, he made breakfast and sat down with his laptop to scroll job listings again.

A music school was hiring guitar teachers, but he *really* didn't see himself teaching. Not enough qualifications for a music therapist. A local theater was looking for an audio engineer, although it was only part time. And a local radio station needed a programming director. Not that he was dying to get back into radio, but at least he was qualified for that one...ish.

He applied for the audio engineer and programming director positions, then sent Kazio a text.

Why do they make you upload your resume, but then put all your work experience in little boxes too?

Kazio's reply came a minute later as Morgan was making tea.

I don't know, that sounds annoying. I like to hire people who come in with a resume and talk to me. Where did you apply?

Morgan told him. *I need more than part time but maybe it'll be a good starting point. It would be fun to work in a theater.*

Yeah, for sure. Good luck with those. Did you get the campfire smell out of your hair?

I think so. I can't smell it anymore anyway. Morgan carried his mug to the living room and plopped onto the couch. *How did the pub do without you?*

Fine, I guess. Tasha says it's less stressful without me there.

Why is that? Morgan blew on his tea and took a sip even though it was still a little too hot.

Apparently some of the kitchen staff are afraid of me.

They are? Although he wasn't that surprised, to be honest. Kazio could definitely seem intimidating at first.

It's fine. I'm not mean or anything, I just like things done a certain way. Like, if you can't remember to hang up the knives in the right order, you're asking to be corrected.

Morgan smiled at his phone. *The knives have a certain order?*

Don't make me correct you too.

He would be lying if he said the idea of a bossy Kazio didn't make his blood pump a little faster. *You'll have to teach me the knife order. I wouldn't want to mess that up.*

I'll make sure to. What are you up to today?

Morgan looked around his apartment still strewn with the clothing he did not pack for camping. *Absolutely nothing.*

Do you want to come by for a drink later?

Sure. Around nine?

See you then.

* * * *

Morgan didn't even get an interview for the theater. The radio station brought him in, but it was a bust after Morgan accidentally let it slip that he hadn't liked working at his last radio station job.

"You didn't...like it?" the man asked, eyebrow raised. He was thin, pallid and clearly unhappy with his life.

"Er..." *Fuck.* "It's not that I didn't *like* it, it's just that...I didn't feel it made the best use of my skills."

He thought he rallied nicely, but Thin Pallid Man gave him a cold smile. "Thank you. We'll be in touch."

They did not get in touch.

Over the next week, he applied for booking agent at the arena, instrument technician at a recording studio and another event coordinator, not just an assistant this time, at a different, moderately less fancy downtown hotel.

He thought he nailed the interview at the arena, but the email said they "ultimately had to go with another candidate who more closely met their needs at this time." The instrument tech application didn't get him a response.

The lack of a job was starting to be a problem.

He was sitting on his couch in pajamas eating instant ramen when an email arrived inviting him for an interview for event coordinator at the Redwood Hotel.

Morgan put his food down and texted Kazio.

I got an interview at the Redwood.

That's great, Kazio replied. *Good luck.*

At this point I need more than luck. Morgan scrubbed his face. *Ugh, why doesn't anyone want me?*

I'm sure someone wants you, Kazio said, encouraging as ever.

Let's hope whoever interviews me at the Redwood is that someone.

* * * *

The someone at the Redwood was Albert, and he was super fucking hot—tall, lean and smiley, with tousled hair and gorgeous green eyes.

"So, Morgan," Albert said, studying his resume with a full, pouty lower lip on display, "what makes you a good fit for this position?"

"Well," Morgan said, admiring the way a single curl flopped onto Albert's forehead, "I can manage all of the AV equipment no problem. I know how to set everything up to optimize the sound quality to make sure the guests—"

"That's not really a huge part of this role," Albert interrupted. "I mean, sure, you would need to plug in some speakers, but we really need someone more for the administrative, organizational side."

Morgan frowned. "Like a secretary?"

Albert tilted his head. "That skill set would be useful. Managing vendors, seating charts, clients… mainly making sure the event goes off without a hitch. You have to do it all."

"Okay, well, I can..." Morgan faded into silence, picturing himself running around a ballroom, headset and clipboard in place, while high-society Karens screamed at him about the temperature of the beef tourtières and shrimp tartlets. "I actually...don't think this is the job for me."

Albert had been tapping a pen against his lip. He paused, raising an eyebrow. "Oh?"

"Yeah." Morgan stood. "Sorry for wasting your time."

Albert stood as well and offered Morgan a handshake, giving him an extra squeeze before he let go. "I'm sorry this won't work, but I appreciate your honesty."

"Thanks."

Albert's green gaze lingered on him as he left.

Morgan stepped onto the sidewalk, dejected. *You are so bad at this,* he told himself. *You are never going to find a job. You're going to be an unemployed loser for life.* The uncertainty of his future overwhelmed him at that moment—he didn't know what to do now, what direction to head—but when he spotted a Hole-in-One across the street, he at least knew that he needed carbs.

An iced vanilla cream coffee and a doughnut later, he didn't feel any better. The lump of sugar hardened in his stomach, and when he got up to go, he somehow spilled the remains of his drink onto his khakis.

The wet brown patch on his thigh mocked him. *Loser.*

Right then a message from Kazio popped up.

How did the interview go?

Worst one yet, Morgan informed him. *And that's saying something.*

You never know, they might still like you.

Oh, no, I took care of that entirely. I told the guy it wasn't the job for me and I left.

Oh.

A caustic laugh bubbled up Morgan's throat. *Yeah. 'Oh.'*

Three dots, then, *Hey, what if I made you dinner tomorrow night? Might cheer you up. I can cook anything you like.*

The kindness nearly brought tears to his eyes. *Wow. That would be awesome. Yes. Yes, please.*

Great. What can I make for you?

Whatever is your favorite thing to cook.

You got it. Six o'clock tomorrow?

I'll be there. Just send me your address.

He blotted at the spill on his thigh one more time and headed for the door. He bumped into a tall man coming in.

It was Albert. His mouth curled into a suggestive grin when their eyes met. "Oh, Morgan. Hi."

"Hi," Morgan said, instantly reliving the shame of bailing mid-interview. "Listen, I'm so sorry about—"

Albert waved it away. "Please, forget about it. If it's not the right job for you then why would you want it?"

"Right."

"So…need another coffee?" he asked, indicating the stain on Morgan's pants.

"Oh, God. No. No, I'm good, thanks. I think I've had all the caffeine I can take today."

"In that case…can I buy you a drink later tonight?"

Record scratch. Freeze frame. The hot guy wanted to go for a drink? Yes, it seemed the hot guy wanted to go for a drink. The hot guy with the long legs and noticeable bulge who was looking at him with those eyes. Blowing off some steam with Albert was probably a really good idea, before he had any more horny dreams about Kazio. "Absolutely."

Those eyes swept up and down Morgan's body. Albert smiled. "Great. I get off at eight."

* * * *

They met at a bar downtown, something all glass and metal with early 2000s club music blaring. Their chemistry was easy and instant, the conversation light and bantery.

On their second drink, Albert leaned over to rumble in Morgan's ear. "I was kind of glad you left the interview today, to be honest."

"Oh yeah?" Morgan said. The heat from the nearness of Albert's body gave him goosebumps.

"Yeah, because I wanted to do this." Albert took Morgan's chin in his fingers and kissed him.

It was a nice kiss. Soft and gentle, but not lacking in heat. Morgan kissed back.

Albert put his hand on Morgan's knee and slid it up his thigh. He pulled away an inch to smolder at him. "Want to get out of here?"

Morgan's dick stirred. "Yes."

They made out in the cab on the way back to Morgan's place, then fell onto the couch, hands and lips wandering, clothes flying. They had sex right there on the couch, then again later in Morgan's bed.

They were lying together, naked and cozy under the duvet, when Morgan sighed. "So happy I walked out of that interview."

Albert laughed. "You don't want to work there anyway. It sucks."

"Does it suck more than looking for a job? I've been rejected everywhere, and they're not even jobs I want. I'm such an utter failure that my friend is cooking dinner for me tomorrow night to cheer me up."

"Friend?"

"Yeah. His name is Kazio. He's been helping me look for a job."

"Sounds like a good friend."

"He is. Sort of a new friend but he's...he's been really supportive."

"Hmm... Are you sure this friend doesn't think cooking you dinner is a date?"

"What?" Morgan went up on an elbow and looked at Albert. "It's not a date."

"Okay. It sounds like it might be though. He's a new friend, been really supportive, making you dinner...at his place?"

"It's not a date. Trust me—we're just friends." Morgan lay back down, resting a hand under his head. It wasn't a date. Was it? No. No, of course it wasn't. Kazio was just a super nice guy who felt sorry for him.

Albert shrugged. "If you say so." He leaned over to kiss Morgan and trailed his hand down his chest. "You got one more in you?"

"I guess that's up to you," Morgan said with an eyebrow waggle.

Albert rolled on top of him. "Then I would say yes, you're about to."

Chapter Seven

Dinner. Date?

Kazio lived in a nice, average house in a nice, average neighborhood. The yard was simple, the landscaping tidy and subdued. He opened the door before Morgan could knock. Kazio smiled, so handsome in a soft, gray sweater.

"Hi." Morgan held out the paper bag he carried. "This is for you."

"Hi. Thanks." Kazio took it from him and peeked inside.

"I didn't know what to bring. You don't have to open it right now." Morgan knew he had to arrive with something, obviously, but he had realized in the store that he didn't have much of an idea of what Kazio might like. So he took a shot.

"Well, thank you. Please, come in."

Morgan wiped his feet on the mat and stepped inside. Warm cherry floors contrasted with white walls and black accents. A large mirror on one side faced bench seating and coat hooks. Not a speck of dust or hint of clutter to be seen. "Your place is really nice," he said.

"Thanks. You can wear a pair of those slippers."

"Oh." Morgan slipped his shoes into the cubby underneath the bench and found a pair of sheepskin slippers. "Cute. Thanks." He followed Kazio down the hall. The mouth-watering aroma hit him full force before they got to the kitchen. "That smells incredible. What are you making?"

"Pierogi."

"Yum!" Saliva flooded his mouth as the kitchen came into view. It looked like the set of a glamorous cooking show—shiny pots and pans steaming and bubbling on a fancy stove, colorful ingredients prepped and ready in white ceramic bowls—the space messy and tidy at the same time. The kitchen was light and airy, a remodel that was a lot newer than the house itself. Open shelves were stacked with simple white dishes, and pots and pans hung from the rack above the huge island. Knives displayed along the wall on a magnetic strip spiked Morgan's anxiety—what if he had to remember the order? "Wow, your kitchen is…impressive."

"Thank you. I renovated a year ago." Kazio rubbed one of the quartz countertops with great affection. "I'll get to the rest of the house eventually." Kazio put the paper bag on the side counter by the wet bar and began pulling items out—a bottle of wine, a box of chocolates, a cooking magazine and a red spatula. He held up the spatula with a questioning glance.

"Um, a lady at the store said it was her favorite spatula."

Kazio didn't look any less puzzled.

"Because, you know…you like cooking."

"Oh. Ohhh. Well, thank you, for all of it. You didn't need to bring anything." Kazio went back to the stove and stirred a pan of onions and mushrooms with a wooden spoon. "Can I get you a glass of wine?"

"Sure, thanks."

"Actually, why don't you go ahead? Glasses are there, wine is in the cooler." He pointed at the wet bar then lifted a lid to peek at the contents of a pot.

"Oh, sure." Morgan opened the beverage fridge and studied the rows of white wine. "Any of these?"

"Sure, grab whatever you like."

Morgan skipped over the Sartini labels, 'cause fuck Breakpoint and their big fancy client, and held up an aromatic white. "How's this?"

"Perfect."

Morgan removed two wine glasses from the rack above the bar and poured them each a full glass. He'd cabbed here, after all. "Here you go," he said, delivering a glass to Kazio, then he sat at the island with his wine and the rest of the bottle.

"Thanks." Kazio paused his stirring and leaned against the counter. "Your hair is getting longer."

"Oh, yeah." Morgan ran a self-conscious hand over his head. "I missed my last haircut." His unemployment had finally started coming in but a haircut still felt like an extra expense.

"It looks good longer."

Morgan's cheeks flushed. "Thank you."

Kazio picked up his wine glass, a tendril of hair falling over an eye. "Sorry about that interview yesterday."

Morgan blinked. The Redwood interview seemed like a hundred years ago. "Oh, it's fine. I actually..."

Morgan chuckled, a little embarrassed. "I ended up sleeping with the guy who interviewed me."

Kazio froze, wine halfway to his lips. "You what?"

"Yeah." Morgan spun the glass stem between his fingers. "I know, kind of slutty. I ran into him at a Hole-in-One across the street and he asked me for a drink. And then, well… something about one in a hole."

"Oh." Kazio took a sip. "Great."

Morgan swallowed a gulp of wine. "Yeah, it was fun. He was really hot."

Kazio turned to a chopping board and began slicing cabbage, knife whisking through the layers in a most satisfying manner.

"You aren't judging me, are you?" Morgan tried to laugh but it came out a little strangled.

"No." Kazio's knife hammered on the board, *thunk, thunk, thunk.*

"It was funny, he — Albert, his name was Albert — said he thought this was a date."

Kazio slowed for half a second, then the chopping resumed. "Thought what was a date?"

"You know…" Morgan waved a hand between the two of them. "*This.*"

Kazio didn't look up from his chopping board. "Hmm."

Morgan gripped his wine glass like it was keeping him afloat in a choppy ocean, while his stomach plunged to the bottom of the watery abyss. "Kazio…this is probably a stupid question, but…this isn't a date, is it?"

There was no pause this time. "Of course not." His knife was a blur through the cabbage.

"Okay, I didn't think so. It's just that Albert said maybe it sounded like one and I didn't want to show up thinking it wasn't and it actually *was*, because that would have been—I mean, it's not like I..." His lungs were desperate for a fresh breath. "But yeah, of course it's not, that's what I told him. Sorry I even brought it up."

"It's fine." Kazio pointed at the fridge with his knife. "Could you grab a red pepper?"

"Yeah, sure." Morgan hopped up and opened the massive fridge, unable to shake the sense that he had done something wrong. "Wow, you could probably get trapped in here too, hey?" He found a red pepper in the crisper drawer and put it down next to the cutting board, careful to keep his fingers far from the blade.

"Yeah, probably." Kazio finished with the cabbage and attacked the pepper. "Are you going to see him again, you think?"

"Who, Albert? I don't know. It sort of felt...one-night-stand-y. When he left he said he'd text me but...we'll see."

"Are you okay with that?"

"Um...yeah? It was just...fun, you know?" *And all I'm good for.* Morgan took another sip of wine, very ready to change the subject, and worried what might happen if Kazio chopped any faster. "In the meantime, the job hunt continues, but I'm not sure where else to apply."

Kazio finally paused his knife and took a sip of wine. "I was thinking—what if we updated your resume?"

"Update it? With what? I don't have any other experience."

"You could do some volunteer work."

"Volun... You want me to volunteer somewhere?"

Kazio raised his eyes to the ceiling for a brief moment. "I mean...the idea of volunteer work is that you do it voluntarily, so it's not about what I want. I just thought it might beef up your resume a little."

"Where would I volunteer?"

"Anywhere you'd like to contribute."

Morgan drained his glass as he considered. "Do you volunteer?"

"I used to help out at the animal shelter all the time. I haven't been as much lately but I just got an email that they're needing more volunteers."

Morgan scrunched his face. "An animal shelter?"

"Yes. I thought you might want to go with me sometime and check it out." Kazio retrieved a cadet-blue ceramic salad bowl from a shelf and started putting the salad together.

"What do you do there?"

"Anything that needs to be done, really. I walk dogs, clean cages—"

Morgan shuddered. "Pass."

"It's nothing major. And it's fun getting to spend time with the animals. Did you never have a pet as a kid?"

"Ha! No. My dad would never. All that hair and slobber and you have to pick up their poop…"

"That's too bad." Kazio's eyes were soft and nostalgic. "We always had a few cats."

A piece of the Kazio puzzle snapped into place in Morgan's brain. "So you're an animal person."

Kazio shrugged. "I like animals. The unconditional love and affection you get from them—" He paused, flushing. "But yeah, they can be messy."

Yup. Animal person. Morgan poured himself some more wine and topped up Kazio's glass. "Why don't you have a pet now?"

"I work such long hours at the pub. I couldn't take care of a pet properly."

"You should get a pet," Morgan decided.

Kazio shrugged again and turned off the elements on the stove. "Dinner's ready. Bring the wine."

* * * *

Kazio had set two places together at the far end of the island, with a candle and small jar of white roses and hyacinths.

"Wow, this is all so amazing," Morgan said as Kazio placed a plate in front of him, the pierogi steaming, topped with mushroom and onion and accompanied by a colorful cabbage salad.

"I hope it's good." Kazio settled next to him.

"I have no doubt." Morgan tore into his meal, proclaiming its deliciousness every bite or two.

After his next glass of wine was emptied, Morgan paused. "I have to ask… This vibe—" He waved his knife at the flowers and candle on the quartz countertop. "This is not what you have going on at the Exchange at all."

"I left the 'vibe,' as you say, pretty much the way it was. I just tried to improve the menu, the bar selection and the way the kitchen was run."

"Interesting." Morgan took another bite, studying Kazio as he chewed. "I'm gonna figure you out one day. God*damnit*, this is good. Feel free to cook for me anytime you want."

"I appreciate the offer. There's lots more if you're hungry."

Morgan ate and drank way too much as the night went on, but those were the best pierogies—sorry, pierogi—he'd ever had in his life.

They were well into their third bottle when thick pieces of chocolate strawberry mousse cake materialized in front of him. "I couldn't possibly," Morgan said, before devouring the entire serving.

The room spun when he got up to pee. "Oh... I...I'm a little drunk."

"You don't say." Kazio moved Morgan's wine glass away from the edge of the counter. "You want to crash here tonight?"

"Nah." Morgan steadied himself on his chair. "I can... I should go home."

The bathroom had a painting of a sandy seashore, whites and blues and greens in thick dabs of paint. Morgan imagined falling right into the waves. They looked so soothing. He'd just float there a while. "You're amazing," he said to Kazio back in the hallway. "So amazing. This was so fun."

"Mm-hmm," Kazio said. "Your shoes, Morgan."

"Right." Shoes.

Kazio's hand on his elbow. "Watch your step."

"Thank you," Morgan said. "You were right. This did cheer me up." His cab waited at the curb, a yellow square of light in the darkness.

"Good." Kazio was a silhouette in the doorway, expression unreadable. "Goodnight, Morgan."

"G'night."

* * * *

He slept until well past noon and woke up with a fucking headache.

"Ugh," Morgan muttered, reaching for his phone. He had a new text waiting from Kazio that said *Water. Please.* Except, oh God. There were more. He scrolled back in the thread. Apparently he had texted Kazio from the cab. A lot.

First he had sent *No but srsly ur Amazing*

So you said, was Kazio's reply.

Thankks for bein g mfy fiend. Then he tried again. *My fernd.* Once more. *my friend!!!!*

You're welcome.

I dont kno why ur so nice to me. Morgan's testicles shriveled at the cringe. *Why. Whyyy.*

Drink some water when you get home, Kazio had replied. *You're hammered.*

But Morgan's next message got worse. *Shold I ask Albert out a giann?*

Kazio, bless him, had used all caps for the first time. *Dear God, Morgan, whatever you do, DO NOT TEXT ALBERT NOW.*

Oh fuck. Please no... Chanting a prayer in his head, Morgan swiped over to his thread with Albert, breath held. *Please, please, please... Shit.* He had texted Albert too. His stomach flipped.

Itt wasnt a daete was all he had sent, thank God.

Could have been so much worse. Albert hadn't responded though, so still...super embarrassing.

He went back to his thread with Kazio, face burning. There was more.

I like ur gay sweater

Gray wsweater. also gay too thoug

"Oh my God," Morgan groaned. "I am such a *loser*." He buried his face in his hand. *Just end me.*

That was when Kazio had sent the final *Water. Please.*

Blessedly, it appeared Morgan had passed out as soon as he got home before he could further embarrass himself.

Morgan got up to pee and have that water before shuffling into the kitchen in his sweats. He paused, frowning, at a puddle on the floor, which puzzled him until he saw the white hyacinths and roses on the counter, with almost no water left in the jar. Weird. He had no memory of carrying them home.

He mopped up the spill, refilled the jar, then made some tea and sat at the table with the flowers. It was time to bite the bullet and text Kazio.

Thanks for the flowers? he sent. *And for dinner. In case I didn't say it last night.*

You're welcome, Kazio replied right away. *You insisted on taking the flowers with you. But you did say thank you last night. Several times. You said a lot of things.*

Morgan's stomach heaved. *Oh God. Yeah, sorry about those texts too.*

It's fine. It was cute.

Cute? His cheeks flared. *Is typo-filled drunken rambling cute?*

Maybe.

I hope Albert thinks so too. I messaged him.

You did?? Morgan! What did you say?

It's okay, it wasn't too bad. I just told him that last night wasn't a date.

Did he reply?

No. Not yet. Morgan took a tentative sip of his too-hot tea.

Good luck. Let me know if he does.

I will.

And let me know when you hear back from the animal shelter.

Morgan paused, then put his tea back down. *What? Hear back from them?*

Yes… You submitted a volunteer application last night.

I did??? Morgan checked his email. Indeed, there was a message from the shelter.

"Thank you for your interest… Your application will be reviewed…"

Oh, I guess I did. I hope they also like typo-filled drunken rambling.

I proofread it for you. You'll be fine. They're just happy to have anyone.

We'll see about that.

Chapter Eight

Drew, Ralph and Grumpy Cat

Kazio picked him up bright and early on Saturday morning.

"This is almost as bad as camping," Morgan proclaimed when he got into Kazio's SUV. "Why does everything you like to do start so early?"

"The pub doesn't open early."

"That makes even less sense then, because you're up both late and early."

Kazio opened his mouth to respond, but paused. "That's a good point, actually. It is a bit weird. I get by on less sleep than most, I think."

"Do you? You're not tired right now?"

"No."

"Well, I'm tired." Morgan fastened his seatbelt with a pout. "At least with camping there were s'mores."

Kazio nodded at a bag and cup from Hole-in-One sitting in the console. "That's for you."

Morgan gasped. "It is?" He resisted the urge to kiss Kazio on the cheek and instead pulled his sandwich from the bag with great delight. "Okay, so far, camping and animal shelter are tied."

The Mountain Meadow Animal Care Center was near the southern edge of the city, where fields and orchards stretched fresh and verdant between the thinning houses, and the purple mountains rose from the rolling foothills in the distance. The center looked a bit like it belonged on a farm, a long, low, narrow building cobbled together and patched up over the years. They parked in the dirt lot. A lone gray cat stretched out on the fence eyed them sleepily.

"Do the cats run wild here?" Morgan asked as they climbed out. He had not imagined animals roaming about.

"That's the owner's cat, Drew." Kazio joined him on the front walk.

"The cat's name is Drew? Or the owner?"

"The cat. What are you wearing?"

"What?" Morgan looked down at his outfit. Kazio had suggested he wear 'appropriate clothing.' What was more appropriate than this?

"Is that Grumpy Cat on your shirt?" Kazio asked.

"Yes."

"Why…why do you have a Grumpy Cat T-shirt?"

"You said to wear clothes I didn't mind getting dirty. I don't mind getting it dirty, and it's got a cat on it. It's perfect."

"No, but like…why do you *have* it?"

"Oh. Someone thought they were hilarious and gave it to me for the Secret Santa my first Christmas at Breakpoint. Pretty sure it was Finn. He's not as funny as he thinks he is."

The corner of Kazio's mouth twitched. "You're right, it's perfect."

Drew hopped off the fence and led them inside.

A soft chime dinged when Kazio opened the door. Morgan wrinkled his nose at the smell.

But before he could say anything, Kazio leaned over and whispered in his ear. "Do not say it smells weird."

"I was going to say it smells *bad*, actually," Morgan whispered back.

Kazio gave him a warning glare as they approached the front desk.

The woman behind the counter burst into a huge smile when she saw them. "Kazio!" She was maybe in her early fifties, in jeans and a faded green staff polo, Black with long box braids tied back and warm, kind eyes. She came out from behind the counter and enveloped Kazio in a huge hug. "It has been way too long!"

"Camella!" Kazio replied. "I know, I know, I'm sorry. Work's been so busy..."

She pulled away and studied his face. "I get it, hon." She turned to Morgan. "And who's this handsome man?"

Morgan flushed. He liked her already.

"This is my friend, Morgan. This is his first time here."

"Morgan, right! We just got your application. And with Kazio as a reference, I had no doubt." Before he knew it, Camella was hugging him too. There was a softness to it that Morgan hadn't felt in a long time. "It's so nice to meet you, Morgan."

"You too." He blinked away the emotion gathering in his eyes.

The gray cat hopped up onto the counter. Camella tsked but gathered him into her arms and stroked his head. "I see you've met Drew. He runs the place."

"Yes, we met Drew." Morgan gave the cat's head a scritch. "He's sweet."

"Hush! His opinion of himself is already much too high, isn't it?" Camella tossed the cat toward the doorway. Drew landed with an offended glance, then strolled out, tail in the air, as if that had been his plan all along.

"So, what's new with you?" Kazio asked, looking around the lobby. A few worn vinyl chairs lined the front wall, accompanied by a rack of animal magazines. The other wall displayed beautiful framed photographs of cats and dogs taken by a photographer who clearly adored those animals, showing their humanity and personality in loving close-ups. They made Morgan want to smile.

"Oh, you know." Camella waved a hand around the room. "Same old. So many animals, never enough time, money, or volunteers, but we do what we can. What about you?"

"Same old for me, too." His eyes shifted over to Morgan. "Mostly."

"And what do you do for work, Morgan?"

"I, er..."

"Morgan's a musician," Kazio said. "You should hear him sing."

Morgan's cheeks flared again. "I..." Why was it so embarrassing having Kazio gush about him?

"Oh, are you, now? Lacy was a singer, too..." Camella trailed off, eyes sad and distant for a moment, then she snapped back to attention. "Well, we're thrilled to have you both here. Why don't you sign in and I'll show you around? A few things have changed since you were here last, Kazio."

"A personal tour?" Kazio whistled. "Don't I feel special."

"You stop." Camella swatted Kazio's forearm. "Let me know when you're ready."

Kazio showed Morgan where to sign in at the volunteer station and handed him an apron.

"Why is your name tag yellow and mine's green?" Morgan asked as he stuck the label to his shirt.

"You're just a baby volunteer." Kazio patted Morgan's shoulder. "You have to log fifty hours to get to yellow." Kazio's name tag hung in a plastic Mountain Meadow lanyard.

"Fifty! That's a lot."

"It goes by fast."

Morgan studied Kazio as they went to find Camella—he was practically bouncing on his toes, eyes bright, smile not far from his lips. He really, really liked it there.

They stopped at the framed photos again. "These are gorgeous," Kazio said to Camella as she came over to join them.

Camella smiled, hands on her hips. "Lacy took them all. I finally got them blown up and framed."

"That's a beautiful idea. She would have loved it."

Camella squeezed Kazio's arm. "Let's start in the kennels."

The smell grew stronger as they followed Camella down a hallway, and so did the sound of a dog barking. It got louder as they approached a door affixed with a red sign warning people, in large, bold letters, not to stick their fingers through the chain link.

"Here we are! If you're dog walking, this is where you pick them up," she explained to Morgan. "We've got a new color-coding system for the dogs—the ones with green cards on the door are available for level one volunteers to walk."

"It smells like wet dog," Morgan couldn't help but say. Kazio elbowed him.

"Ooh, yes it does," Camella agreed. "We gave a few baths this morning. Not my favorite day. Now, we've expanded our walking area out back…" They peeked through the door to check out a large fenced-in field. A chocolate lab, tail wagging a mile a minute, tongue lolling, danced around a volunteer. "Poop bags are here," Camella continued, "there's a sink there by the door for washing your hands before and after… Then down this way is the laundry…"

"New machines?" Kazio said as they shuffled in.

"Yes, finally! That old set was on its last legs. We got these donated from a hotel chain. This load is almost done" — she patted a humming dryer — "so maybe you can come fold in a bit."

"You got it, boss," Kazio said.

She breezed through the rest of the building — office, staff room, veterinary clinic, cat room — and left them at the kitchen. "How about you two start here? Someone bailed on their shift this morning, we had a pack of puppies dropped off yesterday and we're out of clean food dishes." She waved and hurried away down the hall.

Morgan lurched to a halt at the teetering mountain of dirty food bowls and litter trays. Crusty bits of food clung to the edges of the bowls, and the trays had all kinds of mysterious substances stuck to them that he didn't even want to think about. And the smell in there… 'hot garbage' was too kind.

"Ew," he said succinctly. "They want me to wash all these?"

"Yup," Kazio said, clearly enjoying the moment. "We scrub first with soap and water, then they soak in disinfectant for five minutes."

Morgan sighed. "Do they have rubber gloves?"

* * * *

An hour later, a fresh stack of stainless-steel dishes gleamed on the metal racks.

Morgan wiped his brow with his forearm. "God. I can only imagine what exactly was in the gunk that sprayed all over me. I'm giving camping a point here."

"You can shower it all off when you get home." Kazio patted his back. "You did a great job."

Morgan sighed. "What's next?"

"Laundry."

They made their way back to the laundry room, dryers now silent.

Morgan pulled an armful out of the dryer and dumped it on top. "This isn't so bad. Blankets are easy to fold."

"Here." Kazio dropped a knot of leashes from the other dryer on top of the pile. "Can you untangle these? You have such nimble fingers."

"Umm... Wait, I have nimble fingers?"

"Yes." Kazio busied himself with the first blanket then added it to a stack on the shelves.

"Well, okay. I'll give it a go."

Blankets folded, leashes untangled and dryer humming again with the next load, they went to the cat room.

It smelled even worse in there, but Morgan's jaw dropped when he got a look at the room. "This is...so cool."

'Magical' was the word that came to Morgan's mind to describe the room, in fact — some sort of carpeted cat fantasyland. There were stairs and ramps, bridges and tunnels, all cat-sized, lining the walls and crisscrossing the room, plus an abundance of scratching posts, cat beds and toys. About a dozen cats lounged around the room in various states of tranquility. An orange cat leaped up a few stairs to a ledge running just below the ceiling and peered down at them.

Kazio smiled and nodded at the wall by the door. "Here's all their names."

Morgan turned to look at the wall of cat Polaroids, with a few notes below each one about their temperaments and personalities. Midnight liked to be scratched behind the ears. Cookie hated his tail being touched. Susi was especially cuddly and Raspberry walked with a limp. Frodo, Puffball, Bitty…so many cats.

Kazio sat on an ottoman and extended a hand to Raspberry so she could sniff him.

Morgan crept toward a chubby brown tabby with ragged ears who was drowsing in a cat bed, eyes open in tiny slits. "Who's this old guy?"

"Oh, that's Ralph. He's been here since I can remember. We figure he has to be at least fifteen years old."

"Do you think he'll mind if I pet him?"

"Go ahead. Just let him sniff you first."

Morgan held out his hand. Ralph opened his eyes a crack more and regarded Morgan for a long moment before touching his nose to Morgan's hand, then he closed his eyes.

"That means you can pet him," Kazio told him, running a hand down Raspberry's orangey-pink fur.

Morgan gave Ralph a few tentative pets, waiting for the cat to hiss at him or otherwise voice his displeasure. But Ralph just sat there, eyes still closed. "He's so soft."

Another voice joined them from behind. "He hasn't been eating much lately. We're not sure how much longer he'll make it." A young woman in a green staff polo with a short black bob knelt next to Morgan.

"Ishi!" Kazio said. "You work here now?"

"I sure do." Her smile was a mile wide. "I graduated in December and Camella hired me right away."

Raspberry was in Kazio's lap now. "She's so lucky to have you. Morgan, this is Ishi. She's been volunteering here longer than me, since the day she turned sixteen. And now she's a vet!"

"So nice to meet you." Morgan shook her hand with a pang of jealousy. *Imagine knowing exactly what you wanted to do in life and getting to do it straight out of college.*

Ralph nudged Morgan with his head.

"Oh, sorry, Ralph." Morgan resumed his petting while Kazio and Ishi chatted. Ralph started to purr. Morgan's breaths fell into a rhythm with his petting. The warmth of the room and Ralph's rumbling wrapped Morgan in a cocoon of comfort, mind blissfully calm and quiet.

A hand on his shoulder startled him.

"Morgan." Kazio's smile was gentle. "Are you ready to move on?"

"Sure, yeah, sorry." Ralph appeared to be fast asleep. "Guess I zoned out for a minute there."

"A minute or thirty," Kazio said. "Ralph looks as content as you did." He held out a hand to help Morgan to his feet. "Let's go walk some dogs."

* * * *

Morgan's dog, Sunny, a mix of a golden retriever and some sort of spaniel, was young and energetic, bouncing along agreeably on her leash. Kazio had Bear, a more stately and subdued mastiff. Bear had a yellow card, so was only meant to be walked by more experienced volunteers like Kazio. The dogs were not permitted to mix since they weren't kenneled together, so Morgan was careful to leave a good distance between Sunny and Bear.

The morning haze had burned off and the mountains looked closer than they had when they arrived. Kazio stopped while Bear sniffed a tree, chin tilted up to the breeze that ruffled his long hair. His biceps flexed as Bear gave the leash a tug.

"I can't tell if you're happier camping or here," Morgan told him.

Kazio turned to him, cheeks faintly pink. "Do I seem happy?"

"Yes."

He petted Bear's head. Bear licked his hand. "Well, I am."

Morgan's phone buzzed. He pulled it from his pocket. It was a text. From Albert. *Oh shit.* The last thing he had sent was the drunken *"it's not a date"* text. He held his breath as he swiped it open while Sunny sniffed at a leaf.

How about another date with me, then? it said.

Another date? Morgan's stomach swirled. Another date. On the one hand, Albert was attractive and the sex was fun. On the other...Kazio had crouched down to play with Bear, who was now on his back on the hunt for belly rubs in a most undignified manner.

Morgan put his phone away. He'd have to think about it.

* * * *

On their way out, shift completed, Morgan stopped to talk to Camella again while Kazio finished washing up.

"Morgan!" She put down the stack of papers she had been shuffling. "How did it go?"

"It was great. Thank you so much for having me."

"Are you kidding me? We're thrilled to have you anytime. Please come back soon."

"We will."

Drew hopped up on the counter. "Look who came to say goodbye."

"How did Drew get his name?" Morgan asked, running his hand along the sleek gray fur.

"Oh." Camella scratched Drew under the chin, to his utter delight. "Lacy named him after Drew Carey. She loved *Whose Line Is It Anyway*? We used to watch it after dinner every day."

"Lacy...?"

"My wife. She passed away two years ago. Cancer. She loved this place more than anything."

Morgan's throat tightened with unshed tears. "I'm sorry."

"Thank you. But it's okay. I'm surrounded by her every day when I'm here."

* * * *

Tired, grimy, covered in dog and cat hair, hungry and happy, Morgan climbed back into Kazio's vehicle.

"Thank you for bringing me here," he said to Kazio as they settled in. "I can see why you love it."

"You liked it?"

"I really did."

Kazio started the engine. "Good."

"Now can we get something to eat? I'm fucking starving."

Chapter Nine

Fever

Kazio laughed into his burger. "Your face when you stepped in the dog shit, though..."

Morgan glared at him across the table. Despite the animal shelter grime, Morgan had declared himself Simply Too Hungry, and they had gone back to the Bitter Exchange for lunch before Kazio's shift. "I didn't see it, okay? And you know what?" He pointed his quesadilla at Kazio. "I'm *actually* picking the next place we go. Let's do something *I'm* good at."

Kazio tilted his head as he chewed. "Okay. That's only fair. Where are we going?"

Morgan smirked. "You'll see."

* * * *

"It's a touch on the expensive side," Morgan allowed as they settled at a small high top in his favorite bar, "but worth it."

Kazio's gaze drifted from the menu to the very attractive server in leather pants gliding by. "Is it?"

"Absolutely. The staff are notoriously rude, and the wine list is exquisite. I love it."

"Hmm. I'm not sure I dressed up enough for this place."

"You look great," Morgan assured him. "Just ignore anyone who says otherwise."

"What? Who's going to say —"

"Welcome to Caterwaul Lounge." A server of indeterminate gender announced their presence, rocking a pixie cut, black lipstick and no smile. "I'm Sharp and I'll be your server this evening."

"You're sharp?" Kazio repeated, confused.

Sharp raised an immaculately groomed eyebrow. "As I was saying, the bar is getting pretty backed up, so if you're ready to order, that would be great."

Kazio snapped his menu closed. "A Long Island iced tea, please."

"Oh, no." Sharp took his menu away. "We don't make those. Too many ingredients."

Kazio covered a laugh with a cough. "You're right. I'm so sorry. I'll take a gin and tonic."

"I'm sure you will. And you?" Sharp turned their derisive stare onto Morgan.

"Paloma, please."

Sharp rolled their eyes and departed.

"I like Sharp," Kazio said. "I get Sharp."

"See?" Morgan said. "This place is the best. Now, the next question." He pulled out his phone and opened his Caterwaul app. "What song are you going to sing?"

"Sing?" Kazio looked around. "Sing where?"

"Karaoke starts at nine. It's the best." Morgan pointed to a small stage in a far corner that couldn't fit much more than the piano it already held. "It's just you and an accompanist. You can climb all over the piano and everyone ignores you, like you're a real Las Vegas lounge act. And if you're really impressive, you get a smattering of applause when you're done. Here, scroll through the songs."

"Oh, no." Kazio pushed Morgan's phone away. "I can't sing."

"Ex*cuse* me," Morgan said, voice climbing an octave, "but what did you just say? You can't sing?"

"Seriously, completely tone deaf."

Morgan put his phone down, lips pressed together. "Kazio. Babe. Guess what. I can't take care of animals. I can't set up tents. Lord knows I can't wield an ax. I can't even *roast marshmallows*, for chrissake. And yet" — he held up a finger — "I did all of those things."

Kazio sighed and stared at Morgan with some sort of glimmer brewing in his eyes. Then he held out his hand for the phone.

Morgan squeaked with excitement. "Yay."

Kazio scrolled for a bit with a wry expression then handed the phone back. "This one."

Morgan blinked. "This one?"

"Yes."

"You…you wanna do *this* song?"

"I do."

Morgan blinked some more. "Freddie Mercury is an icon."

"I'm aware."

"I was Freddie for Halloween last year, you know. It didn't end well."

"I do know, you told me about it."

"All riiiight. If you're sure." Morgan filled in the rest of the form, then he signed himself up too.

"What song did you pick?" Kazio asked when Morgan put his phone down again.

"*Fever*. One of my karaoke standards for the quieter places. I totally kill it."

"I have no doubt."

Sharp dropped off their drinks without a word.

Morgan held up his Paloma. "To trying new things."

Kazio tapped his glass. "*Na zdrowie.*"

"Say that again?"

"*Na zdrowie.*"

"Na zdrov-ye," Morgan tried.

"Very good."

They each took a sip.

"Phew." Kazio blew out a breath. "That's strong."

"I told you. Worth it."

They chatted and sipped for a while as nine o'clock approached, until, with no fanfare, a screen beside the stage turned on displaying the line-up.

Kazio curled his lips in a wry smile. "You put my name as 'Kazoo'."

"What? I did not!" Morgan craned his neck to see the screen.

"You sure did."

There it was. *Kazoo Z*. "Gah! Autocorrect," Morgan fumed. "Hang on, I've got to be able to fix that." He grabbed his phone and opened the app again.

Kazio chuckled. "It's fine. Not the first time that's happened, actually."

"There must be an edit button somewhere…"

"Morgan." Kazio put his hand on Morgan's. "It's okay."

Morgan looked up and met his gaze.

"It's okay," Kazio repeated.

"I just feel bad," Morgan said, tequila flushing his cheeks. "Your name should be spelled correctly."

"I'll survive. And, to be honest, I sort of sound like a kazoo when I sing."

Morgan snorted. "Now that's an image."

"You won't have to wait long to experience it. But you're up first."

"I'm *first?*" Morgan had forgotten to look for his own name. Yup, there he was, at the top of the list. "Okay then." He stood and drained the last of his drink. "Here we go."

"Good luck," Kazio said.

"I don't need luck." Morgan winked and turned to cross the bar.

He fucking loved this moment.

The excitement thrummed in his blood as he stepped onto the stage. He perched on the piano waiting for the music to start. The Caterwaul patrons steadfastly ignored him, as they should.

He didn't look at Kazio.

The accompanist—Val, a crusty old broad who'd been doing this for years—gave Morgan a nod, with no sheet music before her and an unlit cigarette dangling from her lips. There was a small screen displaying the lyrics, but Morgan didn't need it.

The opening bass line shivered through his blood. He started soft, a little breathy, teasing, but as the song went on, he deepened his notes, rich and syrupy. The audience tried to ignore him, but the appreciative glances were hard to miss. Even Sharp paused with a full tray to watch for a moment.

As the heat built, his small movements got bigger— knowing glances, shoulder wiggles. He finished strong, the flames inside licking at his core and warming his voice, rich and fiery.

He inclined his head gracefully at the substantial round of applause, more than he'd ever heard anyone get at Caterwaul before. Not surprising, since he'd absolutely crushed it.

Morgan didn't find Kazio's eyes in the crowd until he was almost back to their table. Kazio was still applauding, mouth open a hair. "Morgan...wow. I haven't seen that side of you before."

"And what side is that?" Morgan sat and took a big gulp of his new Paloma.

"Um...sort of...sultry."

"Sultry?" Morgan dabbed his brow with a napkin.

"I mean, like..." Kazio fidgeted, casting about for the word. "That was very subdued and still... You're just incredibly talented. You're a star, truly."

"Thank you." The warmth in Morgan's chest climbed into his cheeks. "I love to perform."

Kazio leaned back, shaking his head. "No one can live up to that now."

Morgan toasted Kazio with his drink again. "They can try."

Kazio toasted him back. "Best of luck to them."

The next person gave it a good go, but her rendition of *Hello* by Adele was weak — derivative and off-key. The bar patrons ignored her completely. A young man did a passable version of *Piano Man* but the bridge could have been so much stronger. Then it was Kazio's turn.

"You've got this," Morgan said. He almost said something about the song selection, but it was too late now. He didn't want to rattle Kazio's nerves. *Bohemian Rhapsody* was a tall order if you weren't Freddie...or Mike Myers and Dana Carvey in wigs. Kazio took to the stage, looking absolutely terrified. Val gave him a 'you sure about this?' look along with her nod. Morgan held his breath.

Kazio began to sing. The first line was flat, and so was the second — then he went sharp.

But Morgan didn't care.

Because look at him up there.

Kazio was doing it...and he was having fun. He smiled as he got more and more into the song. Morgan sang along with him, quietly, hands clasped under his chin.

Morgan clapped loudly when Kazio was done, much louder than a Caterwaul patron was supposed to, but he didn't care.

Kazio came back, face glowing. He sat, smoothing his hair.

Morgan beamed at him.

Kazio chuckled nervously. "Was it terrible?"

The smile hurt Morgan's cheeks. "I'm proud of you."

"Oh." Kazio blushed a shade of bright pink. "Thanks."

"No, I mean it. You were...amazing."

"I was not amazing. I told you I can't sing."

"I don't mean singing, the singing was, well, it was fine. But you...you were beautiful."

Kazio whooshed out a breath. "Thanks, Morgan. It was really fun. And thanks for getting me up there."

"You're welcome." They stared at each other until Morgan cleared his throat. "You know what you should sing next time..." He held his phone in the middle of the table so they could both see while he scrolled the song list.

A text notification popped up. It was from Albert. *Right. Albert. Shit.*

Morgan swiped it away with his thumb by reflex.

There was an awkward pause.

"You can read it, if you like," Kazio said.

"No, it's fine." Morgan felt a little bad that he hadn't replied since he got Albert's text at the shelter. He didn't want to ghost the man, but he also wasn't sure if he —

"Go ahead." Kazio sat back and picked up his drink.

"Okay." Morgan pulled his phone closer and swiped it open.

Hard to get, hey? I see it, I respect it. But I want to take you out again. No need to be coy with me.

"Everything okay?" Kazio's gaze flicked from around the room, anywhere but Morgan.

"Oh, yeah. It's just... He wants to take me out again."

Kazio finished the rest of his drink and set his empty glass down with a thump. "You should go."

"Yeah?"

"Yeah. Why not?" He signaled another round at Sharp, who glared at them from the bar.

"Well, I...I guess you're right." Morgan finished his drink too. "Why not?"

Kazio nodded at the stage. "This lady is rocking *You Belong With Me.*"

"Oh, yeah, I've seen her here before." Morgan put his phone away. He'd reply later.

The time flew by as they talked and drank, and later, as they walked to the train station, the performance buzz still tingled in Morgan's veins. When they stopped at Morgan's platform, he closed his eyes. The rumble of the approaching train sounded just like a waiting audience. He sighed.

"You need to get another band together."

Morgan snapped his eyes open. Kazio was watching him. Hands in his pockets, stray blond hairs drifting in a gust of warm tunnel air. Goosebumps raked over Morgan's skin. "Yes. I do."

"You do. Let me know what I can do to help."

"Any chance you're secretly a drummer?"

Kazio shook his head with a gentle smile. "I'm afraid not."

"Do you know any drummers?"

"No. But I'll help you find one."

The rumble reached a crescendo as the train roared into the station.

It screeched to a stop and the doors hissed open. At this hour, no one got out.

"Thanks for a fun night, Morgan," Kazio said.

"You're welcome. You were brilliant." Before he could think about what he was doing, Morgan leaned forward and left a soft kiss on Kazio's cheek. It came with another whiff of pine and musk and gin.

Kazio took a slow breath. "Goodnight."

"Night." Morgan got on the train and waved through the window as it pulled away.

Kazio lifted a hand, a pale slice of moonlight in the grimy station.

* * * *

Morgan texted Albert from the train.

Sure, that sounds fun. When were you thinking?

Hey sexy. Glad to hear from you. How about now?

Now? Morgan checked the time. *It's one in the morning. That's not really taking me out. That's a booty call.*

Yeah. You free?

Morgan pondered, drumming his fingers on the edge of his phone. Then a text from Kazio came in.

I don't have a lot of friends and I'm grateful you're one of them, Morgan.

The warmth spread from his heart, right down to his fingers and toes. He replied to Kazio.

Same. Talk to you tomorrow.

Then to Albert he sent, *I'm heading to bed, but let me know if you actually want to go out sometime.*

He hummed *Bohemian Rhapsody* on the way home, not caring if he was annoying the other scattered passengers, not caring if Albert was put out.

Not caring that he had kissed Kazio's cheek.

Chapter Ten

Seriously, Love Me

Find a job and start a band...again. No problem. Easy-peasy.

Step one — plug in the kettle.

Step two — Morgan sat at his kitchen table and fired up his laptop. "All right," he murmured, "who wants to not hire me today?"

More fucking music teacher jobs popped up, but he wasn't desperate enough to apply for those yet. Almost, but not quite. Hmm, what about a media manager for a restaurant chain? Not especially musical, but might be fun. And whoa. A composer for the Oakport Community Theater. Interesting. He clicked on the ad for more details. They were looking for a musician to write a song for the theater and perform it for them at an upcoming summer street festival. It was just a contract gig and the pay was crap but...might be fun. Something to fill the hours. Get paid for writing a song, at least.

The kettle whistled. Morgan got up to brew his tea and poked through the sink in search of a bowl clean enough to require only a quick rinse. Back at the table, and armed with Cheerios, he added his recent volunteer experience to his resume, then uploaded the file, along with a rough cut of *Cherry Tree*, a song he had written for the band—sort of bouncy and fun, something that might appeal to the theater. He applied for the media manager job too, just to feel productive.

Next up—putting a band back together. He scrubbed his face and thought about his former bandmates...then he thought about switching to tequila. Suffice to say, his Felix Bridge was a smoking ruin at the bottom of Drummer Canyon. But maybe Todd and Andre still wanted to be in a band with him. Maybe in the last month, they had already found a new drummer and were just waiting for him to step in as lead singer again. He plunged ahead with a text to the two of them.

Hey guys. How are things? Hope you've been good. I miss playing with you. I've been doing some thinking and...do you two have any interest in getting the band going again?

Todd's reply came right away. *Sorry, man, We're expecting again, and my wife's on bedrest. I can't commit to anything right now.*

Congrats, Morgan replied. *I hope she's doing well.*

Andre's reply came next. *Sorry, I already found another group. Good luck.*

No problem. Good luck to you too.

Fuck. Fuck fucking fuck. Morgan cursed himself for ending up here. From three decent bandmates to zero. Why did he have to be such a prick sometimes?

The hunt for Felix had been painful. He'd lost track of how many bad drummers he'd auditioned, who couldn't even keep 4/4 time…who didn't even know what 4/4 time was. The idea of starting the hunt from scratch… Well, it made him want a drink. He sighed and clicked over to the main classifieds page and searched 'drummer,' just to see what came up.

Three 'drummer wanted' ads, but one was for a high school group, and one was death metal. The other just said 'rock' and would probably be in direct competition with him. He put his own ad together.

Experienced musicians wanted for pop/arena rock band. Drummer must have own kit. Rehearsal space a bonus.

He stared at it for a moment and deleted 'experienced.'

Before he could click 'submit,' his phone buzzed with a text from Kazio.

Morning. How's it going?

Uh, let's see. My bass player's out, my guitar player already found another band, and I just applied to be the social media manager for Chicken Hut.

Oh.

Yeah.

Well, if you're not busy, I just talked to Camella and they could use some help at the shelter this afternoon. You want to go?

Yes, he did want to go. *Please.*

Great. Meet me at the Exchange? We can head out after the lunch rush.

The scratchy edges of Morgan's morning softened. He was so grateful for his friend. *See you then.*

Sounds good. Oh, I saw this and thought of you. Kazio sent a camping meme—the caption "Oh fine, I'll go camping" over a shot of a sumptuous glamping setup.

Morgan sent a laughing emoji. *Exactly. That's my kind of camping.*

Smiling, he posted his ad, downed the cereal-flavored milk left in the bowl and went to go find Grumpy Cat.

* * * *

"Hey." Morgan sat on his usual stool, inhaling the familiar Exchange air—beer, grease and a hint of pine.

"Hey." Kazio threw a bar rag onto his shoulder and leaned on the bar, forearms flexing. The navy blue of his button down was such a good color on him. "So. Chicken Hut, hey?"

Morgan covered his eyes with one hand. "I don't know. Might be fun, right? Posting about nuggets all day? To be honest, I just want someone to love me."

"Give me a second," Kazio murmured.

Morgan looked up at him, confused, but Kazio was sliding over to an older couple who sat one stool over from Morgan.

"Afternoon," Kazio greeted them.

"A chilled white wine," the woman said, fussing with her purse. "Extremely chilled."

"What lagers do you have on tap?" the man asked.

Kazio paused, annoyance resonating through every hard line of his body. "The wines are listed in the menu, and the beers on tap are right here in front of you and on the chalkboard above you."

The man peered at Kazio over his glasses, trying to decide if he was being insulted or not.

Kazio smiled, fake as hell. "You just let me know which one you'd like. I'll be right over here when you're ready."

Morgan fought off a grin as Kazio slid back over. "Should I have applied there, though?"

Kazio collected glassware for the couple. "Do you think you'll have to, like, wear a chicken suit or something?"

Morgan snorted. "I'm sure I won't have to wear... Oh, God. You don't think I'll have to wear a chicken suit, do you? What if they want me to wear a chicken suit?"

"Then you know what, you wear it with pride." Kazio's voice dropped to a private rumble. "After all, who doesn't love a confident cock?"

"I—Wh—" Morgan sputtered, cheeks flushing.

"Excuse me," the man one seat over interrupted. "We're ready to order now, if it's not too much trouble."

"What can I get you?" Kazio snapped, no longer interested in passive-aggressive games.

Ten minutes later, once Kazio had topped up the customers around the bar, Tasha came to relieve Kazio.

"I just have to check on one thing in the back," Kazio told Morgan, "then I'll change and we can go."

Morgan followed him through the swinging doors and into the kitchen. This time, the place was full of kitchen staff, a whirl of food prep all around him.

"Rudy," Kazio barked at a beleaguered young man who looked more like a linebacker than line cook. "What did I say about the carrot curls?"

Rudy looked up from his peeler, eyes wide. "Six inches. But that's imposs—"

"Six. Inches," Kazio repeated.

Rudy sighed. "You got it, boss."

Morgan tried to smile encouragingly at Rudy as they continued on their way to Kazio's office. He examined the small room as Kazio tapped on his keyboard. The space was both what Morgan expected and not at all what he imagined a restaurant office looking like. It was meticulously tidy, one wall covered in shelves of books and binders labeled with neat, block printing in black marker. *Suppliers, Purchase Orders, Staff, Budget…*

Morgan ran his finger along the spines. "Wow, look at you, very *The Bear*—"

Kazio stood and whipped his shirt off.

Morgan froze. He didn't know where to look. Only a few, fine blond hairs interrupted the smooth, pale expanse of Kazio's skin, dusting his chest and trailing down to his waistband. The curves of his pecs and deltoids were…exquisite. The perfect ridge to slide a tongue down…if one were so inclined to think that way looking at their shirtless friend. Kazio put his dress shirt on a hanger and hung it up in the closet, then retrieved a T-shirt from a bag on the floor. His abs flexed as he bent over.

Morgan licked his lips. "Um," he said.

Kazio pulled the shirt over his head and fluffed his hair out. "Sorry, what about *The Bear*?" Their eyes met.

Morgan tried to swallow but he had no saliva. "He... You... Very...organized."

"Oh, yeah, I don't know how anyone can run a restaurant with a desk buried in papers... Are you okay?"

"Fine," Morgan gasped. "Could I just grab some water?"

"You bet."

Kazio filled a Bitter Exchange-branded reusable water bottle for him — "You can keep it, just use it around town lots for some advertising, okay?" — and they hit the road. Morgan did not think about shirtless Kazio for most of the ride.

When they pulled into Mountain Meadows, Drew was waiting for them on the fence again.

"Hi, Drew," Morgan said, giving him a scratch. Drew pushed his head against Morgan's hand, demanding more.

"He likes you," Kazio said.

"I like him," Morgan murmured. "You want to come inside with us, Drew?" He picked the kitty up and gave him a nuzzle on their way through the door.

"Kazio, Morgan!" Camella came out to hug them both when she saw them. "Thank you so much for coming in."

"We're happy to," Kazio said. "What can we help with today?"

"The puppies need some attention," Camella said. "Could you play with them for a bit? Then maybe take a couple dogs for a walk and see what else needs to be done?"

"You got it."

They said goodbye to Drew and signed in, then Camella came with them to the 'meet and greet'—a simple room near the kennels with a few chairs and a box of dog toys, currently filled with four wiggling brown and white puppies with fluffy, curly fur. They charged at the three humans when they came in.

Morgan's heart swelled. They were just about the cutest fucking things he had ever seen. Before he knew it, he was sitting on the floor getting mobbed by balls of fluff with tiny pink tongues.

"These are Cavachons," Camella said. "That's Toffee licking you, and her sister, Honey, has the more golden fur. The one with the white face is Frosty, and the other boy we haven't named yet."

Morgan stroked the fourth one in his lap, smaller than his siblings. He was almost entirely brown and looked up at Morgan with plaintive eyes. "Well, he's a little peanut, isn't he?"

Camella smiled and bent down to scratch the pup's head. "Peanut. Perfect. That's his name."

"Wait, I got to name him?"

"You sure did."

Peanut licked his hand.

"Hello, sweet puppies," Morgan muttered into his armful of soft, soft fur. "Can I take pictures of them?" he asked Camella.

"Of course. In fact, we encourage you to post them to social media and tag the shelter."

Morgan dug out his phone and tried to snap a few pics but they were all blurs of brown fur.

"Here, can you take one of me?" Morgan handed Kazio his phone, scooped up Toffee and Peanut in each hand and held them next to his face.

"Sure. So cute," Kazio said, snapping a few. He handed Morgan's phone back. "Are those good?"

Morgan studied the pics. The puppies were impossibly adorable, of course, but he looked really happy...and hot. His eyes were shining, a dimple winking on one cheek. "Yeah, these are great, thanks."

"Here, let me take one of the two of you," Camella offered.

Morgan handed his phone to her and scooted next to Kazio until their shoulders touched. Kazio put his arm around Morgan, resting his hand on Morgan's hip. Honey squirmed in his lap and he held Frosty in his other hand.

"You two look great," Camella said, holding the phone up.

Kazio's hand was on his hip.

"Hang on..." Camella's eyebrows pinched together. "Let me see if I can get one with all the puppies looking this way. Over here, puppies!"

The hand on his hip felt really nice. Morgan leaned a little heavier into Kazio's side. Was... Was his thumb now *stroking* his hip? It felt like maybe his thumb was —

Peanut let out a little squeak of a bark, squirming in Morgan's hand, and they all laughed.

"Okay, sorry, Peanut, I'm done. I think I got a few good ones." Camella passed Morgan's phone back.

He put both puppies into his lap and took it from her. "Thanks." He flipped through the photos. Kazio dropped his head to look too, but otherwise didn't move.

Morgan didn't really see the pictures, to be honest. It was so warm and comfortable, tucked under Kazio's arm like that.

"Oh, you should post that one," Kazio said.

"Yeah?" Morgan blinked the picture into focus. It was a great photo. Kazio looked amazing, indigo eyes crystal clear, jaw chiseled, and Morgan looked just as hot in this one. Combine that with four adorable puppies… "Yeah, okay."

He opened it in a new Instagram post and added the caption 'Indulging in some sweetness with Toffee, Honey, Frosty and Peanut.' He tagged Kazio and the shelter and added a few hashtags.

Camella checked it out on her phone and rapidly liked, commented and shared it. "Thanks for posting that, Morgan. What a gorgeous pic. I love it."

Morgan picked up Peanut for another snuggle. "You're so welcome."

"Now I have some things I need to do. You guys can sign the puppies back in when you're done."

"Will do," Kazio replied.

Morgan didn't want to move, but it was sort of becoming awkward, cuddled as they were on the floor without having a reason for it any longer.

Honey solved the problem by hopping out of Kazio's lap and coming back with a chew toy. "Oh, you want to play, do you?" Kazio asked, unwinding his arm from around Morgan.

The cool air hit his side and he wondered what the fuck was going on in his brain right now. Why was he so obsessed with having someone's arm around him? Such a simple thing that should not be such a big deal.

He was probably just touch-starved, he decided. He probably just needed another good fuck from Albert. That was all it was.

In the meantime, the puppies wanted attention. Tug-o-war and fetch proved to be a nice distraction for a while, until Toffee fell asleep in Kazio's lap.

"I think this crew is due for some downtime," Kazio said. "We should bring them back to their kennel."

Morgan's heart twinged when he was saying goodbye to the puppies. He knew they'd be adopted quickly and, as he patted each head one last time, said a silent wish that they'd go to good homes. Puppies safely signed back in, they took a couple of older dogs out for walks—Morgan was much more careful where he put his feet this time—folded some more laundry and mopped a few kennels, before they had time to pop into the cat room again.

"I have to see Ralph, of course," Morgan said. Ralph was in the same spot he had been last time, half asleep, tail twitching in his elderly cat dreams.

"Hey, Ralph," Morgan murmured as he sat. "How are you today?"

Morgan gave him one slow stroke down his back and Ralph was purring again.

"Sweet boy," Morgan whispered.

Kazio smiled. "Morgan—don't look now—but I think you're an animal person."

"What? No I'm not."

"The animal fur all over you and big goofy smile on your face say otherwise."

"Well…" Morgan ran his hand along Ralph's back. "It's easy to be an animal person here. It's so…calming." He actually couldn't remember the last time he had felt this relaxed. His band and job stress from the morning had melted away, a distant problem from another life.

"Yeah, it is." Kazio reached over to pet Ralph too. Their fingers brushed.

Morgan's head turned on its own volition, nose toward Kazio's neck, taking a deep inhale of his scent. His heart rate spiked as his stomach swirled.

Oh fuck.

Maybe he wasn't that calm.

Chapter Eleven

Empty Stage

Back in the car, Morgan checked his email. He gasped and clutched Kazio's forearm. "Oh my God, I got an audition at the theater on Friday! They said to bring my guitar."

"That's amazing! Good for you." Kazio put his car into gear.

Morgan bit his lip. "Do you think I should try to write something in advance?"

"Couldn't hurt."

He realized he was still holding Kazio's arm and let go. "But what do I know about theater?"

"Morgan." Kazio cast his eyes sideways as he paused at the parking lot exit. "Theater is performance. And you know all about performance."

"Yeah, I guess." Morgan's fingers twitched, eager for the feel of guitar strings under them. "I have some ideas."

"I'm sure you do."

They drove in silence for a while as the chords gathered in Morgan's head.

"Do you want to come for dinner tomorrow?" Kazio asked at a red light.

"Again? I feel like I should make dinner for you next."

"I've already bought groceries and stuff. You can host another time."

"Then sure, if you don't mind."

"I don't mind."

Kazio insisted on driving him home too, even though Morgan could have taken a train from downtown.

"Thanks, Kazio," Morgan said as they pulled up to his front door. Kazio's shirtless chest and warm hand on his hip flashed through his mind. "It was fun."

"You're welcome. See you tomorrow. Let's say seven?"

"I'll be there."

Morgan's clothes went straight into the wash, then he showered and dug through his fridge in search of dinner. Not much in there, just some cheese, milk and expired salad dressing.

Settling onto his couch with a plate of cheese and crackers, he found he had a reply to his ad for bandmates. He clicked it open, breath held.

Hey, what's up, it read. *I'm Cal, I play guitar, what kind of music u into?*

Morgan let out his breath slowly as he replied. *Hey Cal. Queen is a major inspiration for me. I also love the Stones, Radiohead, Arcade Fire, Adele...* He listed off a few more, then dropped his own question. *Have you been in a band before?*

Cal replied only a couple crackers later. *Ya those r ok. Never been in a band, but been taking guitar lessons for a couple weeks now.*

Morgan dropped his next cracker and groaned. *Looking for someone with a bit more experience, but thanks,* he typed.

Then he went to edit his ad and put 'experienced' back in. Then added 'Eighteen+' for good measure. *Christ.*

Once his plate was empty, he pulled out his guitar. He warmed up with a quick version of *Crazy Little Thing Called Love,* then closed his eyes and thought about the feeling of stepping onto a stage. It was perhaps the very best feeling there was. He tried out the chords that came to him, scribbling down the ones that worked. He was just finishing putting words to the first verse when his phone buzzed.

It was Albert. *Hey sexy, you busy?*

Morgan sighed. Another booty call. *Yeah, working on something right now. But another time.*

No reply.
Oh, well. He went back to his song.

* * * *

Kazio opened his front door.
Morgan stood there, clutching his guitar like a life preserver. "Okay, I wrote something."
"Great." Kazio moved aside so Morgan could enter.

He didn't move. "It might suck."

"I'm sure it doesn't. Are you going to come in?

"Yeah." Morgan stepped in and kicked off his shoes. "Do you want to hear it?"

"Of course I do."

They sat in the living room. Kazio's couch was a thing of beauty, a huge sectional, big enough for three adults to stretch out. Morgan perched on the edge of one side and took his acoustic guitar out of its case. "This is just a rough draft. It still needs work." He checked the tuning with a couple strums and cleared his throat. "Ready?"

Kazio nodded.

Morgan began.

"The empty stage is waiting
It's waiting for a heart
Waiting for the moment when
That magic feeling starts.
When everybody's watching
And there's a part to play
A story to be told
It can't wait another day."

"That last line is still a little rough," Morgan said over the guitar. "Then the chorus.

"The spotlight, it will find you
It will warm you through
The empty stage is waiting
Oh, it's waiting there for you."

"I'll probably sing it twice?" he mused. "And the bridge, something like…

"We need your heart, we need your light
We need your passion, tonight's the night."

He went through the second verse and the chorus two more times before wrapping it up with a final strum. The living room was very silent. "Or something," he babbled, filling the void. "It needs a stronger finish and probably another verse but...it's a start."

Kazio, for some reason, looked like he'd just witnessed the resurrection of Freddie Mercury. "I love it."

Morgan wiped his sweaty palms on his pants. "You do?"

"Of course. It's perfect. Catchy, poignant... They'll love it, too."

"I hope so. Thanks."

"You're really amazing, Morgan. You should know that. And I love that you're writing songs that make you happy — that mean something to you."

Morgan busied himself putting his guitar back in its case, cheeks hot. "Thank you. It's almost like writing jingles was slowly killing my soul." He straightened up, running a hand through his hair. "So...what's for dinner?"

"Just something simple — chicken penne."

"That sounds delicious. Can I help?"

"Could you sauté some onions for me?"

"I can try."

He forgot about onions making him cry though. One slice and the tears were rolling like...well, he didn't really want to think about an emotional moment it might compare to. But he was crying a lot.

"There, there," Kazio said, handing him a tissue.

Morgan laughed, blotting at his eyes. "Shut up. I can't believe you made me cry."

Kazio stilled. "I would never make you cry."

Morgan met Kazio's gaze and, in that moment, had never felt anything to be more true. "I know."

Kazio hemmed and busied himself with the chicken. "You want some wine?"

"Yes, please."

When dinner was ready, they sat at the end of the island again, this time decorated with a jar of pink roses.

"These are pretty," Morgan said as he settled. "Didn't really take you for a rose guy."

"I'm not normally, but I thought you'd like them."

"I do." Morgan raised his glass. "*Na zdrowie.*"

Kazio smiled and tapped Morgan's glass. "*Na zdrowie.*"

Kazio told Morgan a funny story about Rudy measuring his carrot curls, and a rude customer who ordered a round of Long Island iced teas and fancy shots for a bachelor party and didn't even tip. "Sharp was onto something," Kazio said with a rueful smile. "Thinking about banning Long Islands. Along with Bloody Marys."

"You know I'd support that." Morgan shoveled in another mouthful of delicious pasta.

When Kazio went to use the washroom, Morgan checked his email. A message from Chicken Hut waited.

"I didn't get an interview for Chicken Hut," Morgan said when Kazio appeared again. He held up his phone like it was evidence in a courtroom. "They said I'm 'overqualified'. I'm too qualified to make posts about chicken nuggets, Kazio."

Kazio picked up the wine to top up their glasses. "I would agree."

Morgan pouted. "Still sucks to be rejected."

"Yeah, but...you want a 'yes' to be the right 'yes,' don't you?"

"I guess."

"You guess?"

"It's just..." Morgan swirled the wine in his glass. "I've heard a lot of nos lately. I really need a yes."

"Are you talented? Yes. Are you going to find something soon? Yes."

Morgan sighed and changed the subject. "Thanks for another amazing dinner."

"You're welcome." Kazio smiled as he cleared their plates. "You want to take these flowers home with you, too?"

"No, you can leave them here and think of me," Morgan said in a breathy, teasing voice.

Kazio let out a half-chuckle. "Thanks. I'll do that."

* * * *

Another reply to his ad from someone named Brett arrived on the train home.

Hey, my brother Ray plays the drums and I play bass. We've been thinking about getting back into a band. It's been a few years but we still jam together all the time.

Morgan sat up straight and made some sort of noise. He ignored the looks his fellow passengers gave him as he tapped out a reply.

Hi Brett. Would love to arrange a jam session for the three of us, see what the chemistry is like.

Dare he hope? Did he actually find two experienced musicians in one fell swoop, including a *drummer*?

His leg bounced as he waited for a reply. Fortunately, it didn't take long. Brett sent Morgan his cell, and they texted back and forth a few times arranging a session on Saturday morning.

Our basement isn't great, but it does the trick, Brett told him.

Sounds perfect. See you then.

Morgan leaned back in his seat and tried to keep his squeal internal. But an older woman got up to move away from him, so he probably hadn't succeeded.

He did not care one bit.

* * * *

The Oakport Community Theater was a heavy brick building with tall windows that had probably looked sophisticated and modern when it opened in the eighties, but now just looked like they were from the eighties. Morgan followed instructions to go around back to the stage door and found it marked 'Festival Auditions'.

A woman with a clipboard and a headset signed him in and asked him to wait on the row of folding metal chairs. An older man with a long gray beard and battered guitar case nodded at him as he sat. Morgan nodded back, willing the butterflies in his stomach to settle. The man was called in next and a young woman with multiple piercings and tattoos came out of the back and ignored them on her way out the door.

He ran through the chords and the lyrics in his head as he waited.

"Morgan?"

His stomach flipped over. He stood and followed the lady with the clipboard into the green room. Three people sat in a row at a table. One of them, a Black man around fifty with kind eyes and an easy smile, stood to greet him.

"Morgan, it's so nice to meet you. Thank you for coming in. My name is Louis and I'm the festival director. This is Megan, the head of the theater board, and this is Conrad, the assistant director." They shook hands all around before Morgan sat in a chair across from them.

"So…" Louis glanced at a tablet screen. "Morgan. As I'm sure you know, Oakport Theater partners with the City Arts Council every summer for this festival. How familiar are you with our work?"

"Er…" Why was he such an idiot? He was so focused on writing a song that it had never occurred to him to learn more about the theater or the festival. "I haven't been, but I'm looking forward to learning more about it."

Louis smiled like he wasn't an idiot, which was nice of him. "Right, well, the theater, of course, has a tent at the festival where we do a season pass giveaway, and there's also several musical showcases. We thought it would be fun this year to have a song specifically about the theater. We loved the sample you sent. You wrote that song?"

"Yes," Morgan said, thrilled to be on a topic where he knew what he was talking about. "I did. For a rock band I was in. Briefly."

"We'd love to hear you perform it."

"You bet."

Morgan retrieved his acoustic guitar and hummed a quick vocal warm up before getting into *Cherry Tree*. He wrote it one summer when he was having steamy sex with a guy he met randomly at a park one day. They didn't have sex *in* the park, to be clear. But the idea certainly inspired his song.

> *"Hot summer day, 'bout a hundred and three*
> *Watching you down in the shade*
> *Lying back, tongue so red*
> *Under the cherry tree."*

Louis beamed at him the whole time, although Megan and Conrad didn't seem quite as impressed. Conrad looked downright bored by the end, in fact. Still, the three of them applauded lightly when he was done.

"We'd love to hear something else you wrote, if possible," Louis said.

"Actually..." Morgan cleared his throat. "I wrote a bit of a song about the theater already."

Louis cast a bit of a smug 'I told you so' look sideways at the other two. "We would be thrilled to hear it."

"It's called *Empty Stage*." He had made a few tweaks on the train on the way here, and he was very happy with how it turned out. It came out flawlessly for his audience now.

The three applauded again, louder this time. "Well, Morgan..." Louis stood, shaking his head. "You're clearly very talented and we don't want to keep anyone waiting. We are seeing a few more people today and will be making our decision as quickly as we can. You should hear from us tonight."

"Great." They shook hands again and Morgan nearly skipped out into the sunshine.

I crushed it, he told Kazio in a text as soon as he got on the train. *The song was perfect. They said they'll be making a decision tonight. I have a really good feeling.*

That's fantastic, Kazio replied. *Fingers crossed for you.*

I don't need luck, remember? Morgan said with a winky emoji. *I'm amazing.*

Of course, my mistake.

When he got home, he blasted Queen and danced around the kitchen cleaning, and even folded and put away some laundry.

He was staring into his fridge, in case any food had materialized since last night, when his phone dinged. Email.

Heart in his throat, he opened the message from the theater. His eyes jumped over the *Dear Morgan* and skipped past the *thank you for coming in blah blah blah...* Then they fell on *Unfortunately...*

What? No...

Unfortunately...
Unfortunately, we have decided to go with another candidate at this time. Please don't take this as any sort of comment on your talent...

Tears flooded his eyes as he slumped into a kitchen chair, stomach hollow ...*as any sort of comment on your talent...*

They didn't want him.

He wrote them a fucking awesome song, he was everything they asked for...and it still wasn't enough. They didn't want him. No one wanted him. He got up to pour a shot of tequila, tossed it back then poured another one.

It was too embarrassing to tell Kazio. He'd wait and tell him tomorrow.

Still, he was half expecting the text that popped up to be from Kazio. But it wasn't. It was from Albert.

Hey Morgan. All right, I'm not one to beg. You free tonight? If not, I'll leave you be...

Morgan wiped a tear from his eye and slammed his second shot. *Perfect timing. I'm free.*

Chapter Twelve

It's Time for a Montage

The sex with Albert was fine.

Okay, better than fine, to be fair. It was good. It was fun, same as the last time.

It was also, ultimately, unfulfilling.

Sometime around three a.m., Albert had kissed him goodbye, put on his pants and left, and Morgan had never felt more alone.

He slept fitfully and woke up in a foul mood, head pounding and only twenty minutes to spare before he was supposed to meet Brett and Ray for a jam session.

Fuck. Part of him wanted to roll over and blow it off, but he didn't think he'd get another chance like this.

He dragged himself into the shower, threw on some clothes and barely remembered to grab his guitar on his way out the door. He texted from the train that he was running behind and Brett told him to go around the side to the basement door. The yard was noticeably less maintained than the neighbors', with a creaking gate and knee-high weeds. A rusty bike leaned against the fence, brambles growing through its spokes.

Morgan tripped down the uneven paving stone path to the sunken door, frame crumbling around it. He knocked and waited.

"Are you gonna get that?" someone hollered from inside.

"Gimme a second!" came a second voice.

"Get the fucking door!"

He waited another long moment, then the door yanked open. A disheveled man in cargo shorts and a faded Nirvana T-shirt stared at him, brown hair hanging in his face, skin pale. "You're late."

Morgan knitted his eyebrows. "I know, I texted..."

The man turned back into the dark basement behind him. "Come in."

The basement wasn't in much better shape than the yard. It was mostly unfinished, with a few rooms half-heartedly framed in but never completed. A mish-mash of old dining room furniture was piled in one corner, the thick, stately kind that had probably sat in a grandparent's house for multiple decades before ending up here. There were boxes and bins stacked in every available space, except for one tiny corner with a drum kit. A lackluster attempt at soundproofing had occurred, a few raggedy blankets stapled between the two-by-fours. Another man sat on a stool with a bass. He looked like a version of the man who had answered the door, just a little younger and not quite as pale.

This one grinned, at least. "Morgan, what's up? I'm Brett and this is Ray."

"Hey." Morgan ran a hand through his hair. His head was pounding. "Sorry I'm late. I...had a rough night."

"It's all good," Brett said while Ray sniffed and took a seat at the drums, twirling a drumstick in his long fingers. Brett rolled his eyes at him. "Don't start, Ray."

"I'm not doing anything."

"Yeah, you are."

"I am not."

"Whatever, man." Brett tucked his hair behind his ears. "Let's just play."

Now Ray twirled two drumsticks. "That's what I'm trying to do!"

"You're the one who keeps talking."

"*You* keep talking."

"I do not."

Morgan stood there, headache worsening. What the fuck was he witnessing? Was this real life? He busied himself removing his guitar from its case, waiting for the inane bickering to stop.

It didn't.

"Look," Morgan finally interrupted. "Is this a bad time?"

Brett and Ray gave him twin looks of confusion.

"What do you mean?" Brett asked.

"You just…" Morgan waved a hand between them. "You haven't stopped arguing."

"Arguing? Nah, man, that's just how we talk. We're ready when you are."

"Do you know *3 am* by Matchbox Twenty?" Ray asked.

"Sure."

But the arguing didn't stop. It continued right through the song.

"You're a half beat behind on the chorus," Brett told Ray.

"Your G-string is out of tune," Ray told Brett.

Headache pounding through every inch of his brain, eyes scratchy and throat dry, Morgan called it a day after two songs.

"I gotta go," he said. "I, uh… I'll be in touch."

The sounds of their bickering followed him out into the rain.

A text from Kazio arrived once he had slouched back onto the train.

Okay, I didn't want to pester you but…I'm starting to worry. Did you hear back from the theater?

Morgan's stomach clenched. He could barely bring himself to type the words to tell Kazio that he was a major fucking failure in every aspect of his life.

It was a no.

Oh, Morgan. I'm so sorry.

It's fine, he replied, even though it was anything but.

What are you doing today? You want to go for a hike? The rain is supposed to clear up.

Not really. I think I'm just going to wallow on my couch and eat…expired salad dressing.

Is it okay if I come over and keep you company?

Tears pricked in his eyes. *If you want to.*

I do. I'll see you soon. Then Kazio added another message. *Please don't eat the salad dressing.*

* * * *

Morgan opened his front door.

Kazio stood there, clutching a takeout bag from Hole-in-One. "I brought food."

"Thanks. Come in." Morgan was aware he looked like shit—rumpled clothing, dark circles under his eyes—but couldn't bring himself to care. Kazio had seen him in worse shape, anyway, in the middle of the woods and covered in animal hair. He turned and flopped back onto the couch.

Kazio followed him in and closed the door behind him. "Honestly, if they didn't hire you, they're idiots anyway."

Morgan let out a skeptical huff.

"At least you still have a meeting coming up with the brothers about the band, right? That might be great."

Morgan's huff turned into an acidic laugh. "That was this morning, actually."

"Oh." Kazio read his face. "Oh no."

"I've never had to use the phrase 'man-child' to describe someone before, never mind two people at the same time. But, I...the sound of them arguing made me want to pluck out my own eyeballs."

"Okay, easy, Oedipus."

"You don't understand. It was painful. I just couldn't do it. I had to get out of there."

Kazio sat on the coffee table and put the food down next to him. "Were they any good?"

Morgan blinked at him. "I don't think they were terrible, but...I honestly couldn't tell you. I was too distracted by the urge to strangle them."

"I get it, I do. People can be...a lot. But maybe it's worth giving them another chance?"

"I don't think so."

"Everyone deserves a second chance, don't they?"

"Ugh." Morgan tipped over, face first into the couch cushions. "I'm the worst," he mumbled.

"Sorry?" Kazio said. "Your voice was all muffled."

Morgan turned his head. "I said I'm the worst!"

Kazio chuckled. "You are not the worst."

"Okay, maybe not *the* worst, but I'm like bottom five, for sure."

"I like bottoms."

"Stop." Morgan tried not to laugh. "I suck."

"I like—"

"Stop!" The laugh escaped this time.

Kazio offered a gentle smile. "Maybe your standards are too high?"

Morgan groaned. "My standards are not too high, trust me."

"What do you mean?"

Morgan sighed. "I slept with Albert again."

There was a long beat of silence. "What?"

"He messaged me right after the theater rejection so...he came over last night."

"Oh."

Morgan pulled at a tuft on a pillow. "He... I... I just wanted to feel wanted."

Kazio stood abruptly. "You want some tea? I'm going to make some tea. There's a breakfast sandwich and a doughnut in the bag for you."

"Sure, tea would be good, thanks," Morgan said, but Kazio was already in the kitchen hunting for mugs.

"Above the sink," Morgan called. "Tea bags in the cupboard above the kettle."

Kazio clattered around and eventually plunked a mug on the coffee table by Morgan, then he sat in the armchair across the way.

Morgan sat up and took a pitiful sip of his tea, wallowing in his situation. "Oh my God, I have to apply for more jobs. Kazio, what if I never get a job?"

"You will."

"But will I? How do you know?"

"I just know," Kazio said abruptly, like it was the final word on the matter.

"I hope you're right." Morgan gave him a weak smile.

"Get your laptop. Let's see what else is out there."

"Do I have to? I'm wallowing."

Kazio gave him a hard look. "Get your laptop."

Morgan sighed and set his tea down, grumbling. "Yes, sir."

* * * *

Over the next few weeks, Morgan applied for a bunch more jobs, a mishmash of ones he didn't actually want, was overqualified for or he knew he'd never get. A few more replies to his band members ad trickled in too, each one worse than the last. It was starting to feel like he was in the montage part of the movie, a blur of increasingly ridiculous interview questions and deluded people with guitars.

"Now, Morgan, can you tell us about a time you leveraged your soft skills and utilized out-of-the-box thinking to organically solve a problem?"

"No, never actually performed on a stage before. The idea kind of terrifies me."

"If you were a tree, what kind would you be?"

"My mom says I can't stay out past nine."

"Tell us why you want to work at CJ's Party Supply Zone?"

"I don't believe in rehearsal. I think it's better if we just...vibe on stage."

"If I was to interview your last manager about your job performance, what would they say about you that you think isn't true, and why isn't it true, and why do you think they would say that?"

It was a long few weeks.

Morgan was so busy juggling cover letters and emails and interviews that he barely talked to Kazio. Kazio seemed busy too—he said they were doing inventory and trying to hire some more kitchen staff, plus Tasha had been sick so he'd been working long hours.

He hung out with Albert a few more times too, and by 'hung out,' he meant fucked in his apartment.

Morgan rolled over late one night and studied Albert's profile. "What are you doing tomorrow?"

Albert didn't look up from his phone. "Who, me?"

"Yes, you."

"Working."

"Hmm. You want to do something after work?"

"Uh." Albert finally looked at him. "I work till late, we have a wedding, but I'll text you when I get off? Like around one, probably?"

"Sure," Morgan said, but when Albert's text came at one-thirty a.m., he was fast asleep.

* * * *

Morgan woke up the next morning, completely content and cozy under his comforter. The sleep gradually lifted from his brain as he arched his back and stretched his legs, but a pleasant haze from his dream remained, something warm and snuggly about Kazio and puppies.

Kazio.

He really missed Kazio. He picked up his phone to fire him a quick text.

Hey, haven't seen you in a while. Are you free for a shelter visit today?

He stared, waiting for a reply. Kazio would have been up for hours by now. Probably gone for a hike and mowed his lawn already. Then there it was. Three dots. He was typing.

Yeah, I could make that work. Pick you up at two?

Morgan wiggled his toes. *I'll be waiting.*

* * * *

"So, how are things?" Kazio asked when Morgan climbed into his SUV. Morgan's heart fluttered at the sight of him, which was…weird. Kazio looked a little tired, but still put together and…so handsome. A tiny strand of hair had escaped his half-pony that Morgan wanted to push behind his ear, which was…also weird.

"Things are about the same," Morgan reported. "More rejection, and more people who think being in a band is just randomly hanging out on occasion, perhaps with instruments." He left out the part about Albert. "It's getting so bad I'm even thinking about" — he shuddered for dramatic effect — "teaching music."

"Gasp," Kazio said. "Say it isn't so."

"Desperate times, and all that..." Morgan looked around for a Hole-in-One bag but there wasn't one. Although to be fair, it was solidly mid-afternoon. "What's new with you? Tasha feeling better?"

The conversation was stilted on the way to the shelter, but Morgan chalked it up to Kazio clearly being a little worn out. A light rain drummed on the windshield, at least filling the silences with a soothing patter.

Drew and Camella greeted them upon arrival as usual, then Camella put them to work cleaning the floors. Morgan swept the reception area then went down the hallway while Kazio mopped behind him. Morgan didn't mind the meditative rhythm, but it was quiet work, since he wasn't shoulder to shoulder with Kazio as he usually was at the shelter.

Once the floors were as swept as they could be, he checked in with Kazio, who wasn't too far behind.

"I'll meet you in the cat room?" Morgan asked.

Kazio nodded, eyes on the even streaks he was leaving on the tile. "Be right there."

Morgan bobbed his head at Ishi as he entered, who was brushing an orange tabby, and looked around for Ralph. He wasn't on his usual cushion, so Morgan wandered the room, peeking in cubbies and tunnels. "Ralph? Where are you, buddy?"

"I'm so sorry, Morgan," Ishi called over to him gently, "but Ralph passed away yesterday. Peacefully, in his sleep."

"Oh. Okay." Morgan's feet stuck to the floor like they were pillars of cement and the warmth drained from his chest, leaving behind a hollow ache. "I'm sorry."

"No, I'm sorry. I know he was special to you."

"Yeah, he was… He was cool." The tears flooded his eyes without warning. Morgan sniffled and, the next thing he knew, Kazio's arms were around him.

He buried his face in the strong, solid shoulder, and let the tears flow onto Kazio's soft T-shirt. "This is stupid." Morgan sniffled. "He was a cat I barely knew."

"It's not stupid." Kazio squeezed him harder.

Morgan cried harder.

And something snapped in him. Because then he wasn't just crying for Ralph, the poor sweet cat who fell asleep and didn't wake up. He cried for Felix and the band he'd destroyed with his temper. He cried for Luka and Breakpoint, and everything he'd ruined there with his selfishness. He cried for the empty nights with Albert and the endless rejections because he just wasn't good enough.

Kazio made a soothing humming noise, rubbing a hand on Morgan's back. "It's okay, Morgan. You're okay."

Morgan took a shaky breath, suddenly aware of how he had melted into Kazio's body, and left a huge wet patch on his shoulder. Once he pulled away, his tears had stopped. "Thank you," he said in a low voice.

"Of course," Kazio replied. His eyes were steady, peering deep into Morgan's.

"And sorry about your…" He gestured at the shirt.

Kazio looked down, the corner of his mouth twitching. "Don't worry about it. It'll dry."

Ishi subtly handed Morgan a tissue. "There's some new cats in," she said. "Do you want to meet them?"

Another deep breath, a little smoother than the last one. "Sure."

A little white puffball named Florence peered at them from a high ledge. Rizzo pawed at a scratching post. The orange tabby Ishi had been brushing was Jake.

"Who's this guy?" Morgan asked. A black long-hair with white markings on his face and chest glared at them from a cubby.

"He doesn't have a name yet. His owners dumped him yesterday."

The cat scowled at him, with more than a passing resemblance to Grumpy Cat. "He looks pretty cranky."

"That he is. He hasn't let anyone touch him yet. Poor guy."

"Oh." Morgan sat down next to the cubby and held out a hand in the cat's direction.

The cat took a tentative step out, whiskers quivering.

"Hey, buddy," Morgan whispered. "I get it. I'd feel cranky, too. You want to come say hi?"

Camella stuck her head in. "Ishi, they're ready for you in the clinic now."

"Oh, great. Kazio, could you grab Raspberry for me?" She held up Jake. "These two need their teeth checked."

"Sure. No problem."

Camella stepped aside to let the two of them leave, then smiled down at Morgan.

The black cat was sniffing his hand.

"Look at that," Camella said. "That's the closest he's let anyone come."

"Hey, Camella," Morgan said. "Can I ask you something?"

* * * *

After the cat room, they folded a load of laundry, then signed out and stopped at reception to say goodbye to Camella.

"You two heading out?" Camella asked. She bent to pick something up off the floor that turned out to be a small animal carrier. She set it on the counter. Grumpy black cat was inside. "Here you go."

Morgan waited for Kazio's reaction.

Kazio frowned. "What do you mean 'Here you go'?"

Morgan beamed. "I'm taking him home."

Understanding dawned slowly on Kazio's face. "You're what?"

"I'm adopting him."

Kazio's mouth hung open.

Morgan stepped closer to smile at the cat. "Everyone deserves a second chance, don't they?"

"They do," Camella said firmly.

"They do," Kazio agreed, after a beat.

"His name…" Morgan said with a dramatic pause, "is Catzio."

Chapter Thirteen

Catzio

"His name is Catzio?" Kazio closed the car door behind him and turned to stare at Morgan in incredulity.

Morgan grinned. "Yes."

"You got a cat..."

"Yes."

"And you named him after me."

"Yes."

"Why?"

"I don't know..." Morgan peered into the carrier. Catzio stared back, still grumpy. "He sort of reminds me of you. And you're my friend, so why not?"

Kazio started the car. "Did you think this through at all, or was it a complete impulse?"

"I absolutely thought it through. Also could you please stop at ShopMart on the way home? I need to pick up a few things."

* * * *

Morgan's cart was full — cat bed, litter and litter box, scratching post, tins of fancy cat food, bags of treats, toys, the whole nine yards and then some — plus Catzio's carrier, of course, because he couldn't leave him in the car.

"Are you sure you got everything?" Kazio asked.

"Hmm..." Morgan studied his cart.

"I was joking. I think you're good."

"Hope so. Hey, you want to come back to my place, help me get Catzio settled? I don't have any food, but... Ooh, we could grab some groceries while we're here. What if I finally made you dinner?"

"I think you have your hands full for the day," Kazio said. "But I could throw something together?"

"Again? I owe you a meal!"

"You don't owe me anything, and you" — Kazio gestured at the cart — "are busy."

"Well, then, sure, if you don't mind."

They got a second cart for a trip through the grocery side and Kazio scooped up the ingredients for nachos.

"Wait..." He paused at the edge of the produce section. "What else do you need? Do you have milk?"

"No."

"Bread?"

"No."

"Fru —"

"Kazio, you can go ahead and assume I don't have anything. Except expired salad dressing."

"First of all, can you please get rid of the expired salad dressing? And second, you need groceries." He turned around to collect some oranges and bananas, then added milk, bread, cereal and a few other basics to his growing pile.

Jennifer Moffatt

Morgan tried to pay for the food but Kazio fought him off. "You're already going to need a line of credit for your cat supplies. I've got this one."

"Okay, but I really need to make dinner for you next time."

"Deal."

When they got back to Morgan's apartment, they forgot about the ShopMart bags for a moment. Morgan carefully set down the carrier in the middle of his living room and opened the door. "Hey, Catzio," he murmured, kneeling a safe distance away. "Welcome to your new home."

Catzio sat hunched against the far wall of the carrier, watching them with wide eyes.

"It's okay. You take your time." Morgan looked at Kazio. "Do you think he'll come out soon?"

"He will — he just needs to get used to the idea. Here, give him some more space and help me put the groceries away."

Morgan turned to check on Catzio's crate status every five seconds, but they got the groceries sorted, then they got to unpacking the cat supplies.

Morgan opened a bag of cat treats and held one out where Catzio could see it. "You hungry, Catzio?"

Catzio scooched his nose out of the carrier.

"There you go." Morgan inched the treat closer. "Come and try it."

Catzio's whole head poked out now. He darted forward and took the treat from Morgan's fingers.

"Good boy," Morgan said, delighted.

Catzio crunched the treat down, then nosed Morgan's fingers again, looking for more.

"You got it." Morgan fed him another one.

153

Catzio took it, then, before Morgan could even blink, darted under the couch.

Kazio smiled. "Well, he's out. He'll get settled in now."

Morgan nudged the cat bed toward the couch. "Here you go, buddy. This is yours too if you want to lie down."

"You should put one of your T-shirts in the bed," Kazio suggested. "Your smell might be comforting to him, over ShopMart."

"Yeah? Sure, I can do that. What about the one I'm wearing right now? It'll smell a bit like the shelter, too." Morgan pulled his Grumpy Cat T-shirt off and tucked it into the new cat bed. "I hope he's not too scared. Do you think—" He turned to look at Kazio, who was staring at him with wide eyes. "What?" Morgan asked. He smoothed his hair in case it was sticking up.

"Nothing," Kazio said rapidly, diverting his eyes to the mouse toy he was unpackaging. "Nothing, I, uh...I was just going to say that, you know what, we forgot to buy a food bowl."

"Oh, right, duh."

"It's okay. We can use a regular bowl for now. I'll start a list of other things we need." Kazio strode into the kitchen and found a pad of paper while Morgan went to go find another shirt.

＊ ＊ ＊ ＊

They ate on the couch, nachos between them, the silly loincloth show on the TV and Catzio still under the couch.

"But like...*why* is the snake so mean?" Morgan asked, frowning at the TV. "I don't get it."

"Have you ever seen a nice snake?"

"This is a fictional snake."

"Fine, have you ever seen a nice *fictional* snake?"

Morgan pondered that while he crunched his next nacho chip. "You make a good point. There should be some nice fictional snakes somewhere. Snakes get a bad rap, if you ask me. And my next question is — " He held up an immaculately loaded tortilla chip, with the exact perfect ratio of cheese to onion to tomato to green pepper. "How are your nachos so fucking good? Mine are never near this good when I make them."

"It's because I dice the veggies so small," Kazio said, without hesitation.

Morgan dunked it in sour cream and took another bite just to be sure, chewing thoughtfully. "But wait...how could the size of the veggies make any difference in the taste?'

"It's a surface area thing, I've decided," Kazio explained. "Like how apples taste better sliced, or sandwiches taste better cut into smaller pieces."

Something clicked in Morgan's brain. "Oh my God. You're right. You're *so* right. I can't believe my whole life I've been eating huge chunks of food like a total — "

"Hey." Kazio nudged Morgan's foot with his. "Look."

Catzio was out, sniffing at the cat bed.

"Hi, Catzio," Morgan said softly. "That's your new bed. Do you like it?"

Catzio flinched and looked up at them, frozen, probably deciding if he should vanish into hiding again.

"It's okay," Morgan soothed. He leaned forward slowly, hand out. "I'm Morgan. I'm your new roommate."

Catzio tensed, but then relaxed again, craning his head forward to sniff at Morgan's hand. Then he pushed his head against his hand.

Morgan beamed. "He likes me," he whispered as he stroked Catzio's head.

"Of course he does," Kazio said. "You rescued him."

Morgan scratched his head again. Catzio leaned his whole body into Morgan, eyes closing into slits. "There you go," Morgan said. "Welcome home."

* * * *

Catzio carefully and tentatively explored his new apartment while they finished eating. Then, once dinner was cleaned up and the rest of the new purchases tidied away, it was time for Kazio to go.

"Thank you for everything today," Morgan said at the door. "Sometimes I don't know what I'd do without you."

"You're welcome." Kazio turned to face him, one hand on the door knob. "And I'm sure you'd be fine."

The words filling Morgan's mouth weren't quite expressing his feelings properly, but since he had no other words, he used them. "It's sort of lonely without you, sometimes." They were even more inadequate once he said them out loud.

Kazio's reaction was not really what he was expecting either. He tilted his head, jaw clenched. "Have you seen much of Albert?"

"Albert?" Morgan frowned. "Why do you ask?"

"Well, you can't be that lonely with Albert around."

Morgan's mind raced with multiple questions. Why was Kazio asking about Albert? Why was Morgan now *lying* about Albert...by omission, anyway. And how could he make Kazio understand how Albert made him feel not alone for a few minutes, then infinitely more alone as the night stretched on after? "What? No, he's —"

Crash. They both jumped a mile. Catzio was up on a side table, tail twitching, picture frame lying on the ground below.

"Catzio Ralph Di Meo, just what do you think you are doing?" Morgan scolded. Catzio didn't look too bothered by the scolding at all. He hopped to the floor, then sauntered off toward the kitchen, tail in the air.

Morgan darted over and picked up the frame. Thankfully, it hadn't broken. It was a picture of Morgan with his parents when he was still young, before his mom had gotten sick and before his dad had run off to start a new family. They were at the coast in front of a carousel on one of the best days of his life. He remembered choosing the purple horse with the golden mane. He remembered the smell of the salt breeze, the tang of the vinegar on the French fries, the hint of sunburn on his shoulders, the way his mom held his hand and they swung their arms together on the boardwalk... Even his dad looked happy in that picture, clutching the fuzzy orange teddy bear he had won at the ring toss. So many moments from that day were so fresh in Morgan's mind they could have been yesterday—moments that lived inside the one small picture, creased and faded from where it had been stuck into his mom's dressing table mirror.

Kazio's voice startled him. "That looks like it was a really great day."

"Yeah." Morgan traced the curve of his mom's face with his finger. "It was. Oh, Jesus. Don't tell me I'm going to cry *again* today." He sniffled.

Kazio put a hand on his arm. "You don't talk about them much."

"Much, or ever?" Morgan asked with a watery smile.

"Ever, I guess."

Morgan set the picture back on the side table. "I'll give you the quick version—my mom passed away when I was fourteen, my dad lived at the office until I was eighteen, then he ran off with his secretary to start a new family. They live in Florida now with like four kids I've never met."

"I'm sorry, Morgan. That's...that's pretty awful."

"Yeah." Now he was crying again, but this time silent tears slid down his face. "He sends me money sometimes." He shrugged. "He paid for Catzio's stuff. Better than a kick in the pants, right?"

Kazio shifted his weight. Morgan looked up at him. He wasn't sure why, maybe something to do with the lighting, but it was like he was seeing Kazio for the first time. His pale hair looked like moonlight, his eyes the deep bluey-purple of distant mountains, and shoulders that looked strong enough to hold up those mountains.

He could certainly lift Morgan up, anyway.

"Do you have any other family?" Kazio asked.

Morgan shrugged. "Not really. My mom's brother never had kids. I've got a cousin on my dad's side that I see every now and then, but he's never in one place for long. It's basically...just me."

"I'm sorry. I know what it's like to feel alone." Kazio checked the time on his phone. "Shit. Listen, I told Tasha I'd head back in tonight to help with a game night that's gotten a bit out of hand, but I could—"

"No, it's fine," Morgan said quickly, wiping a tear. "You should go help her."

Kazio looked uncertain, fiddling with his phone.

"It's really fine." Morgan smiled. "I've got Catzio now."

"Right. Okay, well..." He stepped forward to hug Morgan again. "Text me if you need anything."

The tears hadn't quite dried up yet, because as he hugged Kazio back, another one squeezed out. *I need more of these hugs,* he thought. "I will," he said.

* * * *

"Salmon or tuna?" Morgan held up the tins of cat food to show Catzio.

Black fluffy tail in the air, Catzio cocked his head.

"The salmon? Excellent choice. That's exactly what I was thinking." Morgan pried open the tin and dumped the meaty cylinder onto a small plate. He set it down on the floor with a flourish. "Bon appétit!"

Catzio looked at it, then looked up at Morgan again.

"No? You don't want it? At least give it a try."

Catzio sat down and stared at Morgan expectantly.

"I don't know what you want me to say. I think you at least need to try it. I can't—Oh. You know what?" He retrieved a fork from the drawer and mashed up the food. "Surface area, am I right?"

Catzio trotted over in the dainty little way he had and devoured the entire thing in what had to be record speed.

"Whoa, easy, you don't want to give yourself a kitty tummy ache, do you?" Morgan ran his hand along Catzio's soft fur.

Plate licked clean, Catzio rubbed against Morgan's leg then headed back to the living carpet for a grooming session.

"All right, fair enough. I like to groom myself in front of the TV after dinner, too." Morgan put the plate in the sink, then made some tea and sat on the couch with his laptop. Time to suck it up and find a job. Or at least, that was his plan, but suddenly there was a black cat in his lap.

"Oh, hello. You want to sit with me?" Morgan put the laptop aside and gave Catzio a few long, smooth pets.

Catzio turned a circle, then settled into a contented ball.

The tea, out of reach now, would cool, but Morgan didn't care. He had a warm cat in his lap, and that was all he needed…for now.

Chapter Fourteen

The *Best* Cocktails

Morgan woke up with a cat inches away from his face.

"Oh. Oh God. Honey, no, it's only..." He fumbled for his phone. "Six o'clock in the morning, Catzio. Oh, no, no, no. I forgot to ask for a cat who likes to sleep in."

Catzio climbed over Morgan's shoulder and circled around his pillow.

"No, this is my pillow," Morgan said, but all he could do was watch helplessly as Catzio burrowed into it. Morgan sighed. "Fine, but...just this once, okay? I'm still in charge here, after all." And since he was already awake, he might as well check the waiting message from Kazio.

How's Catzio? it said.

Catzio is good, Morgan replied. *He's currently commandeering my pillow.* He held his phone up and snapped a selfie of him next to the cat to send.

You're up already???

Yes, the large cat on my pillow had something to do with that.

I seriously can't believe you named him Catzio.

It's actually the perfect name. The more I get to know him, the more convinced I am.

Oh? Please elaborate.

You two have so much in common. First of all, the long flowing hair, obviously.

Obviously.

Second. Morgan wiggled into a more comfortable texting position. *Man of few words.*

I feel like he's a little quieter than I am.

Third. Morgan ignored his protestations. *He stares at me sometimes like he's a little bit worried about what I'm going to do next.*

Accurate.

Fourth, he's very cuddly.

Um...am I cuddly?

No, but... Morgan paused and wondered if he should say it. *You give the best hugs.* Then he dove right into his next message. *Anyway, what are you up to?*

There was a slight pause before Kazio's next reply. *Nothing exciting, did some laundry. Going to head into work pretty soon to get caught up on paperwork. Hey, I had an idea…* Kazio sent a link for some sort of cooking class. *I was thinking…what if we padded your resume a little more?*

Ummmm. *With chef training???*

No, not chef training! Actually read the link.

K fine.

Morgan sighed and sat up in his bed. It was a little early for reading, but for Kazio he would do it. Catzio made a little "meowrp" sound. Morgan stared at him. "I think that's the first thing you've said."

Catzio blinked at him, then started grooming his paws.

Back to the reading. The link was for a community cooking class — it was free and open for anyone needing a little bit of extra help learning how to cook the basics, like students away from home for the first time or developmentally delayed adults. The program was run by volunteers.

I can't teach anyone how to cook though, Morgan texted. *Remember the marshmallow incident?*

Keep reading. Click the 'Volunteer' button.

Kazio was bossy in the morning. Morgan clicked on the 'volunteer' button anyway. Yes, they needed volunteer chefs, but also assistants who helped prep, clean and support the students.

I thought it would be fun to do together, Kazio added. *There's another round of classes coming up and there's training ahead of time.*

And maybe I could learn some cooking skills, Mogan thought to himself.

And maybe you could learn some cooking skills, Kazio added.

Rude, Morgan replied. *I know how to cook. I just choose not to.*

Do you, though?

No.

Morgan imagined Kazio rolling his eyes in response.

Just think about it, Kazio said. *We would need to sign up by the end of the month.*

Okay, I will. Have fun at work. I need more sleep!

Good luck.

Morgan wiggled around in bed for a bit, but it was too hard to sleep without a pillow, so he finally got up with a mildly annoyed huff. "We'll have to get you your own pillow," he told Catzio.

Catzio, fast asleep, ignored him.

Breakfast was more exciting with a kitchen that actually had an assortment of food in it. Morgan had a bowl of cereal and a banana, then opened up his laptop to find some more fucking jobs to apply for. But he got a little sidetracked cleaning out email first, and an old message from Brett caught his eye.

Right. Brett and Ray, Bickering Brothers Extraordinaire... He had been meaning to reach out again. Second chances and all that. And it wasn't like he had any other options for bandmates at the moment.

He pulled out his phone and texted Brett.

Hey Brett. Sorry about the delay getting back to you. Was wondering if you and Ray wanted to get together and jam again?

No instant reply, so he put his phone aside and opened up the job classifieds. Again. Forehead resting in his palm, he began scrolling.

A few temporary gigs caught his attention—someone looking for background guitar music for a business reception, a musician needed for a kids' birthday party, a DJ for a corporate event—plus, yup, a guitar instructor at a local music school.

He'd apply for the background guitar and the DJ—he figured he could mix a playlist together well enough—but the birthday party was a hell no. The guitar player application required a video of him playing background guitar music, which he did not have. "All right then," he sighed. "Guess we're doing this."

First, he needed a good spot for filming. His guest room was full of sound gear and could basically serve as a recording studio, so he pushed some furniture and wires aside to create a plain backdrop and set up his microphone. Staring at the blank off-white wall, he determined that it was a little too plain, so dragged in a potted snake plant from the living room for some ambiance. Satisfied with the space, he showered, coiffed his hair into something sleek and stylish, and put on navy trousers with a white dress shirt and gray blazer over top. And the final piece, his acoustic guitar.

With the camera set up, he hit record. "Hi, I'm Morgan Di Meo," he said, "and this is me playing the guitar." Nope, that was dumb. "Hi, my name is Morgan Di Meo, and I'd be happy to play the guitar for you."

Catzio appeared in the doorway and sat to stare at him.

"Don't judge me," he told the cat. "Sometimes being a human is degrading. You're lucky you're a cat."

Catzio blinked and moved on.

Morgan tried again. "Hi, my name is Morgan, and this is a sample of my guitar music for you." Good enough. He improvised some lilting tunes for about two minutes, as requested, then smiled and said "Thank you." It only took him a few minutes to edit the video and send it off with his resume.

He sent Kazio a shorter clip, just of him playing, not with the awkward introduction.

Would you hire me to play soothing background guitar music at your business reception?

Am I having a business reception?

Like, hypothetically.

Then yes, I would. You look great.

Let's hope… Morgan checked the name of the person he had emailed… *Victoria Barrett agrees.*

He was about to fire off an application to the DJing job, but made himself pause and create a version of his resume that emphasized his sound design training, and sort of tweaked a college project to sort of sound like a DJing job…sort of. He sent that off, too.

Feeling quite proud of himself, he hovered his cursor over the guitar teacher job… But mercifully he was interrupted by a reply from Brett.

Hey Morgan, yeah it's been a while. We thought you'd moved on. Ray has actually decided to quit drumming and pursue his dream of falconry. But I'm still interested if you'd like to meet up.

"Hell yes!" Morgan pumped his fist in the air. Normally he'd be devastated to lose a drummer, but when that drummer was a bit of a weirdo who wouldn't stop arguing with the bassist…

"Meowrp?" Catzio was at his feet.

"Oh, don't mind me. Just got some good news… Am I talking to myself too much now? I guess it doesn't count as talking to myself if I'm talking to you, does it?"

Catzio lifted a leg and started licking his belly.

"Well, okay then."

Yeah, that would be awesome, he replied to Brett. *When are you free?*

* * * *

Brett came over to Morgan's place this time. "Thanks for having me over. It's probably better if I don't bring you around our place with Ray there just now. He's a little sensitive."

"Oh?"

"Yeah, I guess the falconry is not going well. It turns out you have to be licensed and stuff…"

"Oh dear. Yeah, we can jam here a bit. We just can't be too loud."

Catzio entered the front hall and sat, staring up at Brett.

"You have a cat," Brett said.

"Yes. Just. I got him a couple days ago."

"What's his name?"

"Catzio."

"What? Catzo?"

"No, 'Cat-zho'."

Brett crinkled his forehead. "I don't get it."

"Well… My best friend's name is Kazio. It's short for Kazimierz. So, you know… 'Catzio'."

"Kazy…mess?" Brett tried to repeat 'Kazimierz' and failed.

"Uh, almost. It's Polish." This was not off to a good start. Morgan almost wished Ray was there. "So anyway, my studio is through here…"

Brett seemed just as relieved to change the topic. "Sweet setup, man," he said, taking in Morgan's gleaming array of equipment. "Wow, you're serious about this." He raised his hand, grubby fingers reaching for the sound board.

"Don't touch that!" Morgan snapped. "Uh, sorry. It's just… That's, like, really expensive."

Brett dropped his hand, trying to look like he wasn't offended. "Cool, whatever. Let's play."

"Yes, please."

* * * *

Brett was really good.

Thank God.

He had nimble fingers — Morgan regretted thinking the word 'grubby' to describe them earlier — excellent rhythm and an instinct for what was needed in the moment.

Morgan grinned at him, relieved, when they brought *Another One Bites the Dust* to a close. "That was tight."

"Yeah it was." Brett offered him a fist bump. "You're a sick guitar player."

"Thanks… You think we can make this work?"

"Hundred percent."

"Awesome." Morgan strummed a few more chords. "You or Ray don't happen to know any other guitar players or a drummer that might work, would you?"

"Don't think so, but I'll ask around."

"Great. You want a drink before you go? Toast our new partnership?"

"Sure."

They sat at the kitchen table, each with a can of seltzer. Morgan made a note to stock a few other things to drink besides low-cal vodka sodas and straight-up tequila.

"Are you single?" Brett asked a few sips in.

"Oh, yes. Very. My last boyfriend…" He paused. God, Luka had dumped him a year ago now. The sting felt fresher than that, what with him getting fired for being a piece of shit much more recently. "Well, it was a while ago now. And I'm not…very good at dating. You?"

"Yeah, got a girlfriend, been together about five months now. She's honestly the best."

"That's great."

"You know what, her brother is gay, and he's single, I could—"

"No, no, I'm good, thanks."

"You don't want to date?"

"It's not that I don't want to date, it's that I'm..." *Selfish? A bad boyfriend? Bound to fuck it up again?* "...busy," he finished lamely. "You know, trying to find a job, get the band going..."

"Sure, man. Well...here's to the band starting today."

As he waved Brett off down the hallway, he didn't know if the two of them were necessarily going to be great friends, but they sure sounded great together.

He took a deep breath. *Bass player...check.*

A celebration was required.

Are you at work? Morgan texted Kazio. *I need a drink!*

Yeah, I am. Is this 'I need a drink' in a good way or a bad way?

The best!

Come on down.

* * * *

"...And I know it's only one other band member," Morgan chirped as Kazio sorted through receipts, "but it's a huge step. Brett is...I mean, we don't totally vibe super well, you know, like, talking and stuff, but when we're playing?"

"Shit," Kazio muttered under his breath.

"What?" Morgan frowned at Kazio over his Paloma. "It's not shit. Are you even listening to me?"

Kazio made a strangled noise at him, eyes darting meaningfully toward the door.

"What are you—?" Morgan started, baffled, but Kazio interrupted him at near-whisper.

"Don't look, but there's a guy who just came in—I said not to look!"

"Well, what else am I gonna do when you say 'don't look'?"

"How about *not look*? Okay, real quick, this guy won't leave me alone and I need you to be my boyfriend."

"What?"

But Kazio shushed him as the man reached the bar.

"Hello, Kazio," he said, climbing onto a stool and leaning against the bar in a way that could only be described as debonair. The man was extremely handsome, Morgan had to give him that. About forty, with an expensive suit, shiny shoes and a watch that probably cost more than all of Morgan's possessions combined. Well…maybe not all his sound gear.

Kazio kept his face neutral but there was terror in his eyes. "Emil."

"And how are you today, sir?" Emil asked.

"Fine. The usual?"

"Yes, please."

Morgan wasn't sure what to do, so he sat there as he imagined Kazio's boyfriend might sit there. Which is to say…on a bar stool.

Kazio mixed a Brawler and cola in record speed and dropped it in front of Emil.

Emil took a sip, then gave a dramatic sigh. "No one mixes cocktails quite like you, sir."

Kazio shot Morgan a 'say something' look.

Morgan panicked. *Like what?* he asked Kazio with his eyes.

Literally anything, Kazio silently screamed back at him.

"You can say that again," Morgan blurted.

Emil turned, seeing Morgan for the first time. "Excuse me?"

"The *best* cocktails," Morgan clarified, holding up his Paloma. "Doesn't he?"

"Emil," Kazio said, the picture of calm. "Allow me to introduce my boyfriend, Morgan."

Kazio had left his hand on the bar near Morgan's, so Morgan put his on top. "That's me," Morgan said. "The boyfriend."

"Oh?" Emil said, disappointment clear on his face. "Boyfriend?"

"That's right." Morgan ran his fingers over the back of Kazio's hand. His very large and...strong hand.

"How...nice." Emil took a sip. "You've never mentioned a boyfriend before," he said to Kazio with a hint of an accusatory tone.

"Oh, you know how it is..." Morgan drawled before Kazio could get a word in. "I tell him not to. Don't want to make the customers jealous, isn't that right, sweetheart?" Morgan patted his hand, then rubbed his forearm. Kazio hadn't moved an inch since Morgan touched him.

"That's right," Kazio said in a strangled voice. He cleared his throat.

"But he comes home to me, doesn't he?" Morgan continued, on a roll. "I'm not interested in sharing." He laced his fingers between Kazio's and lifted the back of Kazio's hand to his lips.

Their eyes met over their clasped hands. Morgan had expected to see an amused twinkle in Kazio's eyes, but instead he was playing the part, gazing back at Morgan as if they were deeply in love. A warm and fuzzy feeling tickled his rib cage. He smiled and rubbed Kazio's forearm some more with his other hand. Pretending to be his boyfriend was not the worst task he'd ever been given.

Emil gave them a wan smile, collected his drink then made his way over to a table with a mumbled goodbye.

Morgan chuckled, their fingers still woven together.

Kazio leaned closer, putting their heads together like they were sharing an intimate moment. Morgan's stomach flipped as Kazio's lips got closer. He wasn't going to—?

But no. Obviously. "Thank you," Kazio mumbled. "I owe you huge. You were perfect."

"Was I?" Morgan gave a rueful grin. "It's too bad I'm a terrible actual boyfriend."

Kazio pulled back a bit. "There's no way you're a terrible boyfriend."

Luka's breakup words washed over Morgan. *"You and I both know there's no real feelings here."* Those words had flattened him, then backed up and run over him again. Because he had cared about Luka…a lot. He had just fucked it up by being himself.

Luka had caught his eye immediately, of course, because how could he not? Everyone loved Luka. Handsome, charismatic, outgoing… Morgan had employed his usual strategy—strutting around in his cutest outfits, trying to find any excuse to talk to Luka. When that didn't work, he had to step it up a notch with a cheesy, overtly sexual pickup line. Luka seemed to like that, at least. So Morgan had followed him into the supply closet a week later and made his move. It had been risky, but effective.

Luka was so gorgeous and so sweet...and Morgan knew it wouldn't take him long to realize he was way out of Morgan's league. So Morgan overthought everything and tried to play it cool, keep it casual, while he waited for Luka to inevitably break up with him...which he did. The restaurant forgot Luka's pad Thai one night, and Morgan, so caught up in his own head, hadn't thought to do anything about it. And that was it—the moment Luka realized he didn't want Morgan anymore. Still, getting dumped had hurt a lot more than he had expected. Then...oh, then...Morgan had made it all so much worse.

"Trust me, I am a terrible boyfriend," Morgan said, letting go of Kazio's hand and picking up his drink again. "Luka could tell you all about it."

"Then I guess Luka wasn't the right one for you."

He snorted, but now Kazio's words ran through his head instead. *Luka wasn't the right one for me.* And again. *Luka wasn't the right one for me.*

Luka...was not the right one. Yes, the great sex, and Morgan liked being with him, but... Luka wasn't the right one for him. As much as Morgan had wished he was...it was never going to work out.

If only he had known that before he had started blackmailing Luka.

He realized he had been silent long enough that Kazio had made him a new drink.

"Thank you," Morgan said, for more than just the drink.

"You're welcome," Kazio said, for more than just the drink.

Chapter Fifteen

Dancing Monkey

"Who's a pretty kitty? Who is? That's you, isn't it, Catzio?"

Catzio stared back from his spot on the carpet, unimpressed.

"Yes, so pretty," Morgan agreed with himself, snapping a few more pics of his cat lying in a beam of sunlight, just so. "Good boy."

He texted a picture to Kazio.

Look how pretty he is! Look!

I'm starting to feel jealous that you like Catzio more than you like me, Kazio replied. *You never tell me I'm pretty anymore.*

A photo of Kazio came through. Morgan snickered. He was lying on his carpet, sun in his hair, pouting.

You are also very pretty, Morgan assured him.

But am I prettier than Catzio?

Let's not go crazy.

I'm not sure I want to come pick you up now. You can walk to the shelter.

Okay, fine. You are prettier than Catzio.

That's more like it. I'll be there in thirty.

* * * *

"Guess what!" Morgan bounced into Kazio's car.

Kazio raised an eyebrow at him. "You just shot-gunned an energy drink?"

"What? No." Mogan scooped up the iced coffee waiting for him in the cup holder. "The background guitar! I got the gig!"

"You did? Morgan, that's amazing! Congratulations!" Kazio reached over to squeeze his knee.

"Thanks." Morgan's cheeks hurt from smiling. The email from Victoria Barrett had arrived only moments before. It was all he could do to keep from wiggling in his seat with glee.

"When is it?"

"Next week. Pay's pretty good and she said it could easily lead to more gigs if they like me."

"That's terrific, Morgan. I'm so proud of you."

The iced coffee could barely get by the sudden lump in his throat. "Thanks."

When they arrived at the shelter, Camella was out front weeding the raised flower beds that were a riot of brightly colored tulips.

"Hi, boys," she called, brushing dirt from her gloves before giving them each a hug. "How are my favorite volunteers?"

"We're good. How's our favorite shelter owner?" Kazio asked.

"I'm just fine. More importantly, how is Catzio doing?"

"So good," Morgan gushed. "Here…" He pulled his phone out to show Camella a few of the eight thousand cat photos on his camera roll. "These are from this morning, he loves that sunbeam. And yesterday…look at him playing with his little mouse toy, so cute…"

Camella put her hand on her heart. "Oh, Morgan. I'm so glad you two found each other."

"Me too." They shared a smile. "So," Morgan said briskly, lest he start crying again, "Where can we help today?"

"I have a special job for you, actually! Follow me." She led them inside to sign in then to the staff room. "You are judging our coloring contest!"

"We're what now?"

"You heard me." Camella winked and pointed at the table stacked with envelopes and coloring pages. "Those envelopes are from schools so you'll need to open them up and sort the entries into age categories. Then pick a winner from each, plus two runners-up."

Morgan sat and started flipping through a stack. "But how do we decide who wins?"

Camella patted Morgan's shoulder. "I'm sure you'll figure it out," was all she said on her way out.

Morgan ripped open an envelope and dumped the contents on to the table. A sea of brightly colored pages stared back at him. "But seriously…half of these look the same. How do we pick a winner?"

"It's a coloring contest, so…" Kazio held up a page completed entirely in shades of pink "…by the coloring?"

Morgan smacked his arm. "That's helpful, thanks." The contest drawing was simple—just a smiling cartoon cat and dog with 'Mountain Meadows Animal Care Center' below in bubble letters. Morgan selected a page that was colored—or scribbled—by a three-year-old named Sage. "Who am I to judge Sage's creation, though?"

Kazio chuckled. "Let's start by sorting them into age categories, and we can see how many stand out."

They got to work. Morgan's knee bumped Kazio's under the table a few times as they sorted, which was a weird thing for him to even notice. He scooted his chair over an inch.

"Check out this one," Morgan breathed, holding up an entry by eleven-year-old Harper. "It's gorgeous." Harper had used pencil crayons, blending all the colors together expertly, and had created a magical shimmering forest all around the animals. The cat was colored in purples and grays, and the dog was green and blue. "This is the best one so far."

Kazio grabbed the sticky notes to make labels for each category. "Here, we'll start piles for our top ones, too."

The next creation that caught Morgan's eye was from nine-year-old Sabar. The execution wasn't quite there, but the idea was a winner—he had turned the cat and dog into pirates and put them on a pirate ship. "Sabar's a front-runner in nine-ten."

"Should we be concerned about Lena?" Kazio asked. Ten-year-old Lena had turned the animals into zombies.

"We're gonna assume she just likes zombies," Morgan said. "No subtext. Bruno, however…" Bruno's entire page was black. "Bruno is going through some things."

"Look how cute Venus' is," Kazio said, holding up the next one. "They're having a tea party."

Morgan squinted. "How can you tell?"

"Look, this is a teapot."

"Is it? I thought it was a car."

"What? It's got a handle and a spout and everything."

The time flew by as they laughed and sorted and oohed and awed. At some point Morgan realized their knees were pressed together under the table. It felt nice. He didn't move away this time.

"Okay," Morgan said, when all that was left was deciding on the winner of the three-four category. "I am once again asking you to consider…" He held up Sage's entry. "Look how she used the green to emphasize humanity's need to find meaning in nature—the tension between taming and respecting. Survival *despite* the forest, versus survival *within*. It's profound."

Kazio laughed. "But…" He picked up Theo's. "This one has hearts."

Morgan sighed. "Trite."

Kazio laughed harder, which got Morgan going. "I'll give you Theo as runner-up over Natia's naked turtles, but I cannot…" He dissolved into his own laughter, hand on Kazio's forearm.

"Naked turtles," Kazio said breathlessly, mid-giggle. "I think they're supposed to be dinosaurs."

Morgan wiped a tear from his eye. "Clearly Natia left it open for the observer to interpret."

Camella appeared behind them. "I had no idea this job was going to be so much fun!"

They tried to tame their giggles down. "They're all so cute," Morgan said. "It was hard to choose. They really should all get a prize."

"All get a prize? Hmm...I kind of love that idea. I suppose we could swing stickers for all of them, on top of the winners' prizes."

"Yay." Morgan clapped his hands. "That's perfect." He shuffled through their favorites again. "You know, it's actually kind of cool that kids create so freely — before it gets all soulless and corporate. Thanks for letting us judge the contest."

Camella and Kazio exchanged a look, but Morgan wasn't sure why.

"You're welcome," Camella said. "Now who wants to mop some kennels?"

* * * *

When they got to Morgan's apartment, Kazio got out of the car and came around to stand on the sidewalk with him. "I'm really so proud of you," he said, hands in his pockets.

Morgan looked up at him. "You are? Why?"

"It can't be easy to keep the job hunt going, but you're doing it, and now you get to show everyone how amazing you are."

Morgan's cheeks heated as he waved away the idea. "I'm just the background music, they probably won't even — "

Kazio stepped in to hug him.

"Oh." It was more a gasp than a word as Kazio's arms went around him. Morgan rested his head on

Kazio's chest and hugged him back. The feeling of warmth and kindness that enveloped him, it was like nothing bad could ever happen to him there.

Morgan let out an audible sigh, but he didn't care. He wanted to stay there forever.

"Morgan?" Kazio said. "I'm letting go now."

"Not quite yet," Morgan said. "Five more seconds. Or minutes."

Kazio's chuckle vibrated through his chest. "I've got to get to work."

"Hmph. I wish you wouldn't."

"Why don't you come by for a drink later? In case Emil comes by again."

Morgan smiled into Kazio's T-shirt. "I'll be there."

He hated letting go.

* * * *

Galerie de Rêverie was in the older part of downtown, on a cobblestoned pedestrian-only side-street that was lined with charming shops and cafés and popular with tourists year-round. The gallery was much larger than it looked from the outside, making use of the basement, second story, and, as it expanded over the years, neighboring storefronts.

Morgan had spoken to Victoria Barrett on the phone and she had seemed a little high-strung, but nothing prepared him for meeting her face-to-face. "High-strung" was about ten levels too low.

"Morgan!" she trilled when she saw him walking in with his guitar. "*Delighted* to meet you in person. Your video was *lovely*. We're going to set you up in room three..." And she was off, dodging the staff with armloads of tablecloths and champagne flutes setting up for the reception. Morgan kept an eye on her pink and black tweed skirt suit as they wound through a few high-ceilinged rooms connected with wide doorways. She led him into one of the larger, main rooms and pointed to a corner.

"We'll put you over here, I think, but you'll be wired up to play throughout the whole gallery. The guests should start arriving in the next thirty minutes or so, but of course most of them will be fashionably late."

"What's the reception for?" he asked as he opened his guitar case.

"Oh, did I not tell you? It's for Barrett Industries. Rebar. Dreadfully boring stuff, but it's my brother's company and I arrange these little dos for him on occasion. We're trying the gallery for the first time." She smoothed her perfect hair, gathered in a complicated twist of some sort, as she looked around. "Do you like it? This room is apparently art done by the gallery members."

Morgan hadn't had much time to actually consider the space yet. The painting next to him was tall and narrow, from the floor almost all the way to the ceiling, and was mostly blank, save for an assortment of tiny red squares clumped in groups of various sizes. He tilted his head back to take it all in. The red squares got smaller toward the top, then the white canvas seemed to dissolve into the wall. It was called *A Progression and a Dissolution*. "Er, yes. I'm no expert or anything but…yeah, it's cool."

Cynthia looked thrilled with his answer. "Well, I'll leave you to set up. The gallery director said everything you need should be here?"

Morgan examined the equipment piled at his feet and nodded. "Looks good."

"Terrif. If you need anything, I'll be around here somewhere. Oh, dear, dear, dear, Hector, no!" She scurried after a poor man in a bow tie.

Morgan got set up quickly, running wires and plugging in the gear, then tested the sound with a few chords. Everything seemed good. He idly plucked at the strings and looked around his space some more. Across from him was a dark, abstract canvas — a figure curled up in one corner, surrounded by blurry shapes. It unnerved him, so he moved on to the next one, a more conventional mountainous landscape. But the more he looked at it, the more it unsettled him too. The mountains loomed, and the forest had an impossible depth to it that drew him in. It almost made him feel claustrophobic, imagining what it would be like to be lost in those woods. *Survival despite the forest, versus survival within.* He smiled. Sage would have liked this one.

"Shall we do a sound check?"

Morgan jumped when Victoria appeared next to him, seemingly from nowhere. "Oh, yeah, sure."

"Keep playing, I'll do a quick tour and make sure I can hear you in every room."

"Got it." Morgan started strumming as the reception took shape around him. Trays of champagne sat ready on small round tables, smartly dressed servers nearby at the ready.

Fortunately, Morgan saw Victoria on her way back this time. "Lovely, Morgan, lovely. It sounds terrific. You take your breaks as we discussed, and let's hope it all goes smoothly. I'll check in when I can."

"Got it. Thanks, Ms. Barrett."

The guests began trickling in at seven, the men in suits and the women in cocktail dresses. His parents would have fit in perfectly with this crowd.

He started to play. And it felt...nice. It certainly wasn't the same thing as being a rock star at center stage, but it wasn't the worst thing ever, letting his fingers wander on autopilot and people-watching as the guests flowed past him.

A tall, muscular man with curly, shoulder-length red hair came into his vision and for a second he thought it was Finn from Breakpoint... It *was* Finn from Breakpoint.

What the fuck is Finn doing here? Morgan averted his eyes but with a sinking feeling realized there was nothing to do but to stand there and continue playing. Finn was obviously going to see him. His fingers stumbled over a chord.

Finn walked right by, Rory on his arm. *Oh Jesus. The two of them. Even worse.* They didn't appear to see him, pausing at the creepy huddled figure painting across the way, chatting and sipping their champagne. Finn said something to Rory and Rory beamed up at him like he was the most perfect human in existence.

Morgan relaxed somewhat as they wandered into the next room, but knew it was inevitable that they would see him at some point. There was no way around it.

He was taking his first break when the moment he was dreading arrived. Finn's voice, giving him shit, of course. "Can't you play something more upbeat?"

Morgan swiveled his gaze up to meet Finn's. "Finn."

"He's kidding, of course," Rory jumped in, still attached to Finn's arm. "Your music has been beautiful."

Now Morgan met Rory's eyes. As usual, there was nothing in them but kindness. Morgan tried to unclench his jaw. And every other muscle. "Thanks. Wasn't expecting to see you two here."

"Oh, my dad…" Rory said, waving a hand.

It hit him. Of course. Rory Barrett. Barrett Industries… Holy shit, Rory was *loaded*. "Oh, right, Barrett…" Morgan trailed off, nodding.

"Yup."

Another awkward pause.

Even Finn let the silence drag on, which was unlike him—a testament to the level of awkwardness they had achieved. "So…how have you been?" Finn finally asked.

Morgan almost had to laugh. *Oh, you know, still unemployed and single,* he wanted to say. Instead he shrugged. "Pretty good. How are you two?"

"Great, actually," Rory said. They took Finn's hand to display their rings. "We got married."

"Oh, wow. That is great. Congratulations." And he was happy for them, he really was. But it was also a knife in the side of the corpse of Breakpoint Morgan.

"Thanks. You know—" Rory started to say at the time Morgan said, "Well, I'd better get back to work. Victoria's got me on a schedule."

"Yes, of course. That sounds like Aunt Victoria. We don't want to keep you." Rory gave him a small smile. "You sound really good, Morgan. Really."

His stomach twisted. "Thanks. Enjoy the party."

* * * *

Morgan slumped onto the bar. "It was so embarrassing."

Kazio frowned at him, polishing a glass. "Why was it embarrassing?"

"I'm like...the dancing monkey, there for their entertainment."

"Morgan..." Kazio set his glass down and placed both of his hands on the bar. "That's literally what musicians do. You entertain people. You're doing what you love."

Morgan made a noise that was one part scoff, one part groan.

"Look." Kazio picked up a new glass. "I know you've managed to avoid the Breakpoint crew in here, but...you can't avoid them all forever."

Morgan covered his eyes with one hand. "It was working for me so far."

"Morgan..."

He peeked at Kazio with one eye. "What?"

"For what it's worth, you're a very talented monkey."

Morgan tried not to laugh.

"Best monkey I know, really."

This time the laugh escaped. "Thanks."

"So how did it go, besides Finn and Rory?" Kazio asked.

Morgan sighed. "Really well. A bunch of people asked for my card, and Victoria said she'd definitely call me again."

"That's great. You're getting out there, making it happen."

"Is it not more soulless, corporate art, though?"

"What?"

"Like, you know—I'm just in it for the money. I'm not...scribbling with a green crayon, or turning a cat into a pirate. I'm playing generic background music for rich people."

"Hey." Kazio set the glass down again and reached for Morgan's hand. "You are an artist. You are a musician. You got to create whatever music you wanted all night. Artists deserve to get paid, and it doesn't mean they've sold out. Plus, your band will be out there soon, too."

Morgan took a deep breath. "Okay. I guess sometimes you've just gotta be a dancing monkey."

"And sometimes you're a naked turtle."

Morgan threw back his head and laughed. "Either way, I need some tequila."

Chapter Sixteen

Stuck

Morgan woke up Sunday morning to three texts. One from Albert had come in at two a.m. Morgan didn't even open it, just marked it as read. One text was from Kazio wishing him good morning. Morgan smiled and replied to that one before he investigated the third, because the third... That one was from Andre, the other guitar player from his failed band. Andre, who had found a new group to move on with.

Morgan opened the text and... *Best. News. Ever.*

That new band had fallen apart.

And Andre wanted back in.

Morgan screeched.

Catzio glared at him from his spot on Morgan's pillow.

"Okay, sorry, I guess it's horrible of me to cheer another band's demise but...I'm fucking *thrilled.*"

Hell yeah, Morgan replied to Andre. *You're in. And...* He had to ask. *Any chance the drummer can come with you?*

That's part of the problem, we didn't really have one.

"Damn it," Morgan muttered. "Where are all the fucking drummers?" he asked Catzio. Catzio didn't know.

I've been jamming with a bass player named Brett and we're meeting at my place today. Are you free at two?

See you then.

"Yessss!" Morgan whooped, kicking his feet. "We're almost there, Catzio!"
Catzio licked his paw.
Another text from Andre popped up.

Also, I have to ask — why is your Instagram like a hundred pictures of a cat now?

* * * *

"Andre!" Morgan said when he opened his front door. He didn't have the words to properly express how happy he was to see him again — the big Black guy with a cool fade and easy laugh. Morgan had missed him so much.
"Morgan," Andre said, who was smiling just as huge. "Good to see you." Andre set down his electric guitar case and gave Morgan a hug. "Ah, so this is the Instagram model," he said over Morgan's shoulder.
Catzio had appeared in the door to the kitchen, head cocked.
"This is him," Morgan said proudly. "Catzio."
"Nice to meet you, Catzio," Andre said. "Thanks for letting me come over."
Morgan sighed. "So it's obvious that he's in charge?"

Andre grinned. "My partner's got a cat. I know what's what."

"Brett should be here soon," Morgan said, gesturing for Andre to have a seat at the kitchen table. "Can I get you a drink? Coffee? Tea?"

"Water would be great, thanks."

"How have you been?" Morgan asked when he sat with two glasses of water.

"All right," Andre said. "I tell you, getting a band to stick is rough."

"Right? Why is it so hard?"

Andre took a sip of water and gave a sly smile. "I think maybe ego has something to do with it."

"Er." Morgan studied his glass. "Yeah, maybe."

"Easy, man, I wasn't giving you shit. I don't blame you for what happened."

"I do," Morgan muttered.

"It's not your fault. Felix clearly wasn't as committed, you know? You can't bail on a gig last minute like that."

"I shouldn't have told him he was a bad drummer, though."

Andre took a thoughtful sip. "Nah, maybe not. But Felix did some name-calling, too."

"Yeah...he was right, though."

"I don't know about that," Andre replied.

"Doesn't matter now, I guess." Morgan shifted in his chair and put on a bright smile. "So what's new with you?"

The two of them chatted about Andre's work—he was a librarian at the public library and had all kinds of good stories, mostly involving adorable children and unhinged parents—until Brett arrived a few minutes later.

Morgan introduced Brett and Andre and held his breath while they shook hands, as if that moment could make or break the nascent band. No explosion. So far, so good.

He led them into his studio. "Obviously not an ideal rehearsal space but I think we can make it work. Your amps can hook up to my sound mixer, and then we can hear each other with in-ear monitors." He handed out the equipment and showed them where to plug in. "The only thing that's going to make noise is the singing so we'll just have to try to keep it down." He set up mics for Andre and himself and did a mic check, then strapped on his electric guitar. "Can you give me a few bars of *Crazy Little Thing* while I adjust the levels?" Morgan cued up a drum track for them too. It sounded even better than he had expected when they put it all together. "How is that sounding to you guys?" Morgan asked as he fiddled with a few knobs.

"Fucking sweet," Brett enthused.

Andrew nodded and gave him a thumbs up.

"Want to start with *Cherry Tree*?" Morgan asked. He had taught it to Brett, and knew it had been one of Andre's favorites.

"Hell yeah," Andre agreed.

Morgan counted them in, and they were off.

"Hot summer day, 'bout a hundred and three
Watching you down in the shade
Lying back, tongue so red
Under the cherry tree."

Morgan grinned through the transition to the next verse. They sounded great, and he forgot how well Andre's backup vocals complimented his.

"I wanna shake off those leaves
Climb your branches high
Flat on your back, look up at the sky
Under the cherry tree."

Brett pointed at Morgan's mic and gave him a 'turn it up' gesture so Morgan fiddled with the controls again.

"Kisses so sweet, so free
Red juice down your chin
Gonna hold me, gonna let me in
Under the cherry tree."

Joy surged through Morgan's veins at the feeling of making music with a group again, he could —

Bam, bam, bam. Someone pounded on the ceiling above them. They stopped and stared up as if it would reveal an angry neighbor peering down.

"Fuck," Morgan muttered. He hollered, "Sorry, Mrs. Bagshaw-Smythe!" Then he groaned to his bandmates. "I'm gonna hear about that later." If she didn't come banging on his door, he was sure to get a note from the strata.

"Shit, I didn't think we were singing too loud," Andre said.

Brett shook his head. "I don't think this is gonna work."

"Are you sure we can't use your basement?" Morgan asked him hopefully.

"Nah, man. Ray sold his kit to pay for his home brewing equipment, so the basement is full of that stuff now."

"He what?"

"Yeah, falconry didn't work out, so he's brewing beer now. He's down there all the time, hammering away at something. Plus it smells like feet."

"Oh."

"We'll find something," Andre said. "Just gotta keep our eyes open."

They finished *Cherry Tree* without vocals and taught Brett the chords for a few of their other songs. Andre was the perfect addition to the vibe. He smoothed over the inherent bumpiness between Morgan and Brett and filled in the awkward silences before they were even a thing.

When they left a couple hours later, Morgan shut the door behind them and smiled at Catzio. "Well, what do you think?"

Catzio stuck his tail in the air and sniffed at the box sitting on the floor.

Oh. His box of shit from Breakpoint was still sitting there. He hadn't even noticed it for months now, like it was a piece of furniture. "I guess I could unpack this now, hey?" he asked Catzio.

Catzio sat back on his haunches and waited for Morgan to pick it up.

He set it on the kitchen table and took a look inside. Right, broken light bulb. He found a paper bag to put the pieces into and threw it away. He took out the lamp, sticky-note dispenser, and page-a-day calendar, stuck on March sixth—almost three months ago. It felt like three years.

The calendar was called *365 Days of Wine* and featured a fact on each page. Morgan cringed, remembering his wine connoisseur phase. March sixth informed him that the most widely planted grape in the world was Cabernet Sauvignon.

"Don't care," Morgan said, and dumped it in the recycling bin.

A handful of notebooks followed the calendar into the recycling, then he found a single glove and a pack of mints in the bottom of the box. And his Freddie Mercury bobblehead. He stashed the lamp and sticky note dispenser in his studio closet and threw out the glove and mints.

But Freddie... He picked up the figure and stared deep into his black plastic eyes. Morgan smiled. Freddie was going to stick around. He sat him next to his soundboard, ready for their next rehearsal.

He did some laundry, fired off another resume and was eating a bowl of cereal when he got a text from Kazio.

Can I talk you into a hike with me tonight? Just a short one. We can even stick to the little loop off the end of Lupine Park or something.

Oh, sure, I guess. If we get ice cream after.

We can get ice cream.

Everything okay?

Fine. Just had a long day and want to be outside for a while. I can come pick you up?

Nah, it's out of your way. It's only one stop on the train. I can be there in twenty minutes.

Okay. Thanks, Morgan.

* * * *

"So how did rehearsal go?" Kazio asked as they started up the trail from the parking lot. He was weirdly subdued, voice low, hands in his pockets. "You think Brett and Andre will be a good fit?" The park was lush and green around them, a product of the late spring rains and the growing hours of sunshine as June approached.

"Yeah, I think so. We sound really good together. Rehearsal space is going to be a problem, though. We've already annoyed the neighbors, and Brett's basement is full of beer."

"What?"

Morgan waved the idea away. "It's not important. You don't happen to have a secret, magical soundproof basement in the Exchange, do you?"

"I wish I did. But we've got to be able to find something."

Morgan noticed that Kazio said 'we'. "Guess it doesn't really matter until we get a drummer anyway."

"You want to put up an ad at the Exchange? There's that bulletin board by the washrooms. You can ask about a drummer and a rehearsal space."

"Sure. That would be awesome, thanks."

"It's no problem."

"So why was your day so long?"

"Oh..." Kazio raised his chin, eyes on the view of Oakport that was steadily improving as they climbed a hill out of the city. "It was just busy. I'm still short-staffed, and some of the customers were a bit much. And lately I've been feeling sort of... I don't know. Blah."

"Blah? Like you're getting sick or something?"

"No. More like I'm sort of...stuck."

"Stuck?" *Stop repeating everything he says, Morgan.* "Like how?"

"Like something is missing or...I should be doing something differently."

"Hmm." Morgan nodded thoughtfully. His breathing was picking up as the city spread below them. "I can definitely relate to that."

"I was thinking..." Kazio paused, then said the rest came in a rush. "Maybe I should try dating again. It's been a while."

"Oh." Morgan stepped carefully to avoid tripping over a wayward tree root. "I mean, yeah, if that feels like something you'd like to do."

"It does. Or...I'd like to be with someone, anyway."

The twinge of jealousy Morgan felt was obviously inappropriate, and hard to ignore, but he wanted to be a good friend for Kazio. "Then you should definitely get back out there and find someone."

"Okay." A gust of warm wind lifted the tendrils off of Kazio's forehead as he looked down at his feet. "I will."

They didn't talk as much after that, what with Morgan's oxygen supply being otherwise occupied, until the way back down when he chatted about Catzio's latest antics and gave Kazio a blow-by-blow recap of his previous encounters with Mrs. Bagshaw-Smythe.

When they returned to the parking lot at the bottom of the trail, Morgan was finishing up his story. "All I'm saying is, there's no way she could smell it from her balcony, and even if she did, who doesn't like the smell of beeswax?"

"Right," Kazio agreed. He had his hands in his pockets and was staring off in the distance down the linear pathway that stretched back toward the city. "You know what, can we take a rain check on the ice cream tonight? Maybe I am coming down with something. I think I need to go home."

"Oh no." Morgan frowned up at him and resisted the urge to touch his forehead to check for a fever. "Yeah, of course, that's no problem. Text me later, okay? Let me know how you're doing."

Kazio nodded and gave Morgan a half-hearted wave, then turned to make his way to his vehicle, shoulders hunched against a gust of wind.

Morgan watched him go, a little worried. Hopefully Kazio would feel better after a good night's sleep.

He took the train home, the events of the day rolling through his head—meshing so well with his new band, breathing in the warm spring air with his friend at his side, Kazio's thoughts about feeling stuck in life… The rhythm of the train lulled him into a half-awake, half-asleep state then suddenly he jolted awake with a complete musical phrase in his head—the words, the melody…everything.

He hummed it under his breath, then again.

Damn, that was good. He pulled out his phone to scribble it down in a song-writing app he had, then the next line and another as they came to him, until he had a whole damn song jotted down.

When he got in the door, he rushed to his acoustic guitar.

* * * *

"I have a new song," Morgan announced to his bandmates. "It's a love song."

"Let's hear it," Andre said.

Brett nodded and folded his hands over his bass, ready to listen.

Morgan had in fact received a notice from the strata, so this version was unplugged. He took a breath, and began.

"When did my grip become a jail?
I'm holding on so tight
I can't escape, can't look ahead
Alone in the hollow night.

Something is missing
A piece that isn't there
There's a hole in my soul,
There's not enough air.

But then, oh then, there was you
You held my hand and showed me the way
You held me so close
And I just have to say
That you…you take care of me.

It's 'Good morning,' and 'goodnight,'
It's 'This reminded me of you'
Always 'we', never 'me'
And 'I'll pick you up at two'
And then…then there was you.

You crack your stupid jokes
Don't want to smile, but I do
You're not that funny
But I do because it's you.

It's 'Good morning,' and 'goodnight,'
It's 'This reminded me of you'
Always 'we', never 'me'
And 'I'll pick you up at two'
And then…then there was you.

Drink some water
Come walk with me
I'll make you dinner
It's clear to see
I don't want to, but I do
'Cause then, there was you."

The last chord faded, Morgan's heart a warm fuzzy ball of happiness.

Andre and Brett stared at him.

"Morgan," Andre finally said. "I *love* it. That's gorgeous."

"Sick," Brett said. High praise from him. "Wish I wrote that."

"Thanks," said Morgan, suddenly shy. "Glad you like it."

"Who's the guy?" Andre asked. "You been holding out on us?"

"What?" Morgan quirked an eyebrow. "There's no guy."

Andre and Brett shared a look.

"There's no guy!" Morgan insisted.

Andre smirked. "Sure."

"I was just thinking about life and something my friend said—"

"Who, Kazio?"

"Yes, Kazio."

"The one you named your cat after? That friend?"

"Yes," Morgan said defensively. "We are just friends. He would never... I'm not his type, okay?"

"Mmhmm."

"I'm not! Believe me."

"Okay," Andre chuckled. "If you say so."

He folded his arms over his guitar. "I do." If these two ever saw him with Kazio, they'd know.

"Well…either way, that song is going to bring out the lighters one day," Andre said. "Great job."

They had a quiet rehearsal, instrumental only, then Morgan settled into his couch once Andre and Brett left, Catzio in his lap and heart still glowing.

Hey, how are you feeling? Morgan texted Kazio. He hadn't heard from his friend since they had parted ways the night before.

Kazio didn't take too long to reply. *Fine.*

So you're not sick?

Guess not.

That's good. So…I wrote a new song.

Awesome. Do you want to text me the wording for your drummer ad and I can post it for you?

Oh, sure, thanks. Morgan sent him something similar to the ad he had posted online before, then added a 'fingers crossed' emoji. *There's gotta be someone out there, right?*

* * * *

The ad didn't help. It was starting to feel like *Groundhog Day*. Apply for jobs, get rejected from jobs or ghosted entirely, hang out with Kazio, rehearse with

Brett and Andre and talk to people who were absolutely, positively not going to be their drummer.

"Is it so much to ask?" Morgan whined one evening at the Exchange. "An adult drummer who can count to four, communicate at least *semi*-effectively, and can commit to rehearsal time?"

"There must be someone."

"There's not, though." The thing that Morgan had been denying could no longer be denied. "Fuck. I think I need Felix back."

"Felix?"

"Our old drummer. Argh, it took me months and months to find him. Then when he bailed on our first gig last minute, I...I didn't handle it well. I told him his drumming sucks and kicked him out of the band and he called me an arrogant prick. We haven't talked since."

"I mean..." Kazio measured a shot of rum. "I've never been in a band. But I've watched a lot of music biopics and I'm pretty sure that's all normal."

"I don't know..."

"It can't hurt to at least reach out."

"What if he tells me to fuck off?"

Kazio shrugged. "Then you're no worse off than you are now."

Chapter Seventeen

Actual Fever

Dear Felix, Morgan typed. Nope. It wasn't a cover letter, for fuck's sake. *Hey Felix.* Better. *I just wanted to say that I'm sorry about what happened...* Ugh.

He swiped out of that thread and over to Kazio. *I don't know what to say to Felix. Are you working today?*

Yup. You want to drop by later?

Please.

As usual, it was a relief to have Kazio's help, but...if Morgan was being totally honest, things had felt a bit off the last couple weeks. Kazio still seemed quiet and maybe a bit sad, and when Morgan had tried to poke around, he was met with "I'm fine," or "Nothing's bothering me," over and over, so he figured it was time to take the hint and stop asking. But he wanted his friend to be happy again — or at least not sad — so he tried to be as cheerful as he could around him.

When he arrived at the Exchange, he sat at the bar and handed his phone to Kazio. "This is what I have so far. I love your shirt, by the way."

Kazio ignored the compliment and read the message Morgan had typed. "'I just wanted to say that I'm sorry about what happened.'"

"No, shit, that sounds even worse out loud. Hang on." Morgan took the phone back, deleted that and typed a new line. "What about 'I'm sorry about what I said. You are a great drummer.' Is that better?"

"I wonder…are you apologizing because you want to get the band back together or because you're actually sorry?"

Morgan blinked. He was probably acting for entirely selfish reasons, but he did feel bad about the way he'd handled the whole situation. "Both, I think."

Kazio nodded. "Okay, then. Let's see what he says."

Morgan stared at the words, stomach skittering.

"While you're thinking about hitting send," Kazio continued, "I meant to ask you — would you be able to reschedule our next shift at the shelter? I have training on Saturday now."

"Yeah, we can move it — training? For what?"

Kazio got busy unloading a crate of clean glasses. "That community cooking class I told you about."

It took Morgan a second to shuffle through the open tabs in his brain. "The cooking — Oh, shit! I missed the deadline, didn't I? I forgot all about it."

Kazio shrugged, still avoiding eye contact. "It's fine. I signed myself up."

"It just completely slipped my mind. You should have reminded me!"

"I figured you would have remembered if it was important to you."

An emotion — something like anger — flared through Morgan's chest and up his throat. It was a familiar feeling… yet one he hadn't felt in a while. He pressed his lips together and swallowed it back down. Because he knew it wasn't really anger. It was guilt.

Guilt because he was self-absorbed and selfish. "I'm sorry. I—"

"It's fine." Kazio moved onto the next crate. "Anyway, can we move our shift? What day works for you?"

"Um, we're rehearsing Friday but I could do Sunday or Monday…?"

"Sure, let's do Sunday. I'll reschedule with Camella."

"Okay. Thanks…" Morgan looked back at the phone in his hand and read the message he had written for Felix again.

"Did you send it?" Kazio asked, pausing his task to glance at Morgan.

"Not quite yet."

"What are you waiting for?"

It was hard to breathe in that moment, crushed by the idea that he was an irredeemably selfish asshole…had always been, and would always be. "Not sure," he forced out. "I'll send it later." He tried to smile. "Thanks for your help."

* * * *

Hey Felix. I just wanted to reach out to say I'm sorry about what I said. You are a great drummer.

The words still sat there unsent, staring back at him. Was he doing this for the right reasons? Did Felix hate his guts? Was it cruel to uncover old wounds? Was trying to mend this fence the right thing to do?

Then again...this was his dream, and he had exhausted every other way forward he could think of. So, if it meant he had to be selfish again by reaching out, oh well. Nothing new here. He pressed send.

Oh God. "Now what?" he asked Catzio, who had hopped up to join him on the couch.

Catzio flopped onto his side.

"Oh, belly rubs. Yeah, I can do that."

He gave Catzio some attention for a while, then thought about tackling the laundry, but instead stayed on the couch with a box of crackers to watch the loincloth show. It was getting really good — he hadn't seen the evil twin coming, and that snake was so —

A text from Felix popped up. The crackers went flying in the mad scramble to grab his phone. He swiped it open, breath held.

Thanks, Morgan, it read. *I'm sorry about what I said, too. Even though you are kind of an arrogant prick sometimes.*

Oof. But also totally fair. He typed a reply. *I was, and I'm really sorry. And I was wondering if you were interested in maybe getting the band back together.*

What about Todd and Andre?

Todd's out, but Andre's in, and I've got a new bass player.

Let me think about it. I've been trying out a few other groups, got lots of other interest.

"Oh, I'm sure you do," Morgan said out loud.

Take your time. I'd love to play with you again. Maybe we can jam sometime just to see how it goes.

Maybe. I'll let you know.

Sounds good. Thanks, Felix.

Morgan exhaled in a whoosh. Now all he had to do was wait. No problem.

* * * *

It was a bit of a problem.

He drove Brett and Andre crazy at rehearsal on Friday—"What do you think he'll say?" he asked at least ten times—and he was so distracted that he fumbled chords and missed a few cues craning his neck to see if he had any new texts.

"You gotta relax," Andre told Morgan on his way out, clapping a big hand on his tense shoulder. "Stressing yourself out won't help at all."

"Here, try one of Ray's beers," Brett said, fishing a green plastic bottle out of his bag. "They're not terrible. I'm gonna need that bottle back from you, though."

Brett was wrong. It was terrible. Morgan dumped it down the drain after a tentative sip gave him a full body shudder—setting aside the empty bottle to return as promised—then he poured himself a drink of something stronger.

* * * *

Saturday morning he woke up out of sorts, sore and with an ache behind his eyes. Texting Kazio would have been a good distraction, but he was at his training. Training that Morgan should have been at. He wondered who Kazio would be partnered with instead. Scowling, he grabbed his laptop.

Morgan scrolled the job boards, cleaned Catzio's litter box, played some guitar, fiddled with their drum tracks and even got so far as thinking about doing laundry. He didn't get to the laundry, but he did drink a lot of tea and finish off season two of the loincloth show.

He was so bored and twitchy that by eight o'clock he decided to just go to bed early, bringing a cup of tea with him for a bit more scrolling. But as he drank the tea, his throat was a little scratchy.

He slept fitfully, waking up too hot, then too cold, then hot again, and by six a.m., when the sunshine began its creep through the blinds, he felt like absolute hell—hit-by-a-bus hell. Everything ached, his sinuses throbbed and it hurt to swallow.

"Oh God." Morgan groaned, pressing a hand to his eyes. "I'm sick." *Fuck*. He burrowed back under his blankets and fell into uneasy sleep.

Sometime later, he woke up to the sound of the front door buzzer on his landline. It took him a few seconds to process what the sound was, then another few to decide he couldn't get out of bed to answer it. He reached for his phone on the bedside table and blinked the screen into focus.

A string of texts from Kazio waited. *I'm on my way* was the first one.

On his way…?

Hey, I'm here.

Why was Kazio... A thought bubbled to the surface of Morgan's brain through the fog... Right. They were supposed to go to the shelter today.

Hello? the messages continued.

You're not answering the buzzer.

Getting worried...is everything okay?

A new one popped up. *Morgan, don't make me call the police.*

Sick, was all Morgan could find the energy to reply.

Are you okay? Then right after, *Someone let me in, I'm coming up. Can you unlock your front door?*

Morgan thought about it for a few seconds, synapses firing like a paddle through molasses. The front door was very far away, but...he had to pee.

Yes, he replied.

Every muscle protested as he got out of bed and shuffled to the apartment door. He left it ajar, stopped in the bathroom then fell back into bed with a groan. He closed his eyes, and suddenly someone was speaking to him.

"Morgan?" a deep voice whispered.

"Mmm?" Morgan tried to swim back up through the haze. Kazio.

"Shhh, keep sleeping." A cool hand touched his forehead and pushed his hair back. "I just wanted to know if you need anything. Have you taken anything for the fever?"

"No," Morgan scratched out through his dry throat. "You'll get sick…"

"I'll be fine. Do you have any ibuprofen?"

"Bathroom…" Morgan murmured.

"I'll be right back."

Then Kazio was there again, helping him sit up and swallow a few pills with ice water, then laying him back down with a cool cloth on his forehead.

The next time Morgan woke up, Kazio was ready with more water and a new cloth. "Are you feeling any better?" he asked.

"No. So tired," Morgan mumbled. "Where's Catzio?"

"I kicked him out so you can get proper rest."

"Thas' right, i's my pillow," Morgan muttered.

He slept.

* * * *

He woke up drenched in sweat and with wisps of a disturbing dream still drifting on the edges of his brain. He sat up, fumbling to pull his shirt off.

"Easy." It was Kazio again, helping Morgan remove his shirt.

Morgan fell back onto the pillow. "The goat had my shirt."

"Shhh." Kazio smoothed Morgan's hair back again with a cool palm. "There's no goat."

"A goat," Morgan insisted. "Can I have water?"

"Here." Kazio put a cup in his hand. "How are you feeling?"

"Dead." He curled up under his blanket again. "I don't like the goat."

Kazio huffed a laugh. "There's no goat. Go back to sleep."

* * * *

Morgan rolled over and reached for his water. He had a clean T-shirt on.

A weight settled on the end of the bed. "I'm going to run to the store and get you some things," Kazio said in a low voice. "Cold meds and tissues and stuff. Is there anything else you want?"

"Gatorade," Morgan mumbled. "Yellow."

Kazio's voice was soft and kind. "You got it."

"And maybe…Popsicles."

"Sure."

"And chicken noodle soup, the gross instant kind."

A low rumble of a laugh. "I'll see what I can find."

The next time he woke up, there was yellow Gatorade on his nightstand and a dose of cold medicine waiting. He swallowed the pills, drank half the Gatorade and was out again.

Sunlight peeked through the curtains the next time Morgan blinked into consciousness. The sharp pain was gone from his throat and the fog had cleared. He stared at his bedroom, confused, because it looked nothing like his bedroom.

Then Kazio appeared in the doorway. "Hey, there he is. How are you feeling?"

"A little better." His voice was rough. "Are you… How long have you been here? What day is it?"

"It's eight o'clock on Tuesday."

"Tuesday? AM or PM?"

"PM."

He sat up for a drink. "Have you been here this whole time?"

"Yeah. Well, I zipped home yesterday to grab some clothes."

"What about the pub?"

"Tasha's got it."

Morgan took another long swallow of Gatorade. "You need to give that lady a raise."

"You're probably right."

Morgan rubbed his eyes and looked around his room again. "Did you…clean in here?"

"No. Well, I didn't *clean*. I just…picked up your clothes."

"How will I ever find anything if it's not laid out where I left it?"

"If by 'laid out' you mean in piles on the floor, there's this invention called a closet and these handy little devices called hangers…"

Morgan squinted at him. "I'm much too sick for sarcasm."

Kazio chuckled. "Are you hungry?"

"No. Yes. A little."

"I'll make you some chicken noodle soup."

"The gross instant kind?"

"The gross instant kind."

* * * *

Kazio placed the tray on Morgan's lap and sat at the foot of the bed.

"Thank you. You even gave me the right crackers."

"Well, of course. What other kind could you possibly have with instant chicken noodle soup?"

Morgan's stomach growled in anticipation. He ate a few bites, then gave Kazio a look. "Are you just going to watch me eat?"

"I already had something."

"Hmm…is my kitchen going to be even cleaner than my bedroom?"

"Sorry, I just started to pick up a few things and…"

"You did all my laundry, didn't you?"

"A few loads."

Morgan waited.

"Okay, I washed everything."

Morgan looked down. "These are clean sheets, aren't they?"

"Those are clean sheets."

"How did you change the bed with me in it?"

"You rolled around a lot."

Morgan chuckled, but then grew serious and studied his next spoonful. "Thank you. So much. I can't believe you took so much time out of your life to look after me." He looked up and met Kazio's eyes. "Really, thank you. It means a lot."

"You're welcome." Kazio's eyes were huge and deep as they studied Morgan's face, blond tendril over one eye. "I like taking care of you, Morgan. You know that, right?"

Morgan's cheeks flushed. Maybe his fever wasn't completely gone. "I don't know what I did to deserve you."

"You don't have to earn or deserve friends. They're in your life because they care about you. I care about you."

Morgan's heart beat faster, the temperature in his face climbing. "I care about you, too." He coughed.

"You've done so much for me. I feel bad you've been here so long. If you want to go home, I'll be okay."

Kazio stood with a small smile. "I've always said that, haven't I? I know you will."

Chapter Eighteen

Breathe

Kazio didn't get far, though, because, as another veil of fog lifted from Morgan's brain, he gasped and clutched his heart. *"Did Felix reply?"*

Kazio chuckled. "I don't know. I didn't look at your phone."

Morgan lunged to check, and yes, there it was. A message from Felix. "Ohmygod. Ohmygodohmygod-ohmygod."

"What does it say?" Kazio asked.

"I don't know. So far I'm just staring at it."

"Okay... You should probably read it."

"I will, I will. I will. I'm...gathering my strength." He swiped it open and read. *"He wants to meet!"* Morgan screeched, then cleared his scratchy throat. "Ouch. He wants to meet!" he said again at a normal volume.

"That's great," Kazio said.

Morgan spoke slowly as he typed a reply. "'Hey Felix, sorry about the delay getting back to you. I've been sick. I would love to meet up. Brett and Andre are coming over on Friday. Do you want to join us? I don't have a kit but you can come hang out and see what you think.' Send."

Kazio leaned on the doorway, smiling. "You're doing it, Morgan."

He shivered. "Am I?"

"You are."

Morgan smiled up at him. "I really am feeling a lot better. Do you want to stay a little longer?"

"I'll make some tea."

* * * *

Morgan finished his soup and had a shower, then came back into the living room toweling off his hair. "You know, I could get used to this whole 'hangers' thing," he said, squeaky clean and feeling human again. "Not to mention..." He whistled and looked around. "Wow. You're hired. This place looks amazing."

Kazio was waiting on the couch with two steaming mugs of tea. Every visible surface gleamed, the throw pillows were expertly fluffed and a vase of sunflowers sat on the kitchen table. "Oh, I didn't do much," he demurred.

"Are you kidding? Everything is perfect. You are seriously the best. Maybe we should be roommates."

Kazio didn't seem to think the joke was funny. He half smiled and shifted in his seat.

"I'm kidding, of course," Morgan said quickly. "I would never subject you to that. I'm, uh, going to have some more soup. You want some?"

Kazio hopped to his feet. "I'll get it. You should rest."

"It's okay, I can..."

But Kazio was already striding into the kitchen.

Catzio came trotting into view from wherever he had been hiding in a beeline for Morgan.

"There's my boy!" Morgan scooped him up.

Catzio rubbed his head against Morgan's chin, purring like a maniac.

"Aw, I missed you too." Morgan buried his face in Catzio's fur. "Although I know that if Kazio looked after you half as good as he looked after me, you've been getting spoiled all week."

"I handed out treats at a very responsible rate," Kazio informed him from the kitchen.

"I'm sure you did." Morgan chuckled, settling on the couch and scratching Catzio's head. Catzio closed his eyes in bliss.

Kazio came back into the living room with a tray. "I've been thinking..." He set the tray on the coffee table and sat next to Morgan. "If it works out with Felix, why don't you use my garage?"

Morgan blinked at him. "Use your garage for what?"

Kazio rolled his eyes, but, to be fair, it was in an affectionate way. "For rehearsal."

"What?" Morgan's jaw dropped. "You — you'd let us use your garage?"

"I know it's not ideal, or long-term, but — "

Morgan hurled himself into Kazio's arms. "Thank you, thank you, thank you! That would be amazing! Oh my God, I could kiss you!"

Kazio laughed and hugged him back. "You're welcome."

"Are you really sure, though? Your neighbors won't mind?"

"We won't ask them. Beg for forgiveness, et cetera."

"You really are the very best. Thank you so much." Morgan collected his bowl of soup from the tray. "I just hope it goes well with Felix. I have to remember to think about what's good for him, too." He nodded to himself as he picked up his spoon. "It's all going to work out. I just know it."

* * * *

"Hey, Felix," Morgan said when he opened his door on Friday.

Felix looked much the same—cool and confident with wavy hair, skinny jeans and sexy glasses.

Morgan had changed his outfit three times.

"Hey." Felix stuffed his hands into his pockets.

"Come on in." Morgan waved him in.

Felix shuffled through the door, like he wasn't so sure he wanted to be there.

"So…how have you been?" Morgan asked.

"Good." Felix nodded. "You?"

"Um…well, I wasn't great for a while. I got fired and then, you know…this"—he gestured between the two of them—"fell apart. And I, uh, still don't have a job but…I'm okay." And, he was pleased to notice, he really meant it. "You still work at Shoe Shack?"

"No, I quit there." Felix half smiled. "They were pretty rigid. I manage a shoe store in the mall now. Better hours."

"That's good."

"Yup."

"Thank you so much for coming," spilled out of Morgan's mouth. "I really appreciate you giving me another chance. And there's absolutely no pressure, I promise..." He trailed off.

Felix nodded tightly.

Thank God Brett and Andre arrived right then, before things could slide from new and uncomfortable into awkward and painful. Greetings were exchanged all around. Felix and Andre hugged, then Morgan introduced Brett.

"Does anyone want a drink?" Morgan asked, leading them into the kitchen and crossing his fingers that Brett didn't have any more of Ray's beer in his bag. "Your bottle is there on the counter, Brett."

"Oh, you can keep it," Brett replied. "The home brewing thing didn't work out."

Morgan pulled a handful of drinks out of the fridge. "It didn't?"

"No. Ray said he bought bad equipment or something, kept having trouble with his batches. Anyway, he sold it all, and he's gold panning now."

"Who's Ray?" Felix asked.

Brett chose a beer for himself. "My brother."

Andre frowned as he took an iced tea. "I'm sorry, did you say...gold panning?"

"Yeah, he's going to pan for gold and make jewelry with it. He said he'd make a ring for my girlfriend. He got a smelter and everything."

"Er...good for him," Morgan said. "I really admire the way Ray...pursues his passions."

Brett shrugged and popped his beer open. "I get a free gold ring, so..."

"Yes, well... Good luck to Ray." Morgan handed Felix a seltzer and took one for himself too. "Should we get to it?"

Morgan led them all into his studio. He had moved out the spare single bed that was usually against the wall to give them a bit more space.

He gave an ear piece to each of them. Morgan had discovered that Mrs. Bagshaw-Smythe had bingo on Fridays — he had seen her getting on the casino shuttle a few weeks ago and since then checked the sign-up sheet in the lobby every Friday — so they could risk a bit of singing.

They warmed up with *Crazy Little Thing* as usual, then went through *Cherry Tree* and a few others. Morgan had introduced *Empty Stage* at the last rehearsal, and they worked on adding another verse. Felix had brought his drumsticks along and tapped the beat on his thigh as they played.

At one point, Catzio wandered in between songs.

"Ah, so this is the famous Catzio," Felix said. "I saw him on Insta."

"Wait, how did you know how to pronounce his name properly?" Morgan asked.

"Oh, my parents are Polish."

"No way! I didn't know that."

"Morgan's boyfriend is Polish," Andre offered helpfully.

"He's not my boyfriend!"

"Who's not your boyfriend?" Felix asked.

Andre grinned. "Kazio. Ooh, let's play the song that's not about Kazio for Felix."

"It is not about Kazio!" Morgan protested.

"I know, that's what I just said." Andre strummed the opening chord from the song, still grinning.

"Sorry, who's Kazio?" Felix asked.

"He's my *friend*," Morgan explained.

"So," Felix summarized, "you have a Polish friend named Kazio, and your cat is named Catzio...and you wrote a song about him? But he's not your boyfriend?"

"Correct...except I did not write a song about him!"

"Hmm..." Felix tapped his chin. "I'll need to hear it to decide."

Morgan sighed and picked up his acoustic guitar. "Fine." He knew where this was headed.

And he was right.

Felix whistled when it was over.

"Don't say it." Morgan groaned.

"I don't know... If it's not about Kazio, who is it about?"

"It's not about anyone. I just...wrote a song about being in love!"

"Well, your last boyfriend was lucky then."

Morgan snorted. "He would disagree."

Andre wiggled his eyebrows. "I don't think Kazio would disagree..."

"Can we please change the subject?" Morgan asked, but he had to laugh at the good-natured ribbing.

Rehearsal continued. The banter and laughter got easier and more comfortable as they went, and, as the session drew to a close, Felix smiling and still drumming on his thighs, Morgan knew that this could actually work. He tucked that hope away for the moment, trying to stay focused on the music. But the hope was there.

And he wasn't the only one feeling that way. The guys had only been gone a few minutes when the text from Felix arrived.

I'm in.

* * * *

Morgan wiggled with excitement as they pulled into Kazio's driveway. Kazio had picked him up to help transport all the gear to their new rehearsal space.

"This is so amazing of you," Morgan babbled, repeating himself. "Really, so amazing. I hope it goes well. Do you think it'll go well?"

"Morgan," Kazio said, calm and steady as always. "Breathe. It'll be fine. Whatever happens, happens. And it'll be okay in the end, either way."

"Right. You're right." Morgan wiped his sweaty palms off on his shorts.

Kazio's garage was, unsurprisingly, the cleanest, tidiest garage he had ever seen. One wall was lined with metal shelves stacked with matching labeled bins, and the opposite wall was covered in hooks holding ladders, a bike, shovels and the like. A workbench ran along the back wall featuring all manner of tools hung up in an impeccably well-organized fashion. There was undoubtedly a correct screwdriver order.

They unloaded Morgan's gear from Kazio's car — his guitars, amps, speakers — and began setting up. It went quickly with Kazio following Morgan's instructions.

"Do you mind if I stick around to listen for a bit?" Kazio asked once they were done. "I'd love to hear what you guys sound like."

"Yeah, no, of course, feel free to hang out."

Morgan had prepared for this moment by threatening his bandmates with bodily harm if they were idiots about Kazio.

I'm begging you, was his final word on the matter in the group text this morning, *please be normal when you meet him.*

Felix had picked the others up, so they arrived in a carload shortly after. They tumbled out and began unloading their own stuff, oohing and ahhing appropriately over the new space.

"This is Andre, Brett and Felix," Morgan said to Kazio, stomach clenched in anticipation of extreme embarrassment. "And this is Kazio."

"So nice to meet you, Kazio," Andre said, shaking his hand with entirely too much enthusiasm. Morgan tried to glare at Andre but he refused to make eye contact. "We've heard a lot about you."

"Oh yeah?" Kazio raised an eyebrow. "I've heard a lot about you guys, too."

"Shall we get started?" Morgan said, an octave higher than normal. He herded them into the garage and Kazio closed the door behind them. They got busy getting set up, Felix putting his kit together and the rest plugging in and tuning their instruments.

Morgan got goosebumps when Felix joined in on the warmup. Having a drummer brought it all together for him. They were a *band*. He was *doing it*.

The smiles on the rest of the faces told him they all agreed.

Kazio sat on the steps leading up into the house, quietly bobbing his head, but clearly trying to be as unobtrusive as possible.

After warming up, they worked on *Cherry Tree* for a while, and just when things were going a little too well...

"How about we do — what's it called again?" Andre said with an unsubtle look at Morgan.

"*Always We*?" Morgan asked, jaw clenched.

Andre pointed. "That's the one." Oh, the amused glint in his eye. This qualified for bodily harm.

"Yeah, let's do it," Felix agreed. "I need to figure out the percussion."

"Er…" Morgan stole a glance at Kazio. "Sure." He swapped his electric guitar for his acoustic as his heart rate accelerated. *Be cool,* he pleaded silently to his bandmates. *Please, for the love of God, just be cool.*

Kazio leaned back on the steps.

Morgan started to sing, pulse racing.

"When did my grip become a jail?
I'm holding on so tight
I can't escape, can't look ahead
Alone in the hollow night."

Felix joined with the drums, a light swish on the snare. Kazio cocked his head, listening intently. Morgan plunged ahead.

"Something is missing
A piece that isn't there
There's a hole in my soul,
There's not enough air."

A flash of recognition crossed Kazio's face. Morgan's stomach flipped again. It hadn't occurred to him that maybe *Kazio* would think the song was about him. Their eyes met, for only half a second, before Morgan ripped his gaze away and stared at the floor. He vamped for a few extra bars, trying to get his heart rate back under control. *Breathe, Morgan.*

"But then, oh then, then there was you
You held my hand and showed me the way
You held me so close
And I just have to say

That you…you take care of me."

A series of images flashed through Morgan's mind. Kazio cooking him dinner. Kazio comforting him at the shelter when Ralph passed away. Kazio buying him groceries and helping get Catzio settled in. Kazio's cool hand on his forehead when he was sick.

Oh.

Kazio…took care of him. It was so painfully obvious that he wondered how he really could have been that dense.

Fuck.

"It's 'Good morning,' and 'goodnight,'
It's 'This reminded me of you'
Always 'we', never 'me'
And 'I'll pick you up at two'
And then…then there was you."

His gut swirled, like it was trying to turn upside down and inside out at the same time. But all he could do was keep singing. Brett added a gentle bass line.

"You crack your stupid jokes
Don't want to smile, but I do
You're not that funny
But I do because it's you."

Morgan's eyes were drawn to Kazio again, as if he had no choice in the matter. Kazio had his hands folded and head down, staring at the floor. Morgan took a deep breath, hoping it would help calm him, but his heart continued to pound. Andre joined in with harmonies on the chorus.

"It's 'Good morning,' and 'goodnight,'
It's 'This reminded me of you'
Always 'we', never 'me'
And 'I'll pick you up at two'
And then...then there was you."

Morgan was no longer in control of his body. His stomach contained a million butterflies searching for an escape route while the blood in his head pounded a rhythm in his temples. Fortunately, his fingers continued to find the notes and the words kept coming out. Kazio's gaze flicked up, beautiful indigo, and found his.

"Drink some water
Come walk with me
I'll make you dinner
It's clear to see
I don't want to, but I do
'Cause then, there was you."

Morgan had no air left, throat clogged with his pounding heart.

The fucking song was about Kazio. Of *course* it was about Kazio. Kazio, who was leaning there against the steps like the amazing, wonderful, *perfect* human he was, not taking his ocean eyes off of Morgan.

Oh *fuck*.

Kazio applauded as Morgan's guitar faded to silence.

Everyone was staring at him, if they weren't staring at Kazio.

"Great song. Did you write that?" Kazio asked him.

"Yeah," Morgan scratched out, despite the total lack of oxygen in his lungs.

"I loved it." Kazio stood. "Anyway, I should…" He pointed at the door with his thumb. "I've got some paperwork to do. I'll let you guys get to it. Thanks for letting me hang out for a bit."

"Okay," Morgan said, watching Kazio turn and disappear into the house. "No problem."

The garage was silent. Three pairs of wide eyes stared at him.

Morgan stared back.

"Are you okay?" Andre asked.

"I…I just need to use the washroom." Morgan made a break for the door and crept into Kazio's house, slipping silently into the powder room.

Morgan closed the door behind him and gripped the sink, staring at himself in the mirror.

"Shit."

Chapter Nineteen

Oh No No No No No

"Shit, shit, *shit*," Morgan whispered, stomach cartwheeling. "I…" He took a deep breath, staring at his reflection. "I…am in love with Kazio." Watching himself say the words was absurd.

He tried again. "I am in love with Kazio."

His reflection nodded back at him. "Yup. Fuck."

He had gone and *fallen in love* with his friend, which had to be the dumbest, most selfish thing he had ever done, and that was saying something. He had managed to take the best part of his life and fuck it right up.

"Now what?" he asked his reflection.

His reflection did not know.

Morgan slinked back into the garage, cheeks hot.

"You good, dude?" Andre asked. "You look like you're going to pass out."

Morgan stared at them haplessly. "Um. That song…might be about Kazio."

The hooting and hollering were deafening, sure to attract Kazio's attention.

"Shut up!" Morgan hissed. "He'll hear you!"

The others muffled their cheers.

"That's great, Morgan," Andre stage-whispered.

"We're super happy for you," Felix agreed.

"That's sick," Brett added.

"But now what do I do?" Morgan asked, twisting the hem of his T-shirt.

"You go in there and tell him!" Andre said.

"Are you crazy?" Morgan squawked. "I can't just walk in there and tell him that song was about him!"

"Why not?"

"Because," Morgan sputtered. "Because we're in his garage in the middle of rehearsal and...he doesn't date guys like me! What if he laughs in my face? What if it freaks him out? What if he regrets having us here? What if we can never come back?"

Andre narrowed his eyes. "You're maybe being a little over dramatic. He's probably just going to be flattered."

"I don't know—I can see Morgan's point," Felix chimed in. "It *might* freak him out. You don't want to ruin a good thing."

"Thank you!" Morgan said. He picked up his electric guitar and slung it over his shoulder. "So can we...please just rehearse?"

The other three exchanged a look but Andre nodded. "All right, man. If that's what you want."

"I do. Let's get back to the new verse of *Empty Stage*."

Rehearsal went on, but Morgan was distracted, to say the least.

"I think that's good for today," Andre said not too much later.

Morgan could only agree, since he was a complete mess.

"So happy you're back, Felix," Andre added.

Felix grinned and slapped his back. "I'm happy to be here." He turned to Morgan. "And thank Kazio for letting us use his garage, yeah?"

"I will."

Andre couldn't help himself. "Yeah, thank him real good."

"I..." Morgan stammered.

"Easy." Andre chuckled, patting his shoulder. "I'm just giving you a hard time. You don't need to say anything to him if you don't want to."

"Don't rush into anything," Felix added. "You can sit on it a bit, see how you feel."

Morgan nodded. "I will. Thanks guys."

Once they left, Morgan stood in the empty garage for a few minutes, trying to get his pulse under control and wondering how to get the fuck out of there as quickly as possible without saying anything stupid to Kazio. Short and sweet would be the best. He climbed the steps up to the door and stuck his head into the house. "Uh, thanks! We're all done! I'm gonna head out."

"Hang on," Kazio called back. Then he appeared around a corner, drying his hands on a tea towel. "So, how did it go? You think Felix is going to work out?"

"Yes! It was great! Really great." Morgan chewed his lip, unsure where to let his eyes settle.

Kazio's forearms were chiseled masterpieces, his hair cascaded over sculpted shoulders, his lips were pink and plump... Morgan had never really noticed his lips before, which seemed an insane thing to miss, given how achingly kissable they looked. The way they would —

"You think my garage will do?" Kazio asked.

Morgan bobbed his head. "It's perfect. Absolutely perfect. I don't know how I can properly thank you." He had a sudden image of how he might thank him and almost choked on his next breath. "Anyway..." He coughed. "I'll, uh, take the train home." The way Kazio's waist tapered, Morgan could hold him tight...

"You want to hang out for a bit?" Kazio tossed the tea towel over his shoulder and nodded toward the kitchen. "I got my paperwork done. I was just making some stew if you want to stay for dinner."

"Uh," Morgan wheezed. "You know, I really need to get back to the job hunt. I've been slacking off. Those jobs aren't going to look for themselves." He laughed in a slightly unstable way and started edging backward into the garage.

Kazio lifted an eyebrow at him. "Okay. Well, I can drive you home."

"No! No. No, you've done more than enough for me today. It's fine. I'll take the train. I couldn't possibly impose—" His back foot found nothing but air, and, off balance and going down hard, he panicked and flailed.

Kazio lunged for him and got a hold of his arm, but it was too late. Morgan's momentum carried them backward and they hit the cement floor hard in a pile at the bottom of the steps.

"Oof," Morgan grunted. His ass took the brunt of the fall. His ankle might have rolled a bit, but he barely noticed because Kazio was on top of him. A delicious, heavy weight that smelled like pine and man and caused goosebumps to leap to attention on his bare skin, not to mention his—

"Morgan!" Kazio was off him and kneeling at his side in an instant. "Are you okay?"

No. No, he was not okay. He was sweating, his heart was pounding, and he was now lying in a heap on the ground all by himself. "Oh, God, yes, I'm fine. Totally fine." He tried to sit up. "I'm so sorry. I'm such an idiot. I don't know what happened, I just totally missed the stair. Are you okay?"

"I'm fine." Kazio gripped Morgan's arms. "Just hang on a sec, make sure you're okay...."

"No, I'm really fine..." Although to be honest, he felt a little dizzy, and it was easy to sag into Kazio's strong hands.

"Here, take a breath with me..." Kazio inhaled deeply.

Morgan tried to breathe along with him. One long slow breath in, then out.

It actually helped his heart calm a bit. He tried it again. Then he made the mistake of looking Kazio in the eye. His heart crashed into his rib cage.

"You know, my ankle, maybe..." Morgan said, looking down at his feet.

"Let me have a look." Kazio put a hand on Morgan's shin and gently cradled his foot with the other. "It's a little swollen maybe... Let me help you up."

Kazio stood, took hold of Morgan's hands and pulled him to his feet.

Morgan tested his weight on his ankle. It wasn't so bad. They were still holding hands though, and Kazio was so close. If he looked up at him, their lips would only be inches apart—

"How does that feel?" Kazio asked, eyes hooded with concern.

"It feels..." Morgan whispered, imagining leaning forward just the tiniest distance to close the gap—*No,*

Morgan, stop. You are fucking stupid. Get a grip. "You know what, it doesn't feel too bad."

"Come inside, let me get you an ice pack. You should rest it for a bit."

"I really don't think—"

"Morgan." The way Kazio said his name, deep and commanding, sent the blood draining south from his cheeks.

"Yes?" he said in a small voice.

"You need to rest."

"Okay."

Kazio helped him limp to the couch and get settled, touching him everywhere—knee, shoulder, hand... Morgan's dizziness did not improve.

"Are you comfortable?" Kazio asked when Morgan was stretched out on the sectional, pillow under his foot.

Sweat beaded on his hairline. *No.* "Yes."

Kazio disappeared behind him into the kitchen, then came back with an elastic bandage and an ice pack. He secured the ice around Morgan's ankle then fussed again with the pillows. "How's this?"

"Great, thank you."

"So..." Kazio studied him, hands on hips. "How about some dinner?"

Morgan covered his face in embarrassment. "I am so sorry to invade like this—"

"You're not invading. I invited you, if you recall."

"Then okay. Yes. Thank you."

Kazio rattled around the kitchen for a few minutes and returned with a tray. He handed Morgan a bowl of thick, meaty stew and set a glass of wine on the coffee table. "Here you go."

Kazio winced as he sat with his own bowl.

"Are you okay?" Morgan asked.

"I'm fine. Just landed on my knee a bit. Well, you and my knee."

"I'm so sorry."

"You can stop apologizing now. I'll be fine." Kazio's gaze met his, his long lashes fluttering, a gentle smile on his face. *So. Beautiful.* "I didn't think I would get to take care of you again so soon."

Heat flooded Morgan's cheeks. "Me neither."

Kazio picked up the remote. "You want to watch something?" He opened up a streaming platform and scrolled through the suggestions.

"Anything is fine," Morgan said.

"Pick something."

"Okay, how about…" He studied the screen until one jumped out at him. "Ooh, *The Sound of Music*?"

"Excellent choice."

Morgan had watched it probably a hundred times as a kid. The sight of Maria twirling on the bright green mountaintop instantly comforted him, just like Liesl must have felt putting on a dry nightgown after the thunderstorm. The stew was delicious, too. Once it was done, he sipped his wine and hummed along with the songs.

Kazio didn't say much, and Morgan almost — almost — managed to forget about his new catastrophic situation.

"You know, when I was a kid," Morgan said as Maria and Captain von Trapp danced their tension-laced folk dance together, "I was obsessed with all the singing, but now… I'm just screaming for them to realize they're in love." As soon as the words were out of his mouth, he wanted to smack himself.

"Well…" Kazio took a sip of wine. "They need time to figure it out. The great love stories always take time."

"Right," Morgan said weakly. "Who doesn't love slow burn, right?"

"I do." Kazio slid his eyes sideways. "Need some more wine?"

"Oh, yes please."

* * * *

Kazio insisted on driving him home, and it was hard to argue he could take the train with a swollen ankle. Kazio even walked him inside to his apartment door.

"Goodnight," Morgan said. "Thank you for everything. And sorry about —"

"Hey," Kazio said softly, eyes skipping over Morgan's face. "I told you to stop apologizing."

Morgan swallowed. "Right. Sorry."

Kazio gave him a lazy grin. "Now you're just doing it on purpose."

Morgan chuckled and pressed a palm to his forehead. "If you can believe it, I'm actually not."

"I do believe it. Goodnight, Morgan."

Morgan watched him walk down the hall, heart in his throat, then closed the door to his apartment behind him and fell back against it. "I've got some bad news, Catzio."

Catzio was grooming himself in the living room. He ignored Morgan, continuing to lick his fur.

"I think I'm in love with Kazio," Morgan told him.

Catzio dropped his leg and stared at him.

"No… I don't *think* I am. I am. I'm in love with him."

Catzio resumed his licking.

Morgan limped over to his couch and fell into a heap. "But it'll be fine. I thought I had ruined everything but…it was okay. We still hung out and had fun. I don't need to blow everything up, right?"

Catzio switched legs.

"Right. I just have to not be an idiot." He studied his bandage wrapped ankle. "Starting now."

* * * *

He woke up to two texts and a voicemail. One text was from Kazio, of course.

Good morning. How's your ankle?

Morgan gave his foot an experimental wiggle. *Morning. It feels pretty good. How are you?*

I'm fine. Just got to work. You want to come by later?

Yes, he did want to come by later, but the more time he spent with Kazio the more likely it was that he would do or say something stupid. But he had pulled it off last night. It was okay.

Sure, he replied.

Great. See you in a bit. And take it easy on your ankle.

The other text was from Albert at midnight. *You up?*

So romantic. *I'm sorry. I can't do this anymore.*

Albert replied right away. *Do what anymore?*

Hook up.

How come?

I think I'm in love with someone else.

Oh yeah? Who's that? That 'friend' who made you dinner?

It took Morgan a second to process. *Good God, did everyone know but me? Yes, that friend. How did you know?*

The way your face lit up when you talked about him.

Why didn't you tell me?

Because I wanted to fuck you, Morgan. Obviously. It would have been bad for business to tell you that you're actually in love with your friend. Although now that I put that into words, it makes me sound awful.

No, that's fair. I wouldn't have believed you anyway.

Cool. Well, sucks for me but happy for you. Good luck! And let me know if you change your mind…

Good old Albert.

The voicemail was a surprise. "Morgan, darling, this is Victoria Barrett calling. How are you? I have some great news. My brother *loved* your work at the reception and now he's planning a staff party this summer. It'll be huge — the whole company is invited, spouses, a few hundred people. He's rented out Harborfront Park for a barbecue and wants to have some live music after dinner, a little concert of sorts, and Rory thought you might have a band available. Do give me a call back at your earliest convenience to discuss. Talk soon!"

Morgan's jaw dropped. A concert? An actual concert? He scrambled to hit the call back button.

"Hi, Victoria, this is Morgan Di Meo returning your call."

"Morgan! Thank you so much for calling me back."

They exchanged the required pleasantries before she got to the point. "So, Rory said you might have a band? Something fun and upbeat?"

"Er, I do, yes. My band." His head spun. So strange that Rory had recommended him... Then again it wasn't strange, since Rory always thought the best of everyone.

"Excellent! We're looking at a Saturday in August. We can nail a date down soon if you're interested."

"I mean...yeah? I'd have to check with everyone but...pretty sure we're interested."

"Excellent." Victoria gave him a few more details, then he hung up the phone with shaking hands. A real gig! A *concert*. His instinct was to text Kazio right away, but instead he messaged the band. It would be more fun to tell Kazio in person.

* * * *

"You won't believe this," Morgan said, dropping onto his stool at the bar. "I got a call from Victoria Barrett, Rory's aunt? The one who hired me for the art gallery? She wants to hire the band! For an actual concert!"

Kazio's face lit up. "What? That's great! When?"

Morgan basked in Kazio's smile. "Not until August, so that gives us time to get our set polished up."

"That's incredible. So excited for you."

Tasha thunked a tray on the bar and shot Kazio a pointed look.

He gave her a begrudging nod and went to check on the orders she had put in. "You guys can add some more rehearsal times if you need to," he told Morgan as he scanned the slip.

"Thanks, yeah, maybe. We can talk about it more on Friday."

Kazio busied himself collecting glassware.

"So what's new with you?" Morgan blurted. "The first cooking class is tonight, right?"

"Yup. Should be good. I'm excited. We're making grilled cheese." He added ice to the highball glasses.

"Nice. And, um, have you been dating at all?"

Kazio measured out shots of rum and distributed them over the ice. "Dating?"

"Yeah, remember, a few weeks ago, you were talking about giving dating a try? You haven't mentioned how it's going yet."

"Oh, right." Kazio frowned, topping up the glasses with cola. "Uh, well, not good, I guess."

"Oh no?" Morgan tried not to sound too happy.

"I didn't get too far. It's just...online dating is scary. Most of the profiles are an immediate hell no, and then the few guys I chatted with quickly *became* a hell no." He sighed, adding limes to the drinks. "It's not easy. Speaking of...how's Albert?"

"Funny you should ask, he texted me last night."

"Oh." Kazio added mint and syrup to a silver cup.

"I told him that I couldn't see him anymore."

"Oh?" Kazio focused on muddling. "Why not?"

Morgan shook his head. "I'm just not interested in meaningless hookups anymore. I want my Captain von Trapp."

Kazio looked up to meet his gaze. "Right. Exactly." A man down the bar snapped his fingers. Kazio barely managed to contain an eye roll. "One moment," he growled at the man as he finished the mint julep in a blur. "Order's up, Tasha." He leaned over to Morgan. "I'll be right back."

"Okay," Morgan said weakly. "I'll be here."

Tasha came to collect her drinks. "Hey, Morgan," she said, loading up her tray.

"Hi, Tasha." Tasha had always struck Morgan as the strong, silent type, an efficient and smart mom of three who took no shit.

"How are things with your band going?"

"Good, thanks. Great, actually. We just booked a pretty big gig."

"That's terrific." Tasha shifted her tray. "You know…maybe it's not my place to say, but you've been so good for Kazio."

"I…what?"

"I know you guys have spent a lot of time together over the last few months and…he's changed. He's nicer. Happier."

"Oh… Wow, I…" Morgan stared at her.

She chuckled and patted his arm. "Just don't mess anything up, m'kay? Or I will have to hunt you down."

Morgan laughed weakly with her, then swallowed hard, wishing he had a drink. "I'll do my best."

Chapter Twenty

Melodies Within

Morgan dreamed about him that night.

A dirty dream, with no words, only desperation — grasping hands, slippery tongues and grinding hips. He woke up aching with longing.

"Oh God," he muttered to himself, scrubbing the sleep from his eyes. "That is…not helpful."

He rolled over to check his phone, hoping for a distraction. A good morning message from Kazio waited, as usual.

Do you have any plans today?

A lot of pining, probably…some longing. Maybe a bit of sweating.

Aside from applying for a few more jobs I won't get, no, not really.

I was thinking we should go check out that art gallery where you did your gig.

Galerie de Rêverie? Why?

I saw that they have an exhibition right now about music. Might be interesting.

I don't know anything about art.

Except for the way Kazio's hair fell over his eyes. That was art.

That's not a prerequisite for entrance, Morgan. Anyone is allowed in. Not to mention, you are an artist yourself. This is just a different way of creating.

Spending the day wandering through a charming art gallery with Kazio sounded pretty great, actually.

Okay. Sure. Let's do it.

They met at the train station closest to the gallery. Morgan hopped out and there was Kazio, leaning against a railing, hands in his pockets, ankles crossed, like a fucking model in a jeans commercial.

"Hey," Morgan said as he approached.

"Hey," Kazio replied, straightening. "How's your ankle doing?"

"Oh, good. Yeah, it's fine now."

"Good."

They turned together and made their way out onto the street. The sidewalks were crowded, lots of tourists out enjoying the summer sunshine with their handfuls of shopping bags and bouncing children.

"The guys are so excited about the concert." Morgan dodged a crying toddler. "I can't wait for rehearsal tomorrow. I've been thinking about our set."

"I'll bet you're excited. I wish I could hang out a bit but I've got to work."

"Don't worry, I'm sure you'll have plenty of chances to listen." Frankly, Morgan was a little relieved that Kazio wouldn't be there. He wasn't sure how he could get through *Always We* again with him watching.

Kazio held the door when they arrived at the gallery. The first wall facing them looked like a giant piece of colorful sheet music with the title *Melodies Within*, the name of the exhibition. As they got closer, they could see that the notes and other musical notations were made of everyday objects tightly packed together — forks, buttons, coffee cups, pencils, eyeglasses, salt and pepper shakers — painted in bright yellow, fuchsia, a rich orange and electric blue. Morgan stopped and stared, reading the notes across the wall. "Hang on, this tune is familiar." He hummed it.

They looked at each other and said at the same time, "*Sergeant Pepper.*"

Kazio shook his head. "The opening guitar riff. Killer."

"That riff... It changed my life." Morgan paused to study the assortment of objects making up the music. "*Melodies Within...* Not gonna lie, I just got goosebumps."

"Off to a good start," Kazio said. "Can't wait to see what else they've got."

They paid their admission and continued into the next room. The first painting that caught Morgan's attention was abstract but made him think of a man holding a guitar and singing his heart out, surrounded by light and stars, shimmering gold, silver and cornflower blue. The piece was titled *Joy*.

"This is…" Morgan said, struggling for words. "The artist got it exactly right."

"What?" Kazio asked.

"The feeling of singing. It—" Then he stopped because he had read the name of the artist. "Finn Owens? *What?*"

Kazio squinted at the label. "Finn Owens, like…Finn?"

"That's the one. Wow. I had no idea he was so talented." Morgan took a step back and studied the painting again. "I mean…wow."

"People have all kinds of hidden talents, don't they?"

"That's for sure."

Through the next doorway there was an installation—a deconstructed piano in about a hundred pieces spread around the room, suspended from the ceiling or held up by clear rods, but arranged so that it looked like the piano could be slotted back together in the center of the room. Morgan read from the placard at the front. "'A piece of participatory art, *Completed Piano* is an exploration of musical consciousness and the innate human desire to create. The artist delves into the themes of expression, expectation and the ephemerality of music. The listener creates melodies by interacting with the sculpture, and is invited to consider how a song can only be experienced once and will never exist again.'"

Each piece of piano had a red button on it labeled "Press for Music." Morgan pushed one button but nothing happened. He tried again. Nothing.

Kazio pressed another with the same result. "I don't get it."

Morgan looked around and noticed two other guests in the room also pushing buttons and looking confused in the ensuing silence. "I think it's broken."

Another man entered, frowning. "Is it still not working?" he asked Kazio, who was the closest to the door.

Kazio shook his head. "I don't think so. We can't hear anything."

Morgan recognized the man immediately but it took him a second to remember where from. It was Louis, the director of the arts festival…who very much did not hire him. Morgan slouched behind Kazio so Louis wouldn't notice him.

It was too late. Louis took a second, then the smile Morgan remembered spread across his face. "Morgan!"

Morgan almost had to turn around to check for another Morgan. "You remember me?"

"Of course I remember you." Louis strode over to shake his hand. "I'm still thinking about that song you wrote for us."

Morgan's mouth fell open. "Really?"

"Absolutely. I pushed hard to hire you but I got outvoted. Conrad's niece got the gig." He gave a resigned chuckle and shook his head. "I'm still bitter about it."

"Oh…" Morgan didn't know what to say, so he turned to Kazio standing at his side. "This is my friend, Kazio."

They shook hands. "Pleasure to meet you, Kazio. Louis Tate. Anway, we can talk more in a bit, but you'll have to excuse me for the moment. I'm having some trouble with the sound on this installation."

"You work here?" Morgan asked.

"Oh, yes. This is my baby, my main gig. I'm the director." Louis walked over to a panel in the wall and opened it, staring at the wiring and sound board. He sighed. "The artist set it all up and it was working fine yesterday. I cannot for the life of me figure out what's wrong with it now. You don't happen to know anything about this stuff, do you?"

"Actually...I do." Morgan hesitated to barge over there and take over until Kazio nudged him. He joined Louis at the open panel. "May I?"

Louis gave him a 'go ahead' gesture. "Please."

Morgan flipped through the configurations on the sound board. "And you said it was all good yesterday?"

"Correct. No problems."

"Hmm... I'm not seeing anything that looks like settings for this piece..." He tapped his chin, lost in thought for a moment. "When was the last time you updated the sound board's software?"

Louis scratched his head. "I couldn't say. All our computers and equipment are updated automatically."

"It's possible someone who wasn't supposed to got in here and messed around with it, or maybe the power cut during an update and everything reset. Did the artist leave you with a backup at all? We could see if reinstalling helps."

"Oh, thank God." Louis clapped a hand on Morgan's shoulder. "Yes, they did leave a USB with me. I totally forgot. Let me go find it." Louis hustled off in the direction of the main office.

Kazio smiled at him. "He's lucky you're here."

Morgan waved away the compliment. "He would have figured it out eventually. And I haven't actually fixed anything yet."

Kazio tilted his head. "I have no doubt that you will."

Morgan flushed as Louis came hurrying back in brandishing a flash drive. "Found it."

He handed it over to Morgan, who inserted it into the board and toggled through a few tabs on the board's screen until he found a backup to install. Some of the sliders moved on their own and the digital labels changed. "There, try that."

Kazio pushed a button on a piece of the piano leg and a trumpet noise sounded.

Louis breathed out a huge sigh of relief. "You fixed it." He tried a few more buttons—a harp and a piccolo. "Morgan, I cannot thank you enough."

"It was no problem."

Louis closed the panel and looked at Morgan, hands on his hips. "You know…it would be amazing to have someone like you around the gallery."

"Well, my schedule is wide open," Morgan joked. "Feel free to give me a call if you need help."

"You're wide open?"

Morgan resisted looking at Kazio. "Yup. Currently looking for work."

Louis studied him, brow furrowed. "Do you want to work here?"

Another harp chord chimed, then the bong of a timpani drum. "Do I want to…"

"I've been meaning to hire an assistant of some kind. Right now, it's just me, and Amanda at the front counter. We're always so busy in the summer, and the art festival starts soon, which is going to take up even more of my time. I could really use another person around here who can do the behind-the-scenes stuff, manage the events, keep things running smoothly. Are you at all interested?"

Morgan wondered if his legs were going to continue holding him up. "I...I mean, yeah. Yes. Yes, I am very interested."

"Amazing." Louis beamed. "Let me sit down and crunch some numbers and I can get back to you later today with a formal offer. How can I reach you?"

Morgan could barely stammer through his phone number and a thank you.

"Not at all. I'm the one who should be thanking you. Kazio, it was great to meet you. You two enjoy the exhibit. I'll be in touch soon."

Morgan turned to stare at Kazio in a state of total shock and joy that was mirrored on Kazio's face.

"Holy shit," Morgan squeaked.

Kazio gripped his arms. "Holy shit!"

"Did he just..."

"He just!"

Before he knew it, Kazio was hugging him while his eyes watered, right there in the middle of the clarinets and tambourines and violins, his world reduced to fizzy joy wrapped in strong arms, the scent of pine in his nostrils, warmth right down to this toes and music all around him.

He took a shaky breath, "Oh my God, a job here? I need to sit down."

Kazio guided him over to a bench and sat next to him. "This is amazing. I knew you'd find something. You're just too talented."

"I shouldn't get so excited. Maybe the pay will be terrible. Maybe the hours won't be enough, maybe—"

"Hey." Kazio searched for Morgan's gaze. "Maybe it'll be amazing."

* * * *

Kazio was right.

Louis offered him a full-time job titled 'Events Manager' with decent pay, starting the next week.

"Thank you, Louis. Really, thank you so much," Morgan said on the phone.

"Are you kidding? I found the perfect person without even having to look. Can't wait to start working with you."

Morgan hung up and leapt to his feet. "I got a jooooob!"

Kazio beamed at him from his spot on the couch with Catzio in his lap. "Yeah, you did!"

"Oh my God, I'm so happy. We need to celebrate."

"You want to go out?"

Morgan danced into the kitchen. "Why would I want to go out when everything I need is right here?"

They ordered Chinese food, drank tequila, took pictures of Catzio playing in the paper delivery bag and watched bad TV.

Morgan ended up more than a little buzzed as the night went on. He sprawled on the couch, full and content, and risked a glance at Kazio. Kazio was dangling a chopstick wrapper for Catzio to bat at. *He really is the handsomest man in the world*, Morgan decided, hair soft and falling over his eyes, chin rugged and strong. Morgan swallowed the need building up in his throat. Life was going so good right now, and risking their friendship was the worst possible thing he could do. Not to mention potentially losing their rehearsal space, when things were finally happening there, too.

"It's getting late. Do you want to crash here?" Morgan offered. "You can take my bed and I'll sleep on the single."

"No, I wouldn't take your bed. I should head home anyway. I was going to go into work early tomorrow."

"Stay," Morgan said, before he could decide whether or not that was a good idea. "A little bit longer," he amended. "The next episode at least."

Kazio hesitated.

"Pleeeease?" Morgan pleaded. "I'll make popcorn."

He relented. "Okay. I can stay. But just one episode."

* * * *

Morgan woke up lying on the couch. Kazio was leaning over him, pulling up his blanket.

"Hey," Morgan said sleepily.

"Shh, it's early. I'm off to work. You should sleep more." Kazio smoothed the blanket over Morgan's shoulder. "Let me know if you have any trouble with my garage code."

"Okay, thanks." Morgan paused, confused. "Did we both sleep on the couch all night?"

"Yeah." Kazio huffed a laugh. "It wasn't bad. You slept like a log."

"Oh, God. Sorry. I didn't mean to pass out."

"It's all good. I passed out, too."

"You want some breakfast?"

"I'm okay." Kazio smiled and pushed a piece of hair off Morgan's forehead. "Sleep."

* * * *

"Wait." Andre sat on his stool and gave Morgan his full attention. "You're telling me that in the last three days, you got us a big gig, you got an awesome job *and* you realized you're in love with your hot best friend? Not too shabby for Morgan!"

"No, being in love with my hot — with my best friend is not good!"

"Why not, again?"

"Because I'm a fucking mess! I don't know how to act around him anymore. Ordinarily, if I was into someone, I'd try to look sexy and give him my best lines, but I can't do that with Kazio."

"Why not?" Brett asked.

"Because he'd be like…'what's with you?' It would be weird."

"You could just kiss him. See if he kisses you back," Andre suggested helpfully.

Felix joined in. "Andre, be serious. You can't just start kissing people."

"Okay, you know what?" Morgan said, determined to put an end to this conversation. "He's my friend. I'm not making a move. And we" — he gestured at the group — "we have a show to put together."

"You're right," Andre said. "You're totally right."

"Thank you." Morgan got back to the set list he had been revising.

"But I'm just saying," Andre mumbled, "a little kiss would go a long way."

Morgan shot him his best death glare. "So we agree we're going to start with *Empty Stage*?"

At the end of the rehearsal Morgan tidied his papers into a folder and packed away his guitars. "You know, it would be nice if we had a small gig or two before the concert."

Felix stood and stretched. "That's a really good point…except where?"

"Anyone have any connections?" Morgan asked.

They stared at each other.

"What about The Sphinx?" Andre suggested. "They were so cool about getting us in last time."

"Um, I believe the manager's exact words to me were '*You'll never play here again, and I'll make sure to tell all the other clubs, too,*'" Morgan informed them.

"Well, shit." Andre steepled his fingers. "What if we apologized and asked for another chance?"

"I don't..." Morgan started, but then he paused to think. "I don't know, maybe." There was something to be said for second chances. Maybe the manager would agree.

"I'll go with you," Felix offered. "It doesn't hurt to ask."

"Okay. Thanks," Morgan said. It would be a little easier with a bandmate by his side.

"Sick," Brett said. "Hey, do you guys want to try some of Ray's sourdough?"

* * * *

Morgan was lying on the couch doing not much of anything Saturday afternoon when he got a text from Kazio.

Are you busy? Can I ask you a huge favor?

He sat up, scratching his chest.

Sure?

He couldn't imagine Kazio asking for anything that he would say no to.

Can you run out and buy a dozen pints of cherry tomatoes and bring them to the community center ASAP? Save your receipt. Sungold tomatoes, if they have them.

Sungold?

The ones that are kind of orange. The tomatoes here are going bad and I don't want to use them.

Yeah, I can do that.

Thank you so much! Room 110. Turn left from the lobby, then it's on your right about three doors down.

Be there as fast as I can.

Morgan changed into slightly more presentable clothes and caught the train downtown. He was able to procure a flat of Sungolds at the big grocery store only a few blocks from the community center. A woman waiting at a corner gave him a strange look. "I really love tomatoes," Morgan explained to her.

Kazio's face lit up when Morgan entered the room, so cute in his white apron and hair all pulled back into a tight knot.

Morgan had to smile at him. "Tomato delivery!" He deposited the flat on the back counter with a flourish.

"Thank you so much! Just in time." Kazio picked up a pint and examined them. "Perfect! You saved the day."

The room hummed with activity and smelled like bacon. Pairs of people worked at the six cooking stations, stirring and chopping. A burst of steam filled the air as one young man dumped a pot of pasta into a colander in the sink. "No problem. What are you guys making?"

"Spaghetti carbonara. Can you help me hand out the tomatoes?"

"You bet." They distributed the pints around the room, then Morgan figured Kazio needed to get back to his students.

"Well, I'll get out of your hair..." he said, edging toward the door.

"No, stay! We're almost done. You can sample some."

It did smell amazing. "If you're sure..."

Kazio's eyes were soft. "I'm sure."

Morgan found a chair and sat at the front near the demo station. Kazio bustled around, checking in with the groups as they chopped their tomatoes and mixed them into the dish. When the students were sitting down to eat, Kazio came back and served Morgan a portion from the sample dish he'd made.

"Amazing, as usual," Morgan said after he swallowed his mouthful. "You never miss."

"Glad you like it."

A woman wearing a full-on chef's coat poked her head in the door. Kazio waved her in.

"This is Aleysha," Kazio said as she approached. "I promised her some dinner." She was beautiful—sparkling dark eyes, light brown skin and a long black braid down her back.

"Hey," she said, with a warm smile. "How'd it turn out?"

"Pretty good, I think." Kazio handed her a bowl. "Aleysha, this is my friend, Morgan. Morgan, this is Aleysha. She teaches the advanced cooking classes. She's an actual chef, not some hack like me."

"Oh, stop," Aleysha said. "It's nice to meet you, Morgan."

"You, too."

Aleysha shoveled in a forkful. "Mmm," she mumbled in appreciation.

Morgan smiled at her. "I know, right? His food is always the best."

Kazio dismissed her compliment. "Nothing compared to what you make."

She swallowed and twirled up another bite on her fork. "Don't be silly — this is fucking delicious."

Kazio shrugged, clearly pleased.

"I've got to run. My evening class is about to start. Thank you so much for dinner! Morgan, nice to meet you."

"You too."

"See you next week," Kazio said.

Aleysha waved her fork and scurried back out the door, eating on the run.

Once he finished his dish, Morgan stood awkwardly with his empty bowl. "Do you need anything else? Help with cleanup?"

"No, it's okay. We've got it." Kazio took the bowl from him. "Thank you again so much for the tomatoes."

"It was no problem."

"I'll pick you up at ten tomorrow?"

"I'll be ready."

On his way out, Morgan had an idea.

He'd have to head back to the grocery store.

Chapter Twenty-One

Surprises

"I'm making you dinner tonight," Morgan announced as he got into Kazio's SUV the next morning. He was quite proud of his cool delivery, because inside his stomach was roiling.

Kazio turned to give him a small smile. "Are you?"

"I keep saying I owe you dinner. So...tonight's the night. You've fed me enough times." He took a sip of the iced coffee that was waiting for him. "You're free, right?"

Kazio shifted into drive. "Yes, I'm free. And thank you." They pulled out of the drive and into traffic. "What are you making?"

"It's a surprise!"

"Not even a hint?"

"No hints. You'll just have to wait." Even though it wasn't a date, it sort of felt like he just asked Kazio out on one. And he said yes. Morgan took another sip of his drink, hoping it would ease the warmth in his cheeks.

July had arrived with blazing heat, and he figured it was fair to blame at least some of his sweat on the sun beating down. When they got to the shelter, Drew was nowhere to be found outside. Instead he was behind the front counter with Camella, curled up in his bed enjoying the air conditioning.

"There are my boys." Camella beamed. "You managing to keep cool?"

"I'm already sweating." Morgan flapped his T-shirt. Drew hopped up on the counter to say hello.

"At least we don't have fur coats, right?" Camella smiled.

"That is true." Morgan gave Drew a head scratch.

"What do you need from us today?" Kazio asked.

"We're drowning in emails. I was hoping Morgan could work on replies for me."

Morgan arched his eyebrow. "You want me to answer emails? Are you sure about that?"

"You've been around here enough that you know the main stuff. About ninety percent of them are answered in our FAQ. You just need to copy and paste and add a pleasant greeting and sign-off. If you're not sure, skip it, and I'll get back to it later."

Morgan had never been one for fluffing up his emails. "Maybe Kazio would be better at that."

"I've got him marked to help with surgery prep. Unless you want to shave a dog's nether regions?" Camella gave him an innocent grin.

Morgan cringed. "Er, I'll take the emails."

"Beautiful. You can use my laptop back here."

He settled at the desk in the office and scrolled down to the oldest unread message. It asked about volunteering. He clicked reply.

Dear Marcy, thank you for your interest in volunteering at Mountain Meadow Animal Care Center. Please see the volunteer page on our website for more information on how to apply for a position. Thank you and have a great day!

He added links for the website and the application and clicked send. Easy.

The second asked the minimum age for volunteering, which was in the FAQ.

Dear Isaiah, thank you for your interest…

He attached the link and fired back his reply.

The third email asked if they were open Sundays. "I mean, check the website. Seriously. You're already on the computer," Morgan muttered as he clicked reply. Next was a question about donating old blankets. Morgan sighed. Nice of them, but that answer was also on the website. Then another email about volunteering. "For fuck's sake, people." He was attaching the link to the volunteering page yet again when a notification for a new message popped up. Morgan's eyes flicked to the preview.

There's a box of kittens behind the ShopMart on 13th was all it said.

"Oh. Um." He got up to find Camella.

She read the email, then reached into the desk drawer for her car keys. "You coming with?"

* * * *

There was indeed a box of kittens behind the ShopMart. Seven tiny little guys squirming around — three brown tabbies, an orange and three white kittens—in an otherwise empty box. Not even a blanket.

Camella put a heating bag in the box with them right away. "It's hot enough out that they're probably warm enough now, but we need to keep their body temperatures up in the A/C or they won't eat."

"Oh my gosh." Morgan's heart ached. "How could someone just dump them here?"

"I don't know, but it happens more than you'd believe."

"How old are they, do you think?" Morgan asked.

"I would say a little over a week. Their eyes are open and their umbilical cords are gone, but their ears are still mostly folded. You got the box?"

Morgan lifted it as carefully as he could. It weighed almost nothing. "Yup."

He didn't remember anything from the car ride back, unless it happened inside that box. The orange tabby was the most restless, nosing at its brothers and sisters and making tiny mewling sounds. One of the brown tabbies, the smallest one, slept the whole way. Morgan trained his eyes on its chest looking for signs of breathing.

"Is it okay if I pet them? Very gently?" he asked.

Camella glanced at him with a smile. "It's okay."

He trailed a fingertip over the small tabby. "Hey, little guy. You okay?"

The kitten's eyelids fluttered.

"Can we feed the small one first?" Morgan asked. "I'm worried about him."

Camella patted his knee. "Sure we can, hon."

When they got back to the shelter, Camella led Morgan into the kitchen. "Can you grab a blanket and heat up the bag again? I'm going to mix up some formula."

Morgan retrieved a clean blanket from the laundry room, then microwaved the heat bag, checking to make sure it wasn't too hot before putting it back in the box. He sat next to them, still keeping a close eye on the small one.

Camella returned with an armful of bottles and formula, and Kazio in tow, carrying a new, cleaner box.

"Can you believe someone would abandon them?" Morgan said, looking up at Kazio.

"I know." Kazio sat next to Morgan on the floor. "It's awful."

Camella pulled a scale and a clipboard out of the box. "We need to weigh them first so we can track their progress." One at a time, she placed the kittens on the scale. Kazio recorded their weight on the clipboard, then Morgan placed them in the new box with the blanket and heat bag.

"If you each want to pick one up for a cuddle, make sure they're warm enough?" Camella said while she began to mix the formula and fill bottles. "Normally we wouldn't wake up a sleeping kitten to eat, but we don't know how long they've gone without food, so I think feeding is more important right now."

Morgan, of course, chose the small one, who fit neatly in his hand, light as a puff of air. Kazio took the orange kitten. Morgan stroked a finger down his kitten's back. The kitten opened his eyes and regarded Morgan gravely. "Hey, little guy. Are you hungry?"

Camella joined them with a handful of bottles. "Let me show you how to feed them." She settled next to them and picked up one of the white kittens. "You want them on their bellies, not their back, and you hold their head steady with your other hand." She demonstrated with the white kitten, who latched eagerly and chugged its formula down, ears wiggling.

The tiny one in Morgan's hand showed some interest in the nipple but didn't copy his sibling's enthusiasm for latching. "You want some food?" Morgan asked him.

The kitten gnawed at the rubber. He looked almost surprised at the formula that ended up on his face.

Morgan chuckled. "There you go... Try again."

It was the cutest thing Morgan had ever seen, the kitten attempting to drink and getting formula all over his fur. He and Kazio shared a smile. "He's sort of drinking out of the side of his mouth?" Morgan said.

"That's okay. If you put a gentle finger on his throat, you'll be able to feel him swallowing."

Morgan followed her instructions. "Oh yeah! He's drinking."

After the little guy appeared to have had his fill, Morgan fed one of the white ones, too.

"Can we come back and visit them again soon?" Morgan asked once they were all fed and cleaned and sleeping curled up in the blanket. The sight of them gave him an immense sense of satisfaction deep in his bones.

"Of course." Camella smiled and rubbed his arm. "Absolutely any time you like."

* * * *

"Would you like a drink?" Morgan asked when they got back to his apartment. "I've got wine." He was tired and sweaty but Kazio was in his apartment and there were things to do.

"You know what?" Kazio said. "Would you mind if I had a shower first? All I can smell is sweat, dogs and kitten formula."

"Of course. Actually..." Morgan tried to subtly smell himself. "I could use a shower, too. Can I go first super quick? Then you can go while I get dinner in the oven."

"Sounds good. I'll pour the wine while I wait."

Morgan preheated the oven, then hurried to his bathroom and peeled his clothes off, intensely aware how naked he was and how close Kazio was to said nakedness. He had a quick, cool shower, then realized he had forgotten to bring fresh clothes in with him. "Damn it." He wrapped a towel around his waist and stared at his reflection in the mirror, hair dripping wet. "Just make a break for it. He won't see you."

He opened the bathroom door as quietly as he could and began to tiptoe to his room, and Kazio appeared in the hallway. Of course.

"Oh, hey, I was going to ask—" Kazio froze, wide eyes on Morgan's bare chest.

Morgan froze too, awkward as hell. "Mm-hmm?"

"Oh, I uh..." Kazio's gaze bounced from Morgan's chest to eyes to hips and back up again. "Um. If I could borrow a clean shirt."

"Of course. I'll just..." Morgan pointed at his room and scurried in.

Kazio followed. Of course. "Wow." He whistled at the clean room. "Look at you. Still using your 'closet' and 'hangers.'"

"Oh, I know, right?" Morgan said weakly, heading into his closet, aware of how he was all towel and water droplets and bare skin. He rifled through a shelf and pulled off a plain black T-shirt that was a little baggy on him. "Here you go." Kazio had followed him to the doorway. Their fingers brushed as Morgan handed it to him.

Kazio stood there, holding the shirt, their gazes locked. "Thanks."

"You're welcome." Morgan swallowed so loud it was like a gunshot in the silent space. "I hope it fits okay." He tried not to let his gaze wander along Kazio's broad shoulders.

"Well. I should shower."

Morgan's heart pounded. "Yes."

Kazio spun on his heel and disappeared into the hallway.

Morgan's thoughts raced. *Was he…? No. No. He was not.* He scurried after Kazio. "There's clean towels in the cupboard, and help yourself to my shampoo and anything else you need…" he called.

"Thanks," Kazio called back. The bathroom door closed.

And now Kazio was getting naked in his bathroom. "Fuck," Morgan muttered under his breath, staring at the door for a few beats longer than necessary, then he went back to his closet to get dressed.

The casserole was already waiting in the fridge, so all he had to do was the topping—cheese and potato chips—and stick it in the oven to heat and crisp up. Morgan sipped his wine as he set the table and adjusted the daisies in their vase.

He was just about to light a candle as the final touch when Kazio arrived, hair wet but still pulled back in his customary half-pony. Morgan's shirt clung to his torso, highlighting his pecs in a rather enticing way.

"I smell like you now," Kazio said.

Morgan paused, lighter flame flickering in the air a moment before he touched it to the wick. "I… What?"

"Your shower gel, I mean. It smells good."

"Right. Well, that's…good. Er, please, sit." Morgan refilled Kazio's glass and topped up his own right as the oven dinged. "Perfect timing." He pulled the casserole out, added a garnish of parsley, then placed the steaming, bubbling dish on pot holders on the table. "Voilà."

"Ooh." Kazio took a deep breath. "This smells amazing. What is it?"

"Tuna noodle casserole. I used to help my mom make it." Morgan served a scoop onto Kazio's plate.

"I've never had this before." Kazio picked up his fork.

"You've never had tuna noodle casserole?"

"Nope."

"That's good. Then you won't know if I messed it up." Morgan gave his own plate a healthy serving.

"I'm sure you didn't."

He did, though. His first bite was a disappointment. The pasta was mushy, the cheese was overdone, and something tasted...off. Too much salt maybe? He had never made it entirely on his own before, but he had assisted his mom many times and had figured it would be a safe choice cooking for Kazio the first time. He had been wrong. But before he could say anything, Kazio made a noise of appreciation.

"This is so good," Kazio said.

"What? No, it's not."

"Yes, it is." Kazio took another bite.

"No, it's... It's not right at all."

Kazio swallowed. "Well, I like it. You did a great job."

"You're just being nice," Morgan grumbled, but the praise curled in his gut and warmed him from the inside.

"Really, it's delicious. You're probably being too hard on yourself."

Morgan took another bite. Well...it wasn't as good as his mom's, but maybe it wasn't terrible.

It didn't take Kazio long to finish the scoop Morgan had served him and help himself to another. "So how are things going with the band? Felix is working out fine?"

"Yeah, so far it's going really well. We're all getting along great." When they weren't actually playing, their time together mostly consisted of good-natured ribbing about Kazio but he couldn't mention that part. "Felix and I are going to talk to the manager we bailed on in March about another gig. We haven't had any luck finding anything else yet."

"Good for you guys. I hope it works out." Kazio paused before he took his next bite. "Maybe this isn't the best time to tell you, but...one of my neighbors made a comment about the rehearsal noise."

"Oh no, really?"

"Yeah. Nothing major yet, but we'll probably need to find you a better rehearsal space soon."

Morgan sighed. "I'll add that to the list."

"But hey, your new job starts in a couple days! Are you excited?"

"Yeah," Morgan replied. "Yeah, I'm really excited." He chewed, considering. "Although it was kind of nice having so much free time."

"No kidding. I hope we can still hang out."

"The gallery is closed Mondays, so maybe that can be our day. I mean, not like *our* day, but...a day I'm available. To hang out." He took a gulp of wine.

"That would be great," Kazio said. Their forks clinked on their plates for a few beats of silence. "Thank you for dinner. I really love it. And the flowers."

They both studied the daisies.

"You're welcome. I don't know if I could make anything else, but I'm glad at least this worked out…sort of."

"I'm sure you could make whatever you wanted."

"No, I really couldn't, I…" He trailed off, a thought taking hold in his mind.

Kazio waited for him to finish his sentence.

Morgan shook his head. "Never mind. You want dessert? I got ice cream."

"I never say no to ice cream."

* * * *

When it was time for Kazio to leave, they stood together at the door.

"Thank you again so much for dinner," Kazio said.

God, he looked good in that tight shirt. "You're welcome. It was the least I could do for you."

"It wasn't the least."

"Well…" Morgan trailed off, finding himself a little bit lost in Kazio's eyes now. "It was a start, I guess."

For a single, stupid moment, the distance between them seemed to be closing, the air crackling with electricity and longing.

Morgan shook himself before he could do anything embarrassing. "Have a good night."

"You too." Kazio's gaze lingered, then he turned and made his way down the hall.

Morgan closed the door and shuffled back into the kitchen, heart skittering a little. He studied the remains of the mediocre casserole and thought about all the amazing food Kazio had made for him.

Maybe the casserole wasn't the *least*, but it was close.

It was time to change that.

Morgan grabbed his laptop.

The leftovers could wait.

* * * *

Tuesday evening Felix waited for him at the train station closest to The Sphinx.

"Hey," Morgan said, hopping up the last few stairs.

"Hey," Felix said. "It's hotter than fuck." He looked like he was melting in the heat, sweat trickling down his temple.

"I couldn't agree more." Morgan was wearing the smallest shorts he thought he could get away with and a light tank top, but it was still entirely too much clothing. He popped his sunglasses on and followed Felix through the crowds toward the seedy end of the street.

The manager of The Sphinx was Zayden Bourne, or at least that was what it said on his business cards, and he was every shitty bar owner cliche rolled into one. Balding, heavy chains around his neck, thin button-down open over a yellowing tank top, but younger than people might otherwise expect. He regarded Morgan and Felix without speaking, rubbing his stubble. Then he jerked his chin at them and led him into his office that stank like cigarette smoke.

"Thank you for agreeing to see us, Mr. Bourne," Morgan said. There were no other chairs in the office besides the one behind the desk, so he and Felix stood fidgeting, like they were in trouble in the principal's office.

"You have one minute of my time," Zayden Bourne said, lighting a smoke.

"Er. Okay. We would first of all like to say how sorry we are for bailing on our gig."

"That was my fault," Felix piped up. "I got stuck at work and I left these guys in the lurch."

Zayden glared at them through a cloud of smoke. "That wouldn't have stopped a pro."

"You're right. I panicked, and said some things I regret, to Felix and to you," Morgan said. "I sincerely apologize. I've learned a lot since then, and I assure you, that would never happen again."

"Same for me," Felix added hurriedly, aware of the ticking clock.

Zayden blew smoke through his nose like a cranky dragon guarding a treasure. "I'm only saying yes" — he coughed up a wad of something and spit it into the garbage can. Morgan tried not to visibly turn green — "because I have an empty opening spot next Friday."

It took Morgan a second to hear the 'yes'. "Wait...next Friday?" He shared a shocked look with Felix.

"Yes, next Friday," Zayden repeated loudly, like Morgan was an idiot.

Morgan resisted the urge to hug him. "Thank you so much, Mr. Bourne. Really, th — "

"Get out of here before I change my mind." He took another drag.

"Yes, sir."

Morgan and Felix tumbled back onto the pavement outside the club. Felix threw his arms around Morgan. "We did it!"

Morgan hugged him back, but it was sticky and uncomfortable in the heat. He peeled himself away. "Yeah, we did!"

"You wanna go grab a drink to celebrate?"

"I actually start my new job tomorrow so I've got to get home. But maybe the four of us can go out after our next rehearsal?"

"Yeah, for sure. Sounds good."

Morgan waved goodbye to Felix at the station then texted Kazio the good news.

So happy for you! Kazio replied. *Can you come by the pub for a drink?*

Sure. Be there in fifteen.

Morgan smiled to himself as he pattered down the stairs.

Chapter Twenty-Two

Tension

Louis opened a door down the hall from his office. "This one's yours."

"I get my own office?" Morgan followed him into the small and sparsely furnished space—not much besides a desk, chair and laptop. But it was his. He ran his hand over the glossy desk.

"You bet. New laptop, too. My IT consultant hooked you up. You should be on our network and set up for email and everything. He left some login instructions on that paper there."

"Thank you. This is great." Morgan sat and powered up the laptop.

Louis looked around, hands on hips. "Man, this place is dire, and we are in an *art* gallery. You need some art in here. What are your tastes?"

"Um…I'm not sure?"

"I'll tell you what—you can pick something out later from storage. For now, go ahead and get settled in. You should find your contract in your email, and the employee handbook, although calling it a 'handbook' is, admittedly, rather generous. There's also PDFs of the gallery guides. Why don't you read all that over, then I'll give you a full tour."

Morgan followed the instructions, signed his contract and read the other information Louis had emailed him. Then he found Louis in his office.

Louis looked up from a stack of papers and smiled. "How'd that go? Any questions?"

"Yes, actually... The contract specifies total hours per week, but doesn't say anything specific about days or anything...?"

Louis leaned back in his chair and folded his hands over his belly. "Honestly? I'll obviously need you here for events and the odd other thing, but otherwise you can pick your hours."

Morgan had to laugh. "I'm sorry, this is almost too good to be true."

"I feel the same." Louis hopped to his feet. "Now let me show you around."

* * * *

My day was amaaaazing, he texted Kazio on his way down the escalator into the train station.

That's great. You want to stop by the pub and tell me about it?

It was after five, and it occurred to Morgan that it would be harder to find time at the Exchange without the Breakpoint crew there, now that he was working something like regular office hours.

Is the coast clear?

A few of them are here, Kazio replied.

Luka? Morgan paused at the train platform that would take him to the Exchange.

Yup. He's here with Thomas, Finn and Rory.

Morgan's fingers twitched, ready to make an excuse not to go, but another message from Kazio arrived.

Please come, Morgan. You've got a job now. A band. A cat! You're not the same person you were when you got fired.

Was he a different person? Different enough that he could face Luka? The train whooshed into the station as he considered.

And I'd like to see you, Kazio added.

Morgan smiled and looked up. A crowd of commuters gathered at the door.
He followed them onto the train.

* * * *

Morgan's stomach had twisted into a ball by the time he arrived at the Exchange. He paused, clutching the door handle, knuckles white, then he took a deep breath and entered. He scanned the pub, trying to make it look nonchalant. But after all that build-up, they weren't there. It was strange that he was both relieved and disappointed.

Kazio was a blur behind the bar, serving a large, jovial crowd who had surrounded Morgan's usual stool. Morgan stood back, trying not to glare at them, until Kazio saw him and waved him over to the server's station.

"Hey," Kazio said. "You just missed them."

"Oh. Okay." Morgan nodded, exhaling. "Good."

"I'm really proud of you for coming anyway, though." Kazio's thin navy T-shirt clung beautifully to his shoulders and chest.

"Yeah, well..." Morgan shrugged. *I mostly wanted to see you.*

Kazio pointed behind Morgan. "You want to grab a table? I'll just get this group settled and join you for a bit."

"Sure." Morgan picked a table and took the seat facing the bar. He pretended to watch a TV screen, but instead he kept his eyes on Kazio, admiring his crisp, efficient manner, firm lines and the glimmer in his eyes that told Morgan exactly what Kazio was thinking.

For example, Kazio hated the loud guy who was leaning on the bar and acting like he was in the middle of his very own standup special. He had a soft spot for the guy's wife though, leaning in to offer her a refill with a half wink. Kazio was also sick of making blended drinks and if one more person called him, "Excuse me," things were going to get ugly.

Finally, crowd appeased, Kazio made his way over, carrying two champagne flutes.

"Bubbly?" Morgan asked, accepting one of the glasses with an amused eyebrow quirk.

"Lots to celebrate lately." Kazio tapped Morgan's glass with his. "Tell me all about your first day."

Morgan described his office and how Louis had let him pick a piece of art for the wall. "There's a storage room in the basement with lots of pieces. I chose a mountain landscape. It's a little bit fuzzy, but bright. Reminds me of when we went camping."

"Good choice." Kazio took a sip. "I can't wait to see it."

"Definitely. Whenever you can come by next. Actually, how about Saturday? The Rotary is putting on an event, but it's open to the public."

"I'm supposed to be on the bar…"

"Oh, don't worry about it. There'll be lots of other chances."

"True. So what else? Do you need anything extra for your office?"

They chatted until their glasses were empty and Kazio had to get back to work. "Champagne is on me," Kazio said, waving away Morgan's offer to pay.

"Are you sure? I feel like I hardly ever pay for my drinks anymore."

"I'm sure. And don't worry about it. I'm just happy you're here."

Before Morgan could untangle his thoughts, then his tongue, to respond, Kazio scooped up the two glasses and carried them back to the bar.

"I'm just happy you're here." No one had ever said anything like that to him, that merely his presence made them happy. Kazio didn't want anything from him. He just liked him. A whimper escaped Morgan's lips. How much longer could he keep his feelings to himself?

* * * *

Morgan worked all day Thursday and Friday morning to ensure he was up to speed for Saturday's event, so he was able to join the band's usual rehearsal time Friday afternoon.

It didn't go quite as expected. Bass still in its case, Brett sat on his stool and frowned. "We need to talk about the band name."

Morgan slung his guitar over his shoulder. "What do you mean?"

"Ray doesn't like it."

"Sorry... *Ray* doesn't like it?"

"He says it's not practical."

Morgan tried to find a response more polite than *Ray can fuck off*, but then Andre joined in. "Morgan, I think Ray might have a point."

It was a slap to the face. "What? You guys all liked the name before."

Andre and Felix shared a look. "We didn't know how to tell you, but...we didn't really."

Morgan opened then closed his mouth. "What's wrong with 'Symphony'?"

Andre scratched his head. "I mean, it's, like, cool, theoretically. But it's hard to search online."

"They'll just get the actual Oakport Symphony," Felix chimed in.

"But..." Morgan floundered. As much as he wanted a cool, iconic name like *Queen*, a part of him knew they were right. 'Symphony' was cool in theory, but, he had to admit, not that functional. "Fine. What's our name, then?"

The other three blinked at each other. "I dunno," Brett said. "Ray suggested Merry Exclamation. Or Merry Sourdough."

Morgan blinked. "Merry...?"

Brett held his hands wide. "Everyone loves sourdough, right?"

"Um, what about Living Titans?" Andre suggested.

Felix piped up. "Ruthless Adventure?"

"Sourdough Adventure?" Brett said.

Morgan pinched the bridge of his nose. "Nothing with sourdough, Brett."

They tossed around a few more ideas, but the clock was ticking, and their first gig was only a week away. "Can we put a pin in this for now?" Morgan finally asked when it was clear they were getting nowhere. "We already have socials set up for 'Symphony,' so I think we should just stick with it until we're sure."

"Sounds fair," Brett agreed. "Let's rock."

* * * *

"Is everyone still up for a drink?" Felix asked once they were packing up for the day. He had floated the idea of heading out to celebrate their gig in the group chat and everyone had said they were free.

"Hell yeah," Andre said.

"Where should we go?" Felix asked.

Brett shrugged. "Wherever."

"You know where we should go?" Andre's face lit up like he had the best idea in the world. "Kazio's pub!"

Morgan wouldn't complain about going to the Exchange, but he narrowed his eyes at the others. "Fine with me, if you guys are going to be cool."

Andre pressed a hand to his chest and fluttered his lashes. "When am I not cool?"

"Never when Kazio's around, that's for sure."

Andre sniffed. "I solemnly swear, I will *continue* to be extremely cool around Kazio."

"Kazio's pub?" Felix frowned. "What's it called?"

"The Bitter Exchange," Morgan replied. "It's right by the ad agency I used to work at. Near the Main Street station."

"Haven't heard of it. Is it nice?"

"It's nice," Morgan said. "You know, your basic pub. But the food is really good, and I know we'll get great service."

"Kazio gives great service, does he?" Andre asked, then dodged away before Morgan could smack him. "Sorry, I just had to get it out. I'll be good, I promise."

* * * *

Morgan wanted it to be a surprise, so he didn't tell Kazio they were coming. The pub was humming with its usual Friday evening business, and it took Kazio a second to see them through the crowd.

When their eyes met, Kazio's smile was like the rising sun, glowing and golden. Then his eyebrows jumped when he saw the rest of the band with Morgan. "Hey, everyone. Thanks for coming in," he said when they reached the bar.

"No problem." Morgan ignored the way his heart rate doubled at the sight of Kazio's handsome face.

"Why don't you guys grab a table, and I'll bring you a pitcher?"

"Sounds good, thanks."

Felix sat next to Morgan on the red vinyl bench and Brett and Andre faced them in the chairs.

Andre looked around. "All right, this place isn't bad."

"Sure, if 'rundown pub' is what you're going for," Felix said with a sniff.

"Kazio wasn't too worried about aesthetics when he took over, just good drinks and food," Morgan explained.

"Those are the most important things," Andre agreed.

Kazio appeared a moment later with a pitcher and four glasses. "Here you go."

"Uh, can I get a vodka soda?" Felix asked.

Kazio hooked his thumbs in his pockets. "Of course. Does anyone need anything else?"

Andre and Brett shook their heads.

"I'm good, thanks," Morgan said. "Oh, actually... Maybe some menus?"

Kazio nodded. "I'll be right back."

Morgan poured glasses of beer for Andre, Brett and himself.

Kazio dropped off the menus and Felix's drink, smiling and holding eye contact with Morgan longer than needed to before he went back to the bar.

Morgan held his menu high and studied it intently to hide his blush.

"Are you going to get some food?" Felix leaned over to peer at Morgan's menu.

"Yeah." Morgan slid a menu over for Felix. "The wings are really good."

Tasha came to take their order. Morgan and Felix asked for wings, Andre ordered a burger and Brett got fish and chips.

"What do you guys think about Porcelain?" Brett asked once Tasha had collected the menus and departed.

"Porcelain?" Morgan wrinkled his brow. "Is Ray into, like...ceramics now or something?"

Brett blinked. "I meant 'Porcelain' as a band name."

"Oh. Ohhhh. Um..."

Andre lifted a shoulder. "Makes us sound...fragile."

"I actually think I saw a band on Insta named Porcelain," Felix said.

"It was just an idea." Brett took a sulky sip of his beer.

"What about Crown?" Andre said. "Sort of a nod to Queen."

Brett shook his head. "People will just think of that boring show."

"*The Crown* isn't boring!" Felix protested.

"Have you *watched The Crown*?" Brett asked.

Morgan smiled and took another sip of his beer. The bickering was good-natured, and at least they weren't giving him shit about Kazio.

Tasha dropped off their food, then Kazio came by with a second pitcher. "Can I grab you another vodka soda, Felix?"

"That would be great, thanks," Felix said, then he added something in Polish.

Kazio narrowed his eyes the slightest bit and replied in Polish.

Felix said something else with a sweet smile.

Kazio smiled in return, but his expression had many layers to it—amused, but also trying not to roll his eyes. He turned his attention to the other three. "Do you guys need anything else?"

"I think we're good for now, thank you," Morgan replied.

As they ate, Felix's knee kept touching Morgan's under the table. Morgan shifted over on the bench. "I'm feeling pretty ready for The Sphinx show. What do you guys think?"

"Definitely ready," Andre agreed. "We're going to kill it."

Brett nodded his agreement as he chewed.

Felix squeezed Morgan's arm. "Thank you for getting us back together."

"I'm glad it all worked out," Morgan said.

Felix's hand lingered. "Me too."

Morgan lifted his arm away to wipe his mouth with his napkin. "How are your wings?"

"They're fine," Felix said.

Just out of habit, Morgan's gaze drifted back to Kazio.

Kazio was watching them.

* * * *

"Remember, three hours early!" Morgan called, waving goodbye to Felix, Brett and Andre as the three of them headed home, then he plopped onto his barstool.

Kazio raised an eyebrow.

"A lime seltzer, please."

Kazio nodded and popped a can for him.

"Thanks. Hey, what did Felix say to you in Polish?" Morgan had been dying to find out all night.

Kazio leaned on the counter. "Oh, not much. He just asked where in Poland I was from." He chuckled. "I think he was trying to insult me, something about a country kid living in the big city."

"Really? That's weird."

Kazio shrugged. "It's fine. It was very Polish."

"Hmm." Morgan took a sip of his drink, considering. "To be honest, tonight I sort of...got the impression that Felix was flirting with me."

Kazio paused his tidying. "Oh yeah?"

"Yeah, I... I don't know. Maybe it was all in my head. But he kept, like, touching me and asking me questions and...he just seemed too interested in me."

"Hmm... So..." Kazio busied himself straightening the wine glasses. "Do you like him?"

"Nooo. No. Definitely not."

"He's cute."

"Yeah, he is, but…I just… I'm not into him. Anymore."

"Anymore?"

"I was interested before but…not now."

"Oh. Probably safer that way. You don't want to Fleetwood Mac the band…" Kazio moved onto the pint glasses. "Is there someone you are into?"

You. The word was on the tip of Morgan's tongue. *Don't do it, Morgan. You'll fuck everything up, just like you did with Luka. You've got a show in a week. Your stuff is still in his garage.* "Um… No. Not really. Pretty busy with my new job and the band and…Catzio."

"Yeah, for sure."

"But listen. I, uh…I wanted to try making dinner for you again."

"Again?" Kazio furrowed his brow. "But you just cooked for me on Sunday."

"It wasn't very good though, plus I figure I owe you several meals anyway. Would Monday night work for you?"

Kazio paused, like he was mentally flipping through his calendar. "Um, yes. Monday works. Thank you."

"Great."

"Great." Kazio cleared his throat. "Ready for your event tomorrow?"

"As ready as I can be, I guess. I don't think I can fuck this one up too badly. Louis basically had everything ready to go." His phone buzzed. It was a text from Felix.

Thanks again for everything plus a heart emoji.

Morgan sighed. Now this… This he could very well fuck up.

Chapter Twenty-Three

One Down

Knock, knock, knock.

Kazio.

Morgan hurried to the door, wiping his sweaty palms off on his pants. He had dressed up even, in dress shirt and trousers, and taken extra care with his hair.

He opened the door.

Kazio held a bouquet of flowers—roses, lilies and hydrangeas in a rainbow of colors. They popped against his gray sweater.

Morgan's heart leapt. "Hi." He stepped aside. "Come on in."

Kazio held the flowers out. "These are for you."

"For me? Why?"

Kazio shrugged. "They were beautiful and...I just wanted to get you some flowers."

"Thank you. I love them." Morgan gave him a quick hug then led him to the kitchen.

Kazio's jaw dropped when he saw the table draped with an elegant white tablecloth—borrowed from Mrs.

Bagshaw-Smythe, who was not so bad after all. Morgan had polished the glassware and cutlery and set the table as meticulously as he could, including candles and linen napkins. The kitchen behind it was, admittedly, a disaster. Pretty much every pot, pan or mixing bowl Morgan owned was dirty. He had been cooking all day.

"Oh my gosh. Morgan, this looks beautiful." Then Kazio saw the mess and widened his eyes. "Wh—holy shit. What did you make?"

"Er..." Morgan busied himself putting the flowers in a vase. "Mushroom-stuffed flank steak roll and Brussels sprouts and broccoli with cranberry *agrodolce*."

"I'm sorry...what? How?"

Morgan's cheeks flushed. "I signed up for a cooking class with Aleysha. So I could make you a better dinner."

"You... You took a cooking class for me?"

Morgan bit his lip and nodded. "Yeah. I made this with her in class last week. So it's kind of cheating making it again, but..."

"It's not cheating. It's—it's amazing. I'm very touched."

Morgan's cheeks got hotter. "Have a seat." He set the flower vase on the side of the table and went to get the wine out of the fridge.

"So Thursday night..." Kazio leaned back and folded his arms. "When you said you were going to just stay home and do laundry and go to bed early...?"

"Yeah, that was when I took the class." Morgan set the wine down next to Kazio's glass.

Kazio's eyes looked a little watery. "I can't believe you went through all this trouble for me."

"It wasn't any trouble." *I'd do anything for you.* "You're my best friend, and...you always do so much for me." They stared at each other in a growing silence. "Er, do you want to pour the wine? I just have to add the sauce to the veggies."

Morgan put the finishing touches on the meal and brought two plates to the table. "I hope I didn't mess these up." He sat and raised his wine glass. "*Na zdrowie.*"

Kazio smiled and tapped their glasses together. "*Na zdrowie.*"

Morgan took a nervous sip.

Kazio dug right into the flank steak. "Oh, God." He closed his eyes, chewing. "Morgan. This is…" He opened them. "This is…fucking phenomenal."

Morgan tried not to wiggle in his seat. "Really?"

"Really." Kazio took another bite. "Jesus Christ. I don't even have words… My mouth has goosebumps."

Morgan would happily sit there and watch Kazio eat all day, but he picked up his fork and tasted the steak. Yeah, it was fucking phenomenal.

Kazio grinned at him. "You know you're smiling right now?"

"Am I?" Morgan pressed a palm to his mouth.

"No, don't hide it. It's so cute. You should be happy that you made this."

"I'm happy that you like it."

"I *love* it."

By the time they had finished eating, they were into their second bottle of wine. "So, ready for your gig?" Kazio leaned back in his chair and swirled his red around the glass.

The anxiety that had been building in Morgan's chest as their show approached came spilling out, loosened by the wine and full stomach. "I think so. I just worry that I'm going to fuck everything up with Felix again."

"What makes you say that?"

"Because I fuck everything up eventually."

Kazio shook his head firmly, lips pressed together. "No, you don't."

Morgan huffed a laugh. "Don't I?"

"Tell me one thing you've fucked up in the last three months."

"How about every single job application I submitted?"

Kazio scoffed. "Those don't count as fuck-ups. You're too hard on yourself."

"I'm not hard on myself. I'm…" Morgan swallowed, mouth dry. "I'm a bad person."

Kazio stilled, searching for Morgan's eyes. "Why would you say that? You're not a bad person."

Morgan stared into his wine glass. "I never told you the full story about why I got fired."

So he told Kazio. Selfishness had led to heartbreak. Heartbreak had turned into sulking, then blackmail. Lying that had nearly gotten Luka fired. And guilt, the weight of the terrible thing he had done resting heavy on his shoulders. "So there you have it." Morgan shrugged and finished off his wine. "Bad person."

Kazio set his glass down. "Listen to me. You are not a bad person. If you did all that and didn't care, *that* would make you a bad person. But you feel guilt about it, and you tried to make things right. That's not something bad people do."

"How would you know? You're perfect."

Kazio snorted and sat back. "Perfect? Hardly."

"Tell me one non-perfect thing you've done." Morgan picked up his wine. "I'll wait."

Kazio narrowed his eyes. "I yell at my staff for putting the knives away wrong."

Morgan chuckled. "That's just an endearing personality quirk."

"Is it? Not sure Rudy would agree."

"Your employees respect you. They know you have high standards but you're fair and working hard right there with them."

Kazio grew serious. "When I left Poland, I cut off all ties with pretty much everyone, except for my parents, and I hardly ever talk to them."

Morgan wanted to reach for Kazio's hand. "That's okay, though. You have to do what's best for you. Sometimes you have to leave people behind."

A smile crept back onto Kazio's face, soft and wistful. "Do you see how you keep finding the best in me? I wish you would do that for yourself. Give yourself the grace to grow."

This time Morgan did reach out and touch Kazio's hand.

Kazio held Morgan's hand for a second. "Can you try to do that for me?"

Morgan smiled back, his heart as full as his stomach. "I'll try."

* * * *

The day of their gig at The Sphinx arrived. He and Kazio were busy in the garage loading their gear into Kazio's car. Morgan was equal parts hopeful and terrified, but with an undercurrent of tension that never went away when he was around Kazio.

Everyone on their way?

Morgan texted the group chat once they were done, leaning on the car door to rest for a moment. He knew he had probably crossed a line into nagging, but he didn't care. He was not risking a thing.

Felix was the first to reply.

I've got some bad news…

"What?" Morgan gasped. His stomach shrank into a ball, head threatening to explode. He clutched his phone, staring at the three dots waiting for Felix's next message.

"What is it?" Kazio frowned.

But before Morgan could reply, Felix sent another message.

Just kidding! I'm on my way.

Morgan clutched his heart and showed Kazio his phone.

"Ugh." Kazio rolled his eyes.

"That asshole," Morgan muttered.

Too soon, Morgan typed.

Lol sorry! I'll see you there.

Morgan grumbled to himself as they got into the car. Kazio had insisted on coming to the gig, and Morgan was so grateful. Not only were the logistics of getting all their gear to the bar much simpler, but Kazio was such a calming, steady presence. It was just what Morgan needed.

"You're going to be great," Kazio said out of nowhere once they were on the highway.

"Hmm?"

Kazio nodded at Morgan's bouncing knee. "Your leg is about to vibrate through the floor."

"Oh, sorry." Morgan pressed on his knee.

"It's fine, I'm just saying...it's going to be okay."

"Honestly, until we're all up on the stage on time with all our gear..."

"I know. We're almost there."

When they pulled up to the loading zone behind the bar, Felix, Brett and Andre were all there waiting. It was a glorious sight.

Once they were unloaded, Morgan went to rap on Zayden Bourne's office door.

"Yeah?" a voice from within barked.

Morgan opened the door and stuck his head in. "Hi, Mr. Bourne. Just wanted to let you know that we're all here and ready to go."

Zayden Bourne stared at him through a cloud of cigarette smoke.

"I'm...Morgan Di Meo? We're opening for you tonight?"

Zayden removed the cigarette from his lips. "Do I look stupid?"

"No, sir."

"Then get out of my fucking office and go warm up."

"Yes, sir."

So warm up they did. Then retreated into the tiny dressing room when the bar doors opened.

"It's going to be great," Kazio said again before he left to go join the crowd out front.

Morgan nodded and blew out a breath. "Thanks."

"Just be yourself and have fun. People are going to love you." He squeezed Morgan's arms.

Kazio's eyes were so intense, like they were trying to convey more than those words. It almost hurt to hold eye contact, but Morgan couldn't look away. "Promise me you'll cheer, even if no one else is?" he joked.

"Just try and stop me." Kazio turned and left, leaving Morgan in the dark hallway.

The show was mostly a blur. They played five songs, leading off with *Cherry Tree*, all fun and upbeat. Morgan was hardly aware of the audience at all, focused solely on the music and his bandmates, but the applause when they were done was solid, if not raucous.

They took a bow and hurried off stage, high fiving and back-slapping, faces shining with sweat and huge smiles.

Morgan's heart threatened to burst when Kazio came around the corner, with a smile just as big as his.

He faced Kazio, arms raised for a hug, but Felix stepped in and wrapped his arms around Morgan instead. "We did it, Morgan. All thanks to you."

"Oh, yeah, we did." Morgan hugged him back, eyes still on Kazio.

Then Felix kissed him.

Morgan broke it off and stepped back. "Um... Wow, I..."

Felix's face flushed, but then he laughed, airy and unaffected. "Oh my God, sorry, just caught up in the moment." He went on to hug Brett and Andre and kiss them on the cheek.

"Okay..." Morgan turned to Kazio, desperate for a life raft in the sea of awkwardness.

Kazio ripped his gaze away from Felix, a flicker of rage replaced with joy as he held his arms out to Morgan, beaming. "That was awesome."

Morgan poured himself into the hug, muscles slack with relief. There was no place he felt safer and more comfortable than in Kazio's arms. He could have stayed there forever, but Andre would have a comment if the hug went on much longer. Morgan pulled away to meet Kazio's soft, shining eyes.

"How did it feel up there?" Kazio asked.

"I barely remember a thing," Morgan confessed. "But I think good?"

"You sounded incredible. And the crowd loved it."

"Yeah?"

"Yeah."

"Thanks." He squeezed Kazio's forearms as his hands slipped from the hug. "Does anyone want to stay for a drink?"

"Yeah, man." Andre wiped the sweat off his brow. "Or two."

"Can't, I should get home. I have to open the store tomorrow." Felix drummed on his thighs with his hands. "But you all have fun. I'll see you at rehearsal Friday?"

They packed up their gear, said goodbye to Felix, then headed out front to the bar. Kazio had a seltzer waiting for Morgan. He handed it over and tapped it with his own can. Morgan leaned against the bar, much more aware of where his shoulder pressed against Kazio's than he was of the next band.

"You're better than these guys," Kazio said, leaning to rumble into Morgan's ear over the noise of the bar.

He was so close their cheeks brushed. Morgan turned his head, inhaling Kazio's scent, whole body tingling. He swallowed the giddiness bubbling up his throat. "I think maybe you're biased…being my best friend and all."

Kazio chuckled and pulled away to take a drink. "Maybe. Or maybe you're just fucking awesome."

Morgan's whole heart swelled, threatening to suffocate him. He took a ragged breath, basking in the warmth of Kazio's words. "Maybe."

* * * *

Late Wednesday morning, Morgan was tearing yesterday's cat from his new page-a-day calendar—a very handsome Siberian studying a goldfish in a bowl—when Louis stuck his head into Morgan's office. "Did you get those schematics from that artist?"

Morgan took a second to mentally flip through his inbox. "For the wood carving installation? Yup."

"Great. And how about the contract from that firm?"

"The staff party for the design agency? All signed."

"Great. Can you come give me a hand with something downstairs?"

"You bet."

Morgan followed Louis down the rickety stairs into the basement. He had only been down there once before to choose his office art from storage. But there were several other mysterious doors lining the dim hallway.

Louis flipped the light on at the bottom of the stairs. "We've got school tours starting next week so I need to haul my program bins upstairs and get them set up in the outreach room."

Morgan followed Louis into one of the mysterious rooms. It was mostly empty, with stale air and a few rows of big plastic tubs. Morgan blinked, studying the soundproofed walls. "You have a *studio*?"

"Oh, yeah." Louis looked around. "The last owner was really into music, too. I've been thinking about renting this room out as a rehearsal space, but..." He shrugged. "One more thing on my plate."

"Um, my band needs a rehearsal space…"

"Do they, now? Well…" Louis held his arms wide. "Here you go."

Morgan laughed. It was too perfect. "Are you serious?"

"Dead serious. You can use it outside of gallery or event hours."

Morgan's jaw flapped as he searched for words. "This is amazing. Thank you so, so much." He shook his head. "I can't believe it."

"I got you, Morgan." Louis offered him a fist bump. "You're going places. I'm just glad to be here along the way."

They hauled the tubs out of the basement and through the gallery into the outreach room at the back, Morgan's body still humming with excitement over the studio. They started packing up their summer programs and pulled out the displays and supply bins for their school tours.

Louis looked around. "Shoot, I left my curriculum binder on my desk. Would you mind running to grab it for me? My hip is acting up after all those stairs."

"No problem." Morgan wound through the gallery on his way back to Louis' office. When he turned a corner, he saw him.

Luka.

As gorgeous as ever, smiling and laughing, in a bright pink shirt, hair flopping and perfect. Thomas, Finn and Rory were with him, the four of them gathered at Finn's painting.

Morgan screeched to a halt, his brain sending conflicting messages to his feet. *Run. Go say hi. No, run.* But before he could decide, Luka looked over and saw him. Surprise flashed across his face, then something else. Maybe pity. "Morgan. Hi."

The other three turned to look at him too.

Okay. Decision made. Morgan crossed the remaining distance to join their group. "Hi," he said, nodding and making eye contact with all of them, then his gaze went back to Luka.

"Fancy seeing you here again," Rory said.

"I, uh…I actually work here now." Morgan pointed at his badge.

"You do?" Rory looked pleased.

"Yup. I just started. And Finn, congratulations." Morgan gestured to *Joy.* "Your work is breathtaking."

Rory beamed and took hold of Finn's arm. "Isn't it?"

"Thanks," Finn said gruffly. "That's actually a portrait of Luka."

"Oh?" Morgan turned to study the painting again. *Of course* it was Luka. He really should have seen that earlier. Luka was magic, and everyone around him felt it. "Yes, I see that now. Beautiful."

"So." Luka cleared his throat. "How are you, Morgan?"

How am I? "I'm…good. I'm really good." The fact that he could answer honestly calmed his jittering heart. "I got a cat."

"Oh?" Luka laughed, but it was kind. "Never took you for a cat guy."

Morgan lifted the corner of his mouth. "It was a surprise to me, too."

"Well, that's great."

An awkward pause. "How are you?" Morgan asked him.

Luka shared a look with Thomas, a silly lovesick look that lit up his whole face. "I'm great." Thomas smiled back at him, his rigid lines softening, eyes warm on Luka's.

Oh. *Oh.* The understanding hit him like a lead balloon in his stomach. The thing that Morgan had tried so hard to convince Luka wasn't going to happen... "So you two are..."

Thomas put his arm around Luka as he placed his hand on Thomas' chest. They both nodded.

Morgan's heart tightened with the memory of Luka touching him like that, before he gave into his worst instincts and ruined it all. "Guess I was wrong."

Luka's smile softened. "Guess so."

"Congratulations. Listen, I'd better get back to work..." Morgan pointed his thumb in the general direction of away from there.

"Great to see you again, Morgan," Rory said.

"Yeah, you too." Morgan swung his eyes around the group, then stopped on Luka. "Really great. Take care."

Morgan walked away, Luka swirling in his brain — the kisses, the laughter...the self-doubt, the heartbreak. But seeing him and Thomas together, and the way they looked at each other... One thing was certain — everything had worked out for the best. He and Luka were not the right fit, and Luka and Thomas were. The tightness in his chest loosened with his next deep breath. He was really happy for them.

And he really wanted that for himself.

* * * *

"Chaotic Crown?"

"Merry Crown?"

"Crown Adventure?"

"Crown of Symphonies?"

"Anyway..." Morgan closed his guitar case with an emphatic thump. "I told Victoria we'd call her once we were done to go over the details for tomorrow, if you're all quite finished."

It was their last rehearsal, and they were ready. Things had admittedly been a little awkward with Felix—he appeared to be doing his best to avoid eye contact with Morgan—but otherwise practice went smoothly. Felix didn't seem to be dwelling *too* much on the awkward kiss.

Once they were all settled, Morgan dialed Victoria's number and set his phone on a stool in the middle.

"Morgan!" Victoria's voice was high and fuzzy on speakerphone. "Thank you for calling. We are so excited for tomorrow night!"

"We are too," Morgan said while the others murmured their agreement.

"Excellent, excellent. I'll be there to meet you at five for set-up—we'll reserve parking for you right behind the stage. The barbecue starts at six and you're welcome to grab yourselves a plate. Jonathan will do a little thank you speech, and we'd like for you to go on at eight. How does that sound? Any questions?"

"That sounds great! I think we're good."

"Lovely. I'll see you tomorrow!"

Right as he hung up with Victoria, a text popped up from Kazio.

I made spaghetti. Do you want to stay for dinner?

Andre laughed. "Did Kazio just text you?"

Morgan looked up. "What? No... How did you know?"

"There's only one reason people smile at their phones like that, man."

Morgan tried to scowl, but he couldn't fight off the smile entirely. "He might have."

Andre snickered. "Say hi for us."

Once the others had cleared out, Morgan knocked on the door and popped his head into Kazio's house. "Hello?"

"Hey! Come on in," Kazio called.

Morgan found him in the kitchen, stirring a simmering pot of marinara sauce. "Smells good."

"Taste it for me?" Kazio scooped a tiny bit on a spoon and held it up.

Morgan ducked his head to slurp the sauce of the spoon. "Yum."

"Do you think it needs more salt? Garlic?"

"It's perfect."

Kazio nodded at the counter. "I poured you some wine."

Morgan picked up a waiting glass of red and took a sip.

"So..." Kazio lifted the lid from the boiling pasta to give it a stir. "Big show tomorrow. You guys ready?"

"I think so. It's a long set, so we'll see how we hold up..." Morgan trailed off. The way Kazio leaned against his counter, wisp of hair across his eyes, was highly distracting. Kazio tilted his head up, and his indigo eyes met Morgan's through his lashes.

Morgan swallowed hard. "You're really beautiful, you know."

Kazio blushed, a rare sight. He had no reply beyond a shy smile.

Morgan resisted the urge to press his hands to his own warm cheeks. "Sorry."

Kazio shifted, brushing his hair back off his face. "Why are you sorry?"

Morgan's cheeks got warmer. "I don't know." His body tilted toward Kazio.

"Don't be sorry." Kazio's voice was molten and sweet, like caramel drizzled over a chocolate cake.

They stared at each other. Morgan's heart thudded.

Kazio cleared his throat. "Did you see the pictures of the kittens Camella posted on Insta today?" He pulled his phone out.

"What? No! How are they doing?" Morgan scooted over to see Kazio's phone. He was momentarily distracted by Kazio's scent, but then saw the first of Camella's photos. "Awwww!" Morgan squeaked. "Would you look at those precious little fuzzballs! They've grown so much!" They all looked like they had doubled in size, from helpless infants to mischievous toddlers, ready to explore the world. The white kittens now had the gray feet and ears of Siamese cats.

Kazio swiped to the next picture. "Look at this one."

It was the tiny brown tabby, Morgan's favorite, looking up at the camera with impossibly big eyes. He was still smaller than his siblings but, Morgan decided, easily the cutest one.

Morgan pressed a hand to his chest. "Stop, I can't. I miss that little guy."

Kazio grinned. "Maybe you should adopt him, too."

"Two cats? I couldn't... I'm home so much less now."

"That's the beauty—he'd have Catzio to look after him."

"Catzio seems much too busy lounging around all day to look after a kitten." Morgan studied the picture some more. "Did Camella say when they would be ready for adoption?"

"I think it was pretty soon."

Morgan sighed, running his index finger along the edge of the phone. "I really shouldn't."

"'Shouldn't' but...do you *want* to?"

Their shoulders brushed together. Morgan looked up, then breathed him in. His heart fluttered. "Yes. But I can't."

Kazio took a sip of wine. "Let's just hope he's still available when you change your mind."

Chapter Twenty-Four

The Big Show

The night of the concert arrived, a perfect late summer evening, warm but not hot, the sun's heat tempered by the season's tilt. A fresh breeze from the harbor wafted over them, pleasant and salty, as they climbed from the car.

Morgan wished Kazio could be there, but the Exchange had a bachelor party filling the place up that night and he couldn't get away.

"It's fine. You need to work. I'll be fine," he had told Kazio.

"I know you will be, but I'd still like to be there."

Morgan had resisted the urge to kiss him on the nose. "I know."

Kazio had insisted they take his car. Andre had met Morgan at Kazio's house to help load their gear. Brett, Victoria and a few other Barrett employees were waiting for them on the sidewalk behind the stage when they pulled in. Felix was running late.

"There's a little dressing room back here for you to use..." Victoria said, leading them toward the stage.

"There's a bathroom and a fridge with a few refreshments and such. Do let me know if you need anything else."

The group carried their instruments and other gear onto the stage. Morgan paused to take in their surroundings. He had been to outdoor concerts at Harborfront Park before, but not from this angle. The stage was surrounded by a flat grassy area and ringed by a hill for seating, already wired for lighting and sound.

"No Felix yet?" Morgan said to Brett once they had everything on stage.

Brett shook his head.

Morgan checked his phone for messages. Nothing there. Surely Felix would be along any minute. But once they had the drum kit set up and Felix still wasn't there, Morgan started to worry.

"Where is he?" Morgan asked his bandmates.

"He must be on his way," Andre said.

Morgan pulled out his phone and realized with a sinking feeling that Felix hadn't said a word in the group chat all day.

Hey Felix, you almost here? Morgan sent. *We've already set up.*

Fortunately, Felix's reply came right away. *So sorry, I got stuck at work. But I'll be out of here soon, I promise.*

You're still at work???

Leaving in a minute, I swear.

Morgan's stomach flipped. "Okay, sound check without Felix, I guess."

Once everything was set up and plugged in and sounding good, Victoria appeared again. "How are we doing? Are you all happy?"

Morgan tried to quell the panic fluttering inside. "Yup, all good."

An older man waited with her, dressed like he had just rolled in from the Hamptons in khakis, a white dress shirt and a blue linen blazer. He was on the shorter side, not much taller than Morgan, with graying dark hair.

Victoria introduced them. "This is Jonathan Barrett, CEO of Barrett Industries."

"It's nice to meet you, sir," Morgan said. "Thank you so much for having us play for you."

"It's our pleasure. Rory said you'd be great. I hope you'll come grab some dinner before the show? The caterers are almost set up."

"Yes, thank you, that would be great."

They joined the thickening crowd milling around the folding tables. The food looked amazing — ribs, corn on the cob, coleslaw, potato salad — but Morgan's stomach was too wound up to eat much. The three of them found a spot on the grass to sit with their plates. He nibbled on a piece of corn and checked his phone. Nothing new from Felix.

Please tell me you've left? he sent when he couldn't wait any longer and his head was going to explode from stress.

Yes! Leaving now!

Morgan tried to take a deep breath but it stalled in his throat. The park had filled around them, several hundred people at least, eating and drinking and having a good time. Pop music played from speakers, adding to the festive atmosphere.

They headed backstage when it was time to get ready.

Morgan brushed his teeth, fixed his hair and changed into jeans and a tank top. Then there was nothing left to do but wait for Felix. He paced the room, either staring at his phone or at the door.

Brett bobbed his head along to the music, strumming the notes on his unplugged bass. Andre examined his hair in a mirror as he did a few vocal warmups.

Every muscle in Morgan's body was wound to its breaking point.

Finally another message from Felix.

Almost there.

"This is fine. It's fine. He'll be here in time," Morgan said, mostly to himself.

The booming echoes of Jonathan's speech reached them, muffled by the cement walls.

When it sounded like Jonathan was wrapping things up, Morgan couldn't wait any longer. He called Felix's number, half expecting Felix to come running into the room before he could answer. But he did answer. "Hi."

"Hey, please tell me you are seconds away. We're supposed to go on in five."

The pause was long...much too long. "I'm not coming," Felix said.

"You *what*?" Morgan plugged his other ear against the dull roar from the party. "What are you... What?"

Felix's voice was flat. "I'm not coming. I'm out."

Morgan's legs turned to rubber. He collapsed into the nearest chair. "What the fuck are you talking about, Felix?"

Felix laughed, a cold, joyless sound. "How does it feel?"

The room spun around him, a dizzying whirl of gray and white lines. "How does what feel?"

"You still don't get it, do you? You're still the same selfish prick you always were, Morgan."

Each word was a knife to Morgan's heart. He could hardly breathe. "Felix, I'm sorry, I... Please. Please come. Whatever I did, I'm sorry."

"'Whatever I did'... You're an asshole, Morgan. And you always will be. Good luck with your concert." He hung up.

The room continued its whirl around him. Bile rose in his throat. "He's not coming." Morgan's voice was hollow.

Andre's and Brett's jaws fell in unison.

"What? Why not?" Andre asked.

"He... I... Because of me, I guess. He says I'm...the same selfish prick I've always been. He... He quit."

Andre scrubbed his face. "Are you kidding me? That's bullshit."

Brett ran a hand through his hair. "Fuck."

The three of them stared at each other. The crowd outside whooped.

"What do we do now?" Andre asked.

Brett shrugged. "I guess we have to bail again."

Morgan closed his eyes and gripped the chair, the only thing keeping him from falling over.

Brett's voice came from a mile away. "I'll go find Victoria."

Morgan imagined her face when they canceled. Saw Jonathan furious, just like Zayden Bourne had been. Hundreds of people staring at an empty stage, their party ruined. Rory disappointed that they had vouched for Morgan. All of Breakpoint knowing he had fucked up again. Having to tell Kazio that he had bailed. That he had destroyed everything he had been building.

"No," Morgan rasped.

"No?"

"No. We're going on." Morgan stood up, teeth clenched, wrestling the spinning room back into control.

"Morgan, we don't have a drummer," Brett protested. "We can't be a rock band without a drummer."

Morgan headed toward the stage.

Victoria was waiting outside the door, eyes on her phone. "There you are! It's almost eight o'clock! Are you ready?"

Morgan nodded.

Victoria ushered him toward the stage.

"Morgan," Andre hissed, following. "What are you doing?"

"I'm gonna go fucking sing and play my guitar."

He walked out onto the empty stage under the bright lights to the polite applause of several hundred employees of Barrett Industries. He picked up his acoustic guitar from the stand and slung it over his torso.

"Hi," Morgan said into the mic as he plugged his guitar in. His voice boomed through the park. "I'm Morgan and we are Symphony. And, uh... Well, this isn't going to go exactly as planned, but..." He shrugged and played the first chord for *Empty Stage*.

"The empty stage is waiting
It's waiting for a heart."

It was only his voice and his guitar and a sea of faces staring at him.

"Waiting for the moment when
That magic feeling starts.
When everybody's watching
And there's a song to play
A story needing to unfold
Won't wait another day."

He licked his lips. This might have been a really bad idea. He had half a mind to turn and run off the stage. Maybe it was meant to be empty. But in that pause, Brett's bass thrummed.

The thrum shivered through his blood. Morgan turned to smile at Brett, who smiled back and nodded at him. Morgan kept going.

"The spotlight, it will find you
It will warm you through
The empty stage is waiting
Oh, it's waiting there for you."

Andre's voice and guitar joined him for the bridge.

"We need your heart, we need your light
We need your flame, tonight's the night."

The three of them wheeled through the rest of the song, voices and confidence growing as they played.

When the song finished, Morgan turned to the other two as the crowd applauded. "Are we doing this?"

Andre chuckled and shook his head. "Looks like it, you crazy bastard."

Morgan faced the crowd with a growing smile, the applause washing over him. "Thank you. That one was called *Empty Stage*." He looked at Brett and Andre. "But it's a little less empty now, isn't it? This next song is called *Always We*." He paused. "I wrote it for a very special person." He began to play.

"When did my grip become a jail?
I'm holding on so tight
I can't escape, can't look ahead
Alone in the hollow night.

"Something is missing
A piece that isn't there
There's a hole in my soul,
There's not enough air."

His gaze drifted over the crowd, smiling, happy families, people laughing with their loved ones, even a few people at the front swaying along to his song. Until his gaze landed on one face in particular.

Kazio's face.

Morgan's breath left him in a whoosh.

Kazio was there.

Kazio nodded when their eyes locked, a shy smile on his face.

Morgan took a shaky breath and continued, only half a beat late on the first word.

"But then, oh then, then there was you
You held my hand and showed me the way
You held me so close
And I just have to say
That you...you take care of me."

He smiled, unable to look away from Kazio. Kazio's smile grew. *I love him so much,* was the thought that came to Morgan. He blinked away a few tears that threatened to fall.

"It's 'Good morning,' and 'goodnight,'
It's 'This reminded me of you'
Always 'we', never 'me'
And 'I'll pick you up at two'
And then...then there was you."

He sang every word right to Kazio. He didn't even care. That man had his whole heart, and it was his song, and he was fucking singing it to him. The final chord faded, but Morgan sang the last line again, just his voice in the night.

"And then...then there was you."

Eyes shining, Kazio applauded along with the rest of the cheering crowd. Morgan felt like he'd run a marathon, heart pounding, blood humming with adrenaline and unable to feel his legs.

"Thank you," Morgan said. "Thank you so much!" The applause faded away as he switched to his electric guitar. "I'm glad you liked that song but, uh...I think it's time to speed things up." Counting off the intro, he crashed into the first verse of *Cherry Tree.*

He was gearing up for the second verse when the drum kit kicked in.

Morgan whirled. Ray. *Ray* was at the fucking kit, grinning like the dumb schmuck he was, pounding away like he'd never left. "Ray!" Morgan howled over the music, letting loose a wild laugh. "Fuck yeah!"

Ray grinned and smashed his crash cymbal with extra enthusiasm. "Let's do this!"

They flew through the second verse like a well-oiled machine, the crowd dancing and cheering. Morgan tore into his guitar solo, shredding it like he never had before.

The audience ate it up, hooting and hollering and cheering wildly when it was over.

Morgan was delirious with happiness. "You guys having fun?" he asked the crowd. They roared back at him. "I thought so! This is going to be a great night. Let's do this."

And they did.

It was the best night of Morgan's life.

The crowd went wild when they were done. Morgan wiped the sweat off his brow and blew a kiss to Kazio, who was standing riveted, hands clasped in front of him, face aglow.

"Thank you, Barrett Industries!" Morgan cried. "We are...Symphony!"

Chapter Twenty-Five

Always We

They held hands and bowed, crowd still roaring, then ran offstage back to their room, panting and laughing.

"Ray!" Morgan cried, throwing his arms around his stupid face. "What are you doing here?"

Brett beamed. "When Felix wasn't here by dinner, I texted him, just in case. He came straight over."

"But you... He knows our songs?"

"Of course." Ray shrugged. "Brett and I practice together all the time. He taught me."

"I thought you sold your drums to buy your... Was it your brewing equipment?"

"Yeah, well...that didn't work out. I was able to get them back. Traded the smelter for them straight up."

"Ray, you beautiful bastard!" Morgan hugged him again, then Brett and Andre. "You guys were amazing. That was incredible, I feel like I could..." He trailed off.

Kazio stood in the doorway.

A thousand words danced across Morgan's tongue, but only one came out. "Hi."

Kazio took a tentative step in. "Hi."

The rest of the room had disappeared from Morgan's awareness. "You're here."

Kazio tucked a piece of hair behind his ear. "I couldn't miss your big show."

"But how...?"

"Rory got me an okay to crash the staff party."

"Rory?"

"You're forgetting that I see them all the time. How do you think they knew you had a band?"

"Oh... I..." Morgan's heart pounded. "I'm so glad you're here."

Kazio looked at the other three, puzzled. "But where's Felix?"

"Felix quit. And he didn't tell us until right before we were supposed to go on. He..." Morgan shook his head. "He said I'm selfish."

Kazio's face darkened. "Then fuck him. You are not selfish. He's the one that abandoned you *again*."

"Hundred percent, Morgan," Andre chimed in. "The way you went out there anyway... You were amazing. And we killed it. We don't need him." He slung his arm around Ray and mussed his hair.

Ray squirmed with delight, cheeks still pink.

"Are you with us, Ray? We'd love to have you," Morgan asked.

"Hmm, I don't know..." Ray tapped his chin. "I've been getting really into glass blowing..."

They stared at him.

"Blowing?" Andre said, after a beat.

"I'm kidding!" Ray guffawed. "I'm kidding. I'm with you."

Victoria and Jonathan burst into the room, all smiles.

"You were amazing, gentlemen!" Victoria trilled. "Absolutely incredible. What a show. Everyone *adored* you! I especially loved how you started with just Morgan and built from there."

"Er...thanks." Morgan grinned, sharing a look with the others.

"Really fantastic," Jonathan agreed, going around to shake everyone's hand, even Kazio's. "We hope you'll stay for a drink or two? You got the party started and it's still going strong. We've got music and dancing, and the park is rented until midnight."

"We would love to," Andre said loudly before anyone else could answer. "Let's go, boys." He rounded up Ray and Brett and herded them through the door with Jonanthan and Victoria.

"We'll be right there," Morgan said, doing his best to not throw up the words that were collecting in his throat.

Andre waggled his eyebrows at him on the way out, shutting the door behind him.

Morgan faced Kazio, pulse thudding in his ears. He couldn't go on without telling Kazio how he felt. Maybe it was stupid, maybe it would ruin their friendship...but maybe it would be worth the risk.

"Morgan..." Kazio reached to hug him. Morgan dissolved into his arms. "You were...absolutely amazing. I can't believe it. I'm so proud of you." He faded into silence, rubbing Morgan's back.

Morgan's heart hammered like never before, so loud that Kazio could surely hear it. It was time. "Kazio, I..." Morgan's hands shook as they pulled apart. His courage fled looking at Kazio's face. "Oh God. I shouldn't even say this."

Kazio's eyes burned into his. "Say what?"

"I… You know that song, *Always We*?"

Kazio smiled softly. "Yeah?"

"That song is… That song is about you." Morgan stared at the floor, face burning. Silence. He risked a glance up.

Kazio's face was carefully neutral, although his eyes betrayed his racing thoughts. "About me?"

Morgan put his hands on his flaming hot cheeks. "Are you going to make me explain it?"

"Yes. Yes, I am." Kazio's body was strung like a bow, nearly quivering with tension.

"So the song is about, um, sort of being lost, and then realizing that the person you love has been right there all along, taking care of you."

Kazio inched closer, eyes aflame. The air between them was thick enough to taste.

"The person you…love?" Kazio repeated.

"Yeah." Tears gathered in Morgan's eyes, emotion that his body couldn't contain anymore. "Shit. I'm sorry. This is probably the last thing you want to hear, and I know it could ruin our friendship, but—"

Kazio took his hand. "Morgan." He grabbed his other hand. "*Morgan*."

"I'm sorry," Morgan babbled. "Oh God, I shouldn't have said anything—"

"Stop," Kazio said. He took Morgan's chin in his fingers, tilted his head up, there was a breath where their eyes met, questioning, then…Kazio kissed him.

A nuclear bomb detonated in Morgan's head, a white flash, heat, fuzz…a shockwave that prevented him from doing much in response.

Kazio pulled away, hesitant.

"What's happening?" Morgan whispered.

"Well, I'm trying to kiss you, but...now you're talking."

"So...you're not mad that I... I haven't ruined anything?"

"Morgan." Kazio rubbed his forehead. "I told myself there's no way you could be this dense, but clearly I was wrong."

Morgan stared at him.

"Jesus Christ, Morgan. I love you. I am *in* love with you. I love you so much that sometimes I can't even breathe."

"You do?" Morgan's legs wobbled. "I need to sit down."

"No, you don't. I've got you." Kazio took him into his arms and kissed him again.

This time, Morgan responded. He wrapped his arms around Kazio, sliding one hand into his hair, and kissed him back for all he was worth. It was all soft lips, slippery tongues, whimpers and gasps and a wild, desperate need for more.

Morgan had to pull back for air, panting, their foreheads and bodies pressed together. "Oh my God," Morgan gasped. "Oh my *God*."

"What?" Kazio trailed his fingers along Morgan's cheek, smiling.

"I can't believe this is happening."

"Why not?"

"I just... I never thought you would feel this way about me."

Kazio tucked his nose under Morgan's ear and murmured into his neck. "Why would you think that?"

"Because, I—I'm selfish. I'm not a good person."

Kazio pulled back and met his eyes. "You are a good person, Morgan. You are."

"Felix didn't think so."

Kazio huffed. "Felix is a fucking asshole. *He's* the selfish one."

Morgan shook his head, pressing his lips together, tears gathering in his eyes.

Kazio took his hands. "You volunteer to help people. You look after animals."

"I only did those things because of you."

"But you chose to come. You…you should have seen your face looking at those kittens, Morgan. You care. You cry when people hug you. You learned how to say my full name properly. No one else has done that. You *care*. This is who you are."

Morgan sniffled. "I don't cry when people hug me."

Kazio tilted his head, mouth softening. "Oh no?" He pulled Morgan in for a hug.

"Okay, fine," Morgan said through tears, half laughing. "Maybe I'm not a bad person. But I am kind of a mess."

Kazio smiled and kissed him again. "Maybe sometimes," he admitted. "But a sweet, kind, adorable mess. A mess I fell in love with."

Their lips met again, slower, more thoughtful, a perfect kiss for a warm late summer night, rich and sweet.

"As much as I could stay here forever…should we head out there?" Kazio murmured at their next break. "Go greet your adoring fans?"

"I don't think I have any fans just yet."

"Oh, I highly doubt that. Clearly you have no idea how fucking drop-dead sexy you were up there tonight." Kazio took his hand.

Morgan groaned.

"What?"

"Nothing, it's just...Andre is going to be insufferable now."

* * * *

It was late when they left, the party going strong until midnight, with lots of new friends from Barrett Industries made along the way. Victoria waved goodbye, promising to help get them as many gigs as she could, and adding a healthy bonus on top of their agreed-upon fee. Kazio and Morgan dropped off Brett, Ray and Andre on the way back to Kazio's house, and parked on his driveway well into the middle of the night.

Kazio turned off the engine. They stared at each other. "I guess we'd better unload all this gear," Kazio said.

"Yup."

"Probably not a good idea to leave it sitting in the car all night."

"Nope."

"...Do you want to leave it in the car all night?"

"Yup."

They fell through the door into the house, kissing, hands fumbling, clothes flying.

They giggled when Morgan tripped on his pants on the way up the stairs, but the laughter faded when Kazio tipped Morgan back onto his bed. He stood, unzipped his jeans and pushed them off.

Morgan gulped, eyes greedily taking in every inch of the man he loved so much, heart near bursting. "Oh God," he moaned, gaze resting on what Kazio's underwear was still hiding...sort of.

Kazio grinned and climbed over top of Morgan, finding his mouth for another long, deep kiss.

Morgan's insides dissolved. He lost all sense of the world, except for the soft, soft lips on his.

Then Kazio pulled away. "Morgan," he whispered.

Morgan whimpered. "Shut up and keep kissing me." He slid his fingers into Kazio's hair and pulled him closer.

Kazio smiled into the kiss, then opened his mouth and pressed his tongue into Morgan's mouth. Morgan wrapped his other arm around Kazio and tried to tug him even closer. Kazio ground his hips up against Morgan's as he slid his lips down Morgan's neck.

"Oh, fuck," Morgan panted, every inch of his skin on fire.

"Morgan," Kazio said again.

"Yeah?"

Kazio stopped, panting, and cradled Morgan's face with one hand. "I've wanted this for so long."

Morgan grinned. "I told you to shut up."

Kazio let out a low rumble, half amused, half irritated. "Oh, are you in charge here?" He took hold of Morgan's waist with one hand and squeezed while he rocked his hips.

Something primal inside of Morgan caught on fire. "No," he gasped.

"Didn't think so," Kazio murmured. He scraped his teeth along Morgan's neck.

"Fuck," Morgan gasped.

"Oh, I will." Kazio brushed his lips over Morgan's. "When I'm good and ready."

* * * *

315

When Morgan finally slept, he slept hard, bone-deep contentment pulling him into a long, dreamless slumber.

When he woke late the next morning, his eyes snapped open at the sensation of a warm body in bed next to him.

Kazio was watching him. "Good morning." He pressed a kiss to Morgan's bare shoulder.

"Good morning." Morgan nuzzled up against his chest. Kazio slid his arm around Morgan's waist. "I still can't believe it."

Kazio rumbled a low laugh and kissed Morgan's forehead. "I can't either. I finally get to take care of you, for real. That's all I want."

Morgan shivered. "You took care of me pretty good last night."

"Yes, I did." Kazio smirked and dipped his head to kiss him. "I was thinking about taking care of you again this morning."

"Oh yeah?"

"Yeah. Would you like that?" Kazio pulled Morgan close, hand drifting over Morgan's hip.

"Please."

Kazio played Morgan's body like an instrument, music sure and sweet.

* * * *

Kazio made waffles for breakfast, although it was more like a late lunch. They sat at the island, ankles woven together.

"When did you fall in love with me?" Morgan asked, between bites.

Kazio lifted Morgan's hand and kissed his knuckles. "A long time ago."

"Really?"

"I couldn't say the exact moment... But I knew for sure when you got fired. You were hurting so badly and you were...so lonely."

"Why didn't you say anything?"

Kazio studied Morgan as he chewed, eyes crinkled in amusement. "I told you I like taking care of you. I literally said those words out loud to you."

"Yeah, but..." Morgan pointed his fork at Kazio. "You should know by now that I'm kind of an idiot."

Kazio laughed. "I didn't think you were ready yet. You were dealing with a lot of stuff and I was waiting for you to figure it out a bit. Plus you kept sleeping with Albert."

"Like I said..." Now Morgan pointed his fork at himself. "Idiot." He took his last bite, thinking. "What if I never figured it out? How long were you going to wait?"

Kazio brushed a soft kiss to Morgan's lips. "I knew you'd get there eventually. And you did."

"I'm glad you had such faith in me. I wouldn't have. Speaking of which...I need to go feed Catzio. He'll be furious with me."

"All right." Kazio stood to clear the dishes.

"You'll come with me, right?" Morgan worried for a second he sounded too desperate, but only for a second.

Kazio leaned over to kiss him. "I'd like to see someone try to stop me."

* * * *

Catzio came running at the sound of the front door opening, then when he saw Morgan and Kazio he stopped and sauntered away, nose in the air.

"I'm so sorry, my boy. Are you hungry?" Morgan hurried to the cupboard to get a tin of cat food out. "I assure you I had an excellent reason for being so late."

Catzio hovered by his dish, uninterested, but he dropped the act once Morgan filled it with food. He attacked his meal, letting loose a loud purr.

"I knew he'd forgive me," Morgan said, running a hand down Catzio's back. "Although he's been holding a bit of a grudge since I got a job."

"Were you planning to work today?" Kazio asked, propping himself against the counter.

"I was going to, but there's nothing pressing I have to get done. You?"

"Yeah, I was supposed to... I might need to give Tasha another raise."

"Hmm." Morgan stood and leaned against Kazio, sliding his fingers into Kazio's belt. "Do you have to go in tonight?"

Kazio bit his lip, raking his eyes up and down Morgan's body. "Oh, I'm gonna go in tonight." He picked Morgan up and carried him down the hall to his bedroom.

Chapter Twenty-Six

I've Got You

Morgan had Monday off anyway, so he didn't have to tear himself away. Kazio, however...

"I'm sorry." Kazio laughed, trying to pry Morgan's hands from his waist and climb out of his bed. "I really, really have to go to work today."

"Don't leave me," Morgan pleaded, tucking his head under Kazio's chin and snuggling even closer. "I can't bear it."

Kazio groaned and relented, finding Morgan's lips instead.

Morgan made a happy noise as they sank back into the mattress. He slid his hands down to Kazio's bare ass.

"Just five more minutes," Kazio mumbled between kisses. "Okay? Then I really have to go."

Twenty-five minutes later, Kazio managed to get out of bed, but only on the promise of a shared shower.

"God, you're so sexy," Morgan said as Kazio stepped under the spray with him. "I can't believe I get to touch you whenever I want now."

Kazio took Morgan's hands and guided them to sensitive areas. "Please do."

Thirty minutes later, they got out of the shower, toes pruned and faces glowing.

"I still don't want to let you go." Morgan pouted as Kazio slid his pants on.

"Come with me." Kazio pulled his wet hair back into a half-pony. "Hang out with me at work."

"Tempting." Morgan bit his lip. "Maybe a little too tempting. I don't know if I can just *watch* you all day."

"I can get you washing dishes," Kazio said with a wink, "if you get tired of watching me."

"Ha. I would never get tired of that. It's just going to be hard."

"Yeah, it is."

Morgan hit him with a pillow.

"So you wanna come? To *work* with me," Kazio added, dodging the pillow this time.

Morgan kissed him on the nose. "'Course I do."

* * * *

Morgan leaned his chin on his hand, twisting his glass of water on the bar. "Was I stupid to try to make up with Felix? Was it always going to end like this?"

Kazio was polishing glasses during a mid-afternoon lull at the bar. He shook his head. "You weren't stupid. Everyone deserves a second chance."

Morgan sighed. "Maybe."

Kazio lifted Morgan's chin with a finger so their eyes met. "You gave one to Catzio, too. That worked out pretty good."

Morgan nodded, blinking a few tears away. "I love you, you know."

"I love you, too." Kazio leaned over the bar to give Morgan a quick, soft kiss. "Hey, would you mind grabbing me some lemons... Maybe five? They're in the walk-in."

Morgan scrunched his face. "It's okay if I just barge into the kitchen?"

"Yeah." Kazio tried to temper his grin. "Rudy just saw me kiss you, so they all know now."

"He did?" Morgan whirled to look at the kitchen door. At least three faces ducked out of view. "Wh —"

"It's fine. It just means that they all know you can go wherever you like."

Morgan slid off his stool. "Are they going to give me shit when I go in there?"

Kazio didn't answer, busy giving a meaningful look in the direction of the door. "They'd better not."

"If you say so..." Morgan crossed to the kitchen, pushed the door open and stuck a tentative head inside. The line cooks were intensely busy, chopping, wiping and avoiding Morgan's eyes. "Kazio wants some lemons," he said to no one in particular.

Rudy nodded, still looking down, lips pressed together, and pointed with his elbow. "In the walk-in."

Morgan hurried past them, heaved the cooler door open then examined the rows and rows of bins and tubs. The door opened again behind him.

"Oh, good, I can't find th..." Morgan's words trailed off when he realized it was Kazio who had joined him. He laughed. "What are you —?"

Kazio cut off Morgan's question by grabbing his hips, easing him back against the metal shelves and probing Morgan's mouth with his tongue.

Morgan kissed him back then broke away chuckling when he needed air. "What are you doing?"

"Helping you find the lemons. You were gone for*ever*."

Morgan poked him. "I was not. It's going to be so embarrassing coming out of here."

"You want to come in here instead?"

Goosebumps prickled his skin despite the chill as heat flared in his gut. "Okay, that has to be a health code violation. You need to settle down." He pointed a stern finger at Kazio. "Don't make me put your knives away in the wrong order, mister."

Kazio pressed his hips into Morgan's. "You wouldn't dare." He scraped his stubble over Morgan's neck.

"Oh, wouldn't I?" Morgan whispered, shivering.

Kazio's next kiss removed all thoughts from his head. "I might have to punish you if you did something like that," he murmured when he pulled away, eyes dark and flashing with desire.

"*Fuck*." Morgan shifted. "Now I really can't go out there."

Kazio gave him one more light kiss then pulled away. "All right. You're right. We'll have to continue this later. But when I get home, I'm going to lie you back on the bed, and…" He shared in explicit detail his plans for the evening.

"Mmmm." Morgan gulped, knees weak. "I— Um—" His face burned in the cold air. "Why were we in here again?"

* * * *

"I'm home!" Morgan called, coming in through Kazio's garage door. "I see Felix picked up his drums?" He slid into his slippers.

"He sure did," Kazio called back. "I managed to not call him any names. How was work?"

"It was good, I—" Morgan stopped at the sight of Kazio sitting on the couch, a furry bundle in his arms. "Wha—?"

Kazio grinned. "Surprise."

A brown tabby kitten blinked up at him.

Morgan gasped, tears flooding his eyes. "Is that...?"

Kazio nodded. "It is. All the others had been adopted. So I..."

Morgan sank down next to Kazio and reached a tentative hand to stroke the kitten. "Does he have a name?"

"I was thinking...Ralph?"

Morgan sniffled, tears now flowing. "That's perfect."

"He's your cat, if you want him. Or he can stay here. Whatever you like."

Morgan rested his head on Kazio's shoulder as he smoothed his hand along Ralph's soft fur. "He can be our cat."

Kazio kissed the top of Morgan's head. "I haven't told you his middle name yet."

"What's his middle name?"

"Meowgan."

Morgan laughed, then sniffled again. "Thank you so much. I love him. I love you."

Kazio gave Morgan another kiss then handed Ralph over "Here, you two cuddle for a bit. I was just making dinner."

Morgan wiggled into Kazio's warm spot on the couch and scratched behind Ralph's ear. "What are you making?"

"Pierogi."

"Like our first date?"

Kazio snickered. "'Our first date'... It wasn't a date!"

"It was, though, wasn't it? It was supposed to be a date?"

Kazio shrugged and picked up his red spatula. "Maybe it was."

Morgan shook his head. "I still can't believe you waited so long for me to figure everything out."

"The thing is...you were worth it. You've always been worth it."

* * * *

Kazio climbed into his bed to join Morgan.

Morgan lifted the covers. "Come under the sheet. I wanna show you something."

"Oh yeah? What are you gonna show me?"

"Look how cute Ralph is."

The kitten peered up at them from the depths of the bed.

Kazio chuckled. "Get up here, Ralph." He tucked the kitten into his arms and Morgan settled into the crook of his other arm.

"I was wrong before," Morgan said, running his hand along Kazio's arm.

"What were you wrong about?"

"I thought that stepping onto a stage was the best feeling there is, but I was wrong. This is."

This time Kazio was the one to tear up. "Thank you."

"Thank you for what?"

"For...going hiking and camping with me. For volunteering at the shelter. For always trying so hard to be the best version of yourself. For letting me be a part of it. Just...for everything."

Morgan tilted his face up to Kazio's. "I couldn't have done any of that without you."

"I know that's not true, but I'm glad I got to be there."

They kissed and cuddled until Ralph wandered off to go explore his new home, then they fell asleep, wrapped together, dreaming of all that was still to come.

* * * *

"Symphony's Crown?"

"Symphony Manor?"

"The Manor of Crowns?"

"Mythical Symphony?"

"Mythical Crown?"

"Waffle Crown?"

"*Waffle* Crown? What—"

Morgan chuckled and shook his head. "You guys let me know when you've settled on one."

Ray thumped the bass drum and twirled a stick. "I still think Sourdough—"

"No!" the other three said in unison.

"Fine." Ray stuck out his lower lip. "You know, for a group of people who sure like *eating* my sourdough..."

"Look, your sourdough is good, but it isn't all that." Brett sniffed.

"Says the guy who demolished an entire loaf last night," Ray retorted.

Morgan picked up his phone. "So, I was telling you all about this new club looking for acts..." He trailed off when an email notification popped up. "Oh my God..." His eyes widened as he read. "You guys!

Zayden Bourne wants us back at The Sphinx...to headline!"

"No way! That's amazing!" Andre crowed. "When?"

"He gave us a few options..." Morgan scrolled, shaking his head. "I can't believe it."

"We should go out to celebrate," Andre suggested. "You guys free?"

"Sorry." Morgan stood to herd them out. "I should get home."

"And by 'home', do you mean Kazio's?"

Morgan shrugged, trying not to smile too big. "Maaaybe."

Andre cackled. "Happy for you, man. Say hi to Kazio for us. Now go get some."

They climbed the stairs and left out the back of the gallery. Morgan waved goodbye to his friends at the train station, whistling *Cherry Tree* on his way down the escalator.

* * * *

When Morgan came out of the bathroom, towel wrapped around his waist, Kazio sat on the edge of his bed scrolling his phone. "Hey. How was rehearsal?" he asked, putting his phone away.

"It was great." Morgan bent over to give him a kiss. "How was work?"

"Oh, fine. I missed you."

"I missed you, too."

Kazio took hold of Morgan's waist and pulled him closer. "So the gallery is going to work for a rehearsal space?"

"Definitely. It's perfect."

Kazio circled his thumbs on Morgan's hips, eyes raking over his bare chest. "Remember that time you came out of your shower in nothing but a towel, and I followed you into your closet?"

Morgan huffed a laugh. "Sure do."

Kazio hooked a finger into Morgan's towel. "You know what I was thinking about doing?"

Morgan's heart quickened. "What's that now?"

"This." Kazio yanked the towel off, eyes dropping.

Morgan slid his hand into Kazio's hair. "Interesting."

Kazio kissed Morgan's stomach, soft feathery touches, then his mouth drifted lower.

"Kaz—*oh.*" Morgan gripped his hair and arched into him.

"I've got you, Morgan," Kazio rumbled, breath warm on Morgan's skin. "I've got you."

"You've got me…" Morgan whispered. He tipped his head back, closed his eyes and let the waves carry him.

It was a first for him—someone who worshiped him, put him first, cared about his pleasure way more than his own. Kazio brought him to the brink, over and over, until he fell beyond it, tumbling through the stars, drifting in clouds, light and mist, ancient and ethereal, all at once.

Much later, after a few hours of sleep, naked and sprawled on the bed, once his senses had come back, Morgan considered that he had never been so completely undone before, left a rubbery mess, spent, sated, and so, so fucking happy he thought he might die.

Kazio curled up behind him. "Morgan," he whispered into the nape of Morgan's neck. "I love you."

"I love you too."

Kazio's hand crept around Morgan's hip and took hold of him.

"Again?" Morgan murmured.

"Again," Kazio rumbled. "Let me take care of you."

"You always do."

"I always will."

Epilogue

I'm Ready

Almost eight months later

Kazio dropped his keys on his kitchen counter. Catzio and Ralph came running to wind themselves around his ankles. "Hey, boys." He reached down to pet them. "Did your mean daddy not feed you dinner?"

Morgan didn't look up from the rosé sauce he was stirring. "Don't believe their bullshit. I did, in fact, already feed them."

Kazio chuckled and came over to kiss Morgan hello. "I got the weirdest email today."

"That's so funny, because *I* got the weirdest text!"

"Was your weird text from Thomas?"

"Yes. Was your weird email from Thomas?"

"Yup." Kazio leaned against the counter. "So, what do you think?"

"What do *you* think? It's your pub."

Kazio lifted a shoulder. "It's not the kind of thing I'd normally do. And we'd have to check with the guys, obviously."

"Yes. And make sure we're not booked. Thomas wanted it specifically on that day."

"Right. But, I guess...if the guys say yes and you're free... Yeah, I can make it work at the Exchange. If it's okay with you."

Morgan stirred the sauce, thinking. Was it weird to be the musical accompaniment for your ex-boss, who helped get you fired, to propose to your ex-boyfriend, who dumped you? Maybe it was weird but... "Yeah. Yeah, it's okay. I'd like to do it."

"That's great." Kazio kissed him again. "I think it'll be really sweet."

So that was how Morgan came to be standing in the kitchen of the Exchange with the rest of his band, peeking out of the window at the Breakpoint crowd gathered around the small stage Thomas had rented. He took a deep breath to steady his nerves.

"You ready?" Kazio asked, squeezing his hand. "You look hot as fuck, by the way."

Morgan had, admittedly, selected his outfit and styled his hair very carefully. He had to crush this. "I'm ready."

"See you out there." One last kiss, then Kazio pushed through the door.

* * * *

Morgan was putting his guitar back in its case in Kazio's office after the show when there was a knock on the door.

It was Luka. He leaned his lanky frame against the door jam, face cautious.

"Hey," Morgan said, straightening and smoothing his tank top.

"Hey."

"You were really —" Luka started to say at the same time Morgan said, "Congratulations on your —"

They both stopped and stared at each other with tentative smiles.

"You go first," Morgan said.

"You were really good. Symphony is really good."

"Thanks, Luka."

He grimaced. "The name though…"

Morgan chuckled. "You've been dying to tell me that, haven't you?"

"I mean…what happens when someone searches for 'symphony'?"

"I hear you, but it's kind of our thing now. And actually, if you search 'Symphony the Band,' you'll get us."

Luka held up his hands. "Okay then. If you're sure."

"I am." Morgan's smile softened. "Congratulations on your engagement. I'm really happy for you two."

"Thank you." Luka's smile dazzled. "I'm really happy too. It was cool that you agreed to play for us. I have to tell you, I did not see it coming."

"It was my pleasure. I was flattered that Thomas asked."

Luka's gaze took in Morgan's outfit. "We've been hearing about Symphony. You guys are really on your way, aren't you?"

It was hard to argue with that. The band's calendar was pretty full. "And you are, too. I saw that you've been doing shows at a coffee house."

"Yeah. It's been…a ride."

They stared at each other again.

Morgan shifted. "Luka, I'm really sorry that I blackmailed you. I'm sorry for everything."

"It's okay. You don't owe me any more apologies. It's ancient history and…it all worked out, you know?"

"I know."

"Speaking of… You and Kazio, hey?"

This time Morgan's grin stretched across his face, cheeks flushing. "Yeah."

"So you're happy?"

Morgan exhaled, his heart giving a gentle throb. "Yes."

"That's great." Luka paused while they held eye contact for another moment. "Listen…the two of you, and the rest of your band, if they want… You should join us for a drink. Hang out for a while."

"Thank you, Luka. I'd like that."

Morgan and Kazio joined Luka, Thomas, Finn, Rory, his bandmates and the rest of the Breakpoint crew around the faded tables. Luka and Thomas glowed like only a newly engaged couple could. Finn cracked inappropriate jokes while Rory grinned and shook their head. Morgan squeezed Kazio's hand as they laughed and drank, a quiet, calm place in his heart. He'd made it. Everything was going to be okay.

It wasn't so hard after all.

Sign up for our newsletter and find out about all our romance book releases, eBook sales and promotions, sneak peeks and FREE romance books!

Want to see more like this?
Here's a taster for you to enjoy!

Cedarwood Pride:
Home to Cedarwood
Megan Slayer

Excerpt

"Hello. Welcome to our single fathers' group. My name is Colin Baker. I own the Books, Comics, Vintage and Memorabilia Bookstore on Main Street. I'm thirty years old, gay and I have a son. I've been single for the last year, and I'm not sure I'm ready to start dating, but I'm positive I'm tired of being alone." Colin rubbed his hands together and stood behind the podium. He hated being the center of attention. Being terminally shy, he preferred to play the role of the wallflower. Then he and his partner had adopted their son. Everything had changed when they'd welcomed Gage into their lives. He gripped the top of the podium.

"I'm glad you're all here." Colin folded his hands to hide the shaking. "I created this group for the single gay parents in the Cedarwood area—especially the guys. As you know, Cedarwood isn't exactly welcoming to the LGBT community. There aren't many of us, but I figured we all need a support system. Feel free to add your name to the outreach list and invite anyone you think might like to attend. In this group, we share our stories and support one another. Now I'll open the floor."

He stepped away from the mic and made his way down the steps of the stage. Meeting in the basement of the former Reserved Church of the Open-Minded worked better than he'd expected. People knew the building, but no one seemed to care if anyone gathered there—unless the people were gay. The church for anyone who wanted to worship had only lasted long enough for a sign to be erected. Bad for the church members but good for Colin and his people, who now numbered only five. He grabbed one of the chairs and listened to the others share their stories.

He'd been asked once if the group was intended to hook up the single fathers. Colin had smiled at the time, but inwardly seethed. God. Yes, they were single, but not everyone wanted to hook up. Okay, that wasn't true. He wasn't interested in a hookup. After Nicolas, he dreaded jumping back into the dating pool. But the loneliness wouldn't go away.

Two and a half hours later, the meeting broke up. He helped put the chairs away, turn off lights and locked the building. The guys in the group were a good bunch. Everyone seemed interested in the problems of the others. Some of the men were making headway in their love lives. Others weren't. Some were happy to be in Colin's not-yet-ready-for-dating camp.

Despite the town's location outside Cleveland, the population numbered only around six thousand. Most people worked in the bigger city and spent their weekends in Cedarwood. People moved to Cedarwood for the schools and the safe small-town feel. The children tended to live idyllic lives. The kids belonging to gay parents were the subject of bullying more than most of the other children. He knew because he'd heard stories from his son.

Colin drove home to the duplex he shared with his brother, Farin. The light shone in the living room of his half of the building. Farin must've brought Gage home for the night. Colin checked his watch. Nine p.m. Shit. He'd stayed out fifteen minutes past his son's bedtime. He preferred to be home before Gage went to sleep to kiss him good night. He strode into the house and dropped his coat and keys on the chair by the door.

"Heya." Farin stood. He rolled his shoulders and groaned. "I've been on that couch for the better part of forty-five minutes. Gage and I read every book he's got on every superhero known to mankind."

"He likes his superheroes." Colin rubbed his temples. "Police too. I don't know why. I tried to get him interested in baseball, but that hasn't worked."

"It's a phase. Remember how I used to get silly over fire trucks?" Farin patted his brother's shoulder. "I was five, but I loved those trucks. But we were talking about Gage. He hit the hay ten minutes ago. He didn't want to go to bed. When I asked him why, he said there's a kid at school giving him hell. He didn't say hell, but you get the idea."

Colin pointed to the chair. "Sit. He hasn't said a word of this to me. What's going on?"

"Okay." Farin perched on the edge of the armchair. "Some kid in his class—he wouldn't say who—has been talking crap to him. Saying his dad is gay, so he must be gay. Kids are rough at that age."

"He's seven." A dull ache grew behind his eyes. The next thing he knew, the kid would be teasing Gage because he was adopted, too. His younger brother had definitely inherited the listening gene. Where Colin moved first and thought second, Farin knew how to get people to talk. Apparently, he'd worked his magic on Gage.

Farin rested his elbows on his knees. "Don't let it bother you. Kids say stupid shit all the time. I talked to Gage, but he wanted me to keep quiet. He just wants to know that Dad has his back, but he's scared to talk to you because he's worried you'll get upset. Let him know you'll go in and talk to the principal, too, if that's what needs to be done."

"You bet your ass I'll talk to the principal." Colin bit back his anger. He hated the way the residents of Cedarwood refused to accept the differences in society. So some people are gay. Who cares?

"Calm down before you do or you'll blow a gasket and get yourself into trouble." Farin left the chair and headed to the front door. "Give Gage a kiss, tell him it's cool and you and Uncle Farin love him. If you need help, I'm right over there." He saluted Colin, then headed out of the door.

Colin jumped up from his seat and ascended the stairs two at a time. When he reached Gage's bedroom, his son was already asleep. The kid did have a talent for crashing once his head hit the pillow. He kissed Gage on the forehead and whispered, "Love you, big boy."

Colin crept out of the room and left the door open a bit. He went back downstairs long enough to lock up and turn off the lights. He paused at the picture window. The lights of Cedarwood twinkled against the dark sky. In the silence of the night, the small town was almost pretty. He should've been happy to live in the community. The schools were all located in one central campus and the sports programs were highly ranked. The graduating classes featured only around a hundred and twenty-five kids each. A person could still shop in town and get everything needed in one trip down the main drag. The cost of living wasn't horrible, either. But the cost of living in Cedarwood as a gay man rose by the minute. He managed to fuck himself over doubly by co-owning the lone bookstore in town. The people wanted the books, comics and collectibles he sold, but that didn't stop them from making derogatory comments.

He raked his fingers through his hair. He wasn't part of the star baseball team and he wasn't the naive kid from high school anymore. He had a kid, a business and a life. He'd worry about Gage's problems at school in the morning. Maybe by then he'd have a fresh perspective or better advice to give his son. Maybe.

* * * *

The next morning, Colin stood at the island in the middle of the kitchen and drummed his fingers on the faux marble surface. Two months into school and his kid was late…again.

"Come on, Gage. You're late." He glanced up the back set of stairs one more time. The light glowed on the wall from the second-story bathroom. "What are you doing up there?"

Gage rounded the corner and bounded down the stairs. "Sorry, Dad." He kept his head down. "My belly hurts."

"Really?" Colin stopped Gage on the steps. "I heard about the kid at school. Besides, you're only a week away from the Halloween parties. You love those parties."

"Harvest parties. We can't have Halloween ones. It's against the law."

"It's not against the law." Probably against something else, but Colin didn't want to discuss that with Gage. "So, talk. What's with the kid at school?"

"Uncle Farin blabbed." Gage ducked under Colin's arm. "He wasn't supposed to talk to you. He promised."

"You do realize your uncle and I talk about everything?" Colin followed his son into the kitchen. "So, spill your guts, kid."

Gage stared at Colin. He might have been adopted, but from the way the kid glowered at him, he could've sworn Gage shared the same gene pool. With the same blond hair, blue eyes and thick lashes, Gage reminded Colin of a mini-version of himself.

Colin squatted in front of his son to put them at eye level. "What did the kid say?"

"That my dad is a fag." Gage stuck out his bottom lip. "Why would he do that? You're a dad."

Colin sighed. "Okay." He needed to explain the situation for Gage to understand. "Some people say mean things. No matter how hard you try to get away from them, they'll always be there." God, did he know that lesson well. He'd tried to shake the memories of the guy from high school who'd insisted on making his life hell.

"What do I do?" Gage rested his hands on his hips. "Uncle Farin said to ignore him."

"That's a good idea. Don't let him know you're upset. It's hard because you're going to be mad, but once he realizes you're not going to react, the kid should stop," Colin said. Unless you have a secret crush on the guy being the dick. He shook his head. He wasn't about to tell his son that little tidbit of information.

"Fine." Gage picked up his tennis shoes. "But I'm already late. Why don't you just let me skip today?" He grinned and batted his lashes. "A mental health day, like you say you want to have?"

Kids were such sponges. He'd have to remember to think before he spoke in the future. "No mental health days. Grab your book bag. You have art today, don't you? You love art."

Gage yanked his bag from the hook. "I do." He hurried past Colin and headed out to the garage.

Colin picked up his tablet, wallet and keys. He'd get Gage to school late, but at least he'd conned the kid into going. He locked the back door, then climbed into the car beside his son.

Once the garage door opened, he backed out of the garage and closed the door. Colin eased the rest of the way down the driveway, then turned onto the street. He glanced at his son's reflection in the rearview mirror.

"I'm going to take you in to school and write the excuse then, okay?" Colin asked. He barreled down the back road to the school complex. The speed limit sign read twenty-five. He snorted. Did anyone actually drive that slow anymore? He checked his speed. Thirty-nine. Fuck. He tapped the brake. He needed to get his head in the game and pay attention. The speed limit was there for a reason, not a suggestion. God. He was a dad and getting his kid to school safely should've been utmost in his mind.

Colin let off the gas and continued down the road, but something in the mirror caught his attention. Red and blue lights. What the hell? Realization washed over him as he recognized the reason for the lights. A cop. Fucking balls. He'd been caught speeding. He pulled over to the side of the road and parked.

"What's wrong, Dad?" Gage asked from the backseat.

"Daddy went too fast on this road and the cop is calling me out. I was wrong. I was speeding." He sighed and leaned back in his seat. Shit. Of all the times to screw up, he had to do it in front of his kid.

"Sorry, Dad." Gage curled up in his booster seat.

"Me too, kid. Now you're super late." Colin pressed the button to roll down the window, then reached across the dash to the glove box and retrieved his registration.

"Excuse me, sir." A shadow darkened the window. "License and registration, please?"

Colin slid the card from his wallet. "Here you go." He refrained from looking at the cop. Not because he disliked cops, but because the shame of his actions washed over him in epic proportions. He'd been speeding, in a school zone more than likely and with his kid in the car.

"Do you know how fast you were going, sir?" the officer asked.

"Probably twenty miles over the limit." He closed his eyes and rubbed his forehead.

"Thirty-nine in a twenty. This is a marked school zone. The lights were flashing."

"I'm sorry, Officer." Colin opened his eyes. The stress was no excuse to be a jerk. "I was trying to get my son to school and wasn't paying attention. I accept responsibility for my actions." And I've learned my lesson.

"I see." The cop paused. "Colin Baker? I knew a guy named Colin Baker when I was in school. We played ball together. Huh. Well, I'm going to give you a ticket. Give me a moment."

Colin slid his gaze to the officer as the man retreated to the cruiser behind Colin's car. He didn't need to read the man's badge to know his name. He'd recognize that body anywhere—Jordan Hargrove. Why in the name of God did the guy who'd featured prominently in all

Colin's high-school fantasies have to be the guy who was currently writing him up for breaking the speed limit?

The dull ache from the night before developed behind Colin's eyes. So much for being a good role model for his son. Horrible fucking luck.

About the Author

Jennifer believes that there are so many more stories to tell than the ones that have traditionally been lined up on bookstore shelves. Her short stories have appeared in several anthologies and literary magazines. Her third novel in the Falling Hard series is on its way, as well as three books from St. Martin's Romance. She lives with her family in BC, Canada.

Jennifer loves to hear from readers. You can find her contact information, website details and author profile page at https://www.firstforromance.com

ENTWINED PUBLISHING